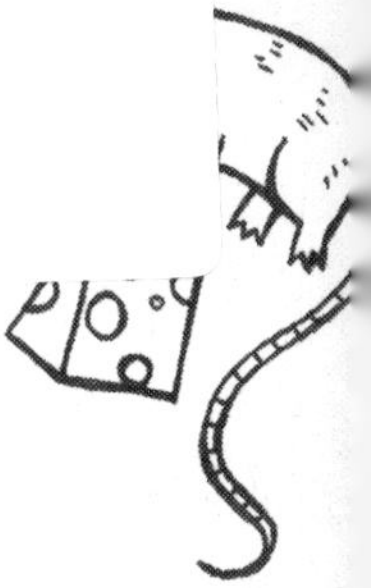

Thanks to my great big sister, who is obviously completely jealous of my artistic genius, my screen time has been banned. FOR A MONTH!!

All this extra free time though has left me free to contemplate life's big mysteries. Like... what if Little Red Riding Hood was a stunt-riding motorbike daredevil, the big bad wolf was a weird werewolf and the brave woodcutter was a stinky cheese cutter?

Now if only I could find a treasured copy of the original fairytale locked away in a secret spot under my sister's bed in a toy safe I just happen to know the code for!

Brace yourself for awesome. I feel another EPIC FAIL TALE approaching!

juice
buddy
hairy
warped
apocalypse
zinger
hot dogs
wheelie
blunder
wrinkly
burped
sucker
ginger
bongos

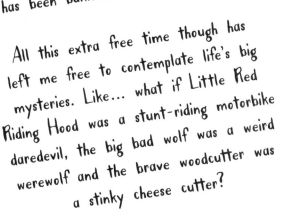

RAT'S TAIL

Dedicated to the guys,
Jay, Dan & Fritz
Woompah!

HE SOUNDS WEIRD!

Koala Books

An imprint of
Scholastic Australia Pty Limited
PO Box 579 Gosford NSW 2250
ABN 11 000 614 577
www.scholastic.com.au

Part of the Scholastic Group
Sydney • Auckland • New York • Toronto • London • Mexico City
• New Delhi • Hong Kong • Buenos Aires • Puerto Rico

Published by Scholastic Australia in 2018
Text and illustrations copyright © Matt Cosgrove 2018
mattcosgrovebooks.com

DO NOT GO HERE!

questionable
The moral right of the author and illustrator have been asserted.

A catelogue record for this
book is available from the
National Library of Australia

ISBN: 978-1-74299-250-1 (paperback)

Typset in Adobe Garamond, Campland Letters and Grafolita Script
by the author/illustrator.

Printed in Australia by Griffin Press.

Scholastic Australia's policy, in association with Griffin Press, is to use papers that
are renewable and made efficiently from wood grown in responsibly managed forests,
so as to minimise its environmental footprint.

10 9 8 7 6 5 4 3 2 1   18 19 20 21 22 / 1

AND I THOUGHT I WAS A SMELLY RAT!

This book belongs to

Smelly

AKA: Dobby McDobber Dobberson

EPIC **FAIL** TALES

LITTLE STUNT RIDING HOOD

PLUS BONUS **SEVEN NINJAS OPERATION: BREAKOUT** STORY

Once upon a

fine, fully sick,

hotted-up motorcycle...

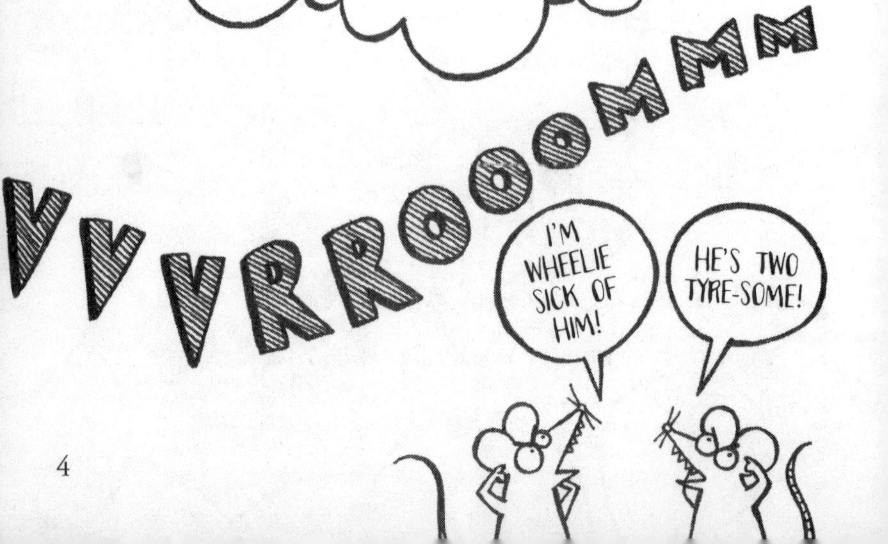
VVRROOOOMMMM
I'M WHEELIE SICK OF HIM!
HE'S TWO TYRE-SOME!

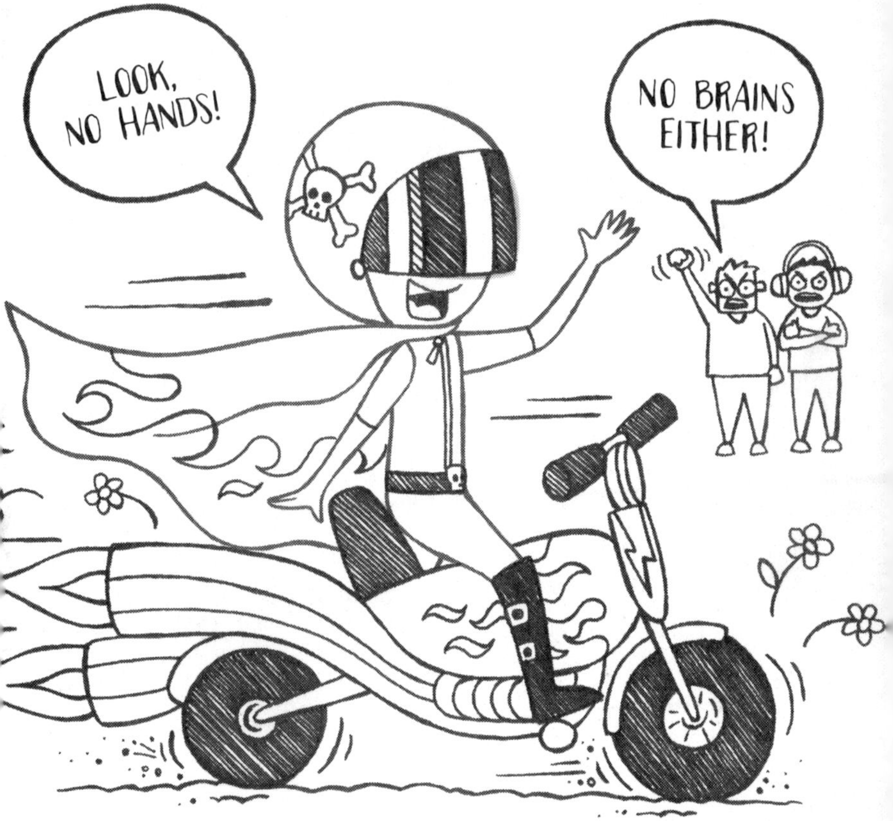
LOOK, NO HANDS!
NO BRAINS EITHER!

… there revved a little daredevil, making the loudest noise you have ever heard!

'Oh, ~~s~~he is so annoying!' the neighbours would proclaim as ~~s~~he roared past on his motorbike.

The little kid lived life on the edge! Of all the riders in the world, he was the bravest idiot you could imagine, with his daring ways.

There was no stunt he wouldn't do for a cheap thrill! Dares. Double Dares. Triple Dares. Triple Decker Double Dares. Challenge Accepted! If you named it, this bike-riding burnout bandit would jump it – backwards and blindfolded!

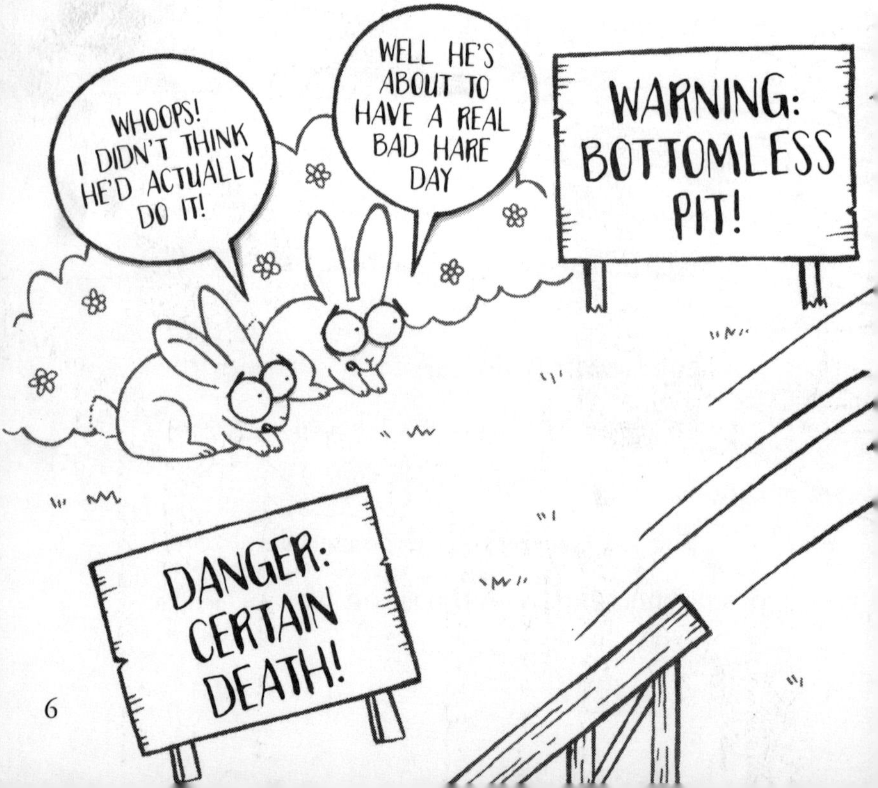
WHOOPS! I DIDN'T THINK HE'D ACTUALLY DO IT!
WELL HE'S ABOUT TO HAVE A REAL BAD HARE DAY
WARNING: BOTTOMLESS PIT!
DANGER: CERTAIN DEATH!

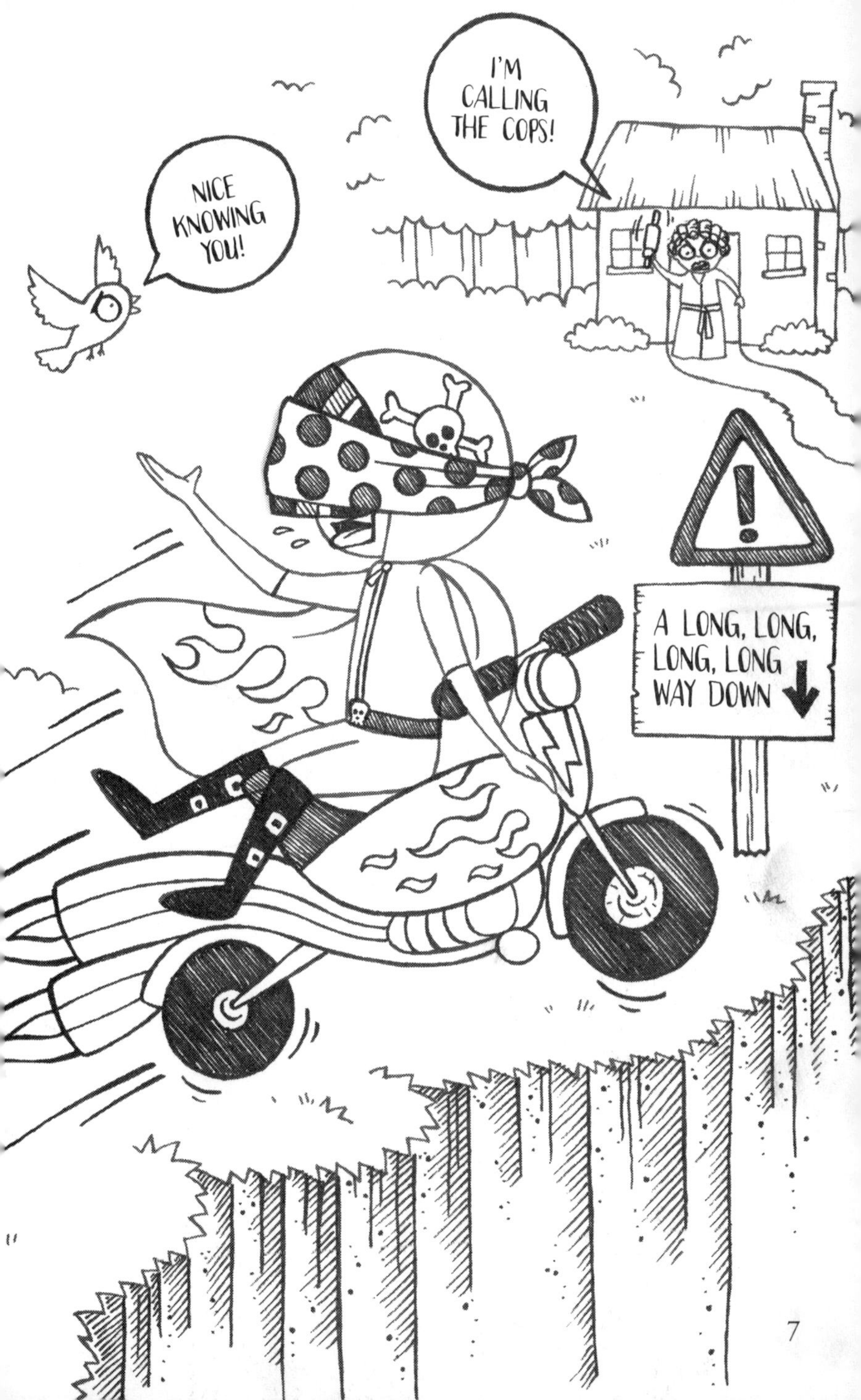
NICE KNOWING YOU!
I'M CALLING THE COPS!
A LONG, LONG, LONG, LONG WAY DOWN

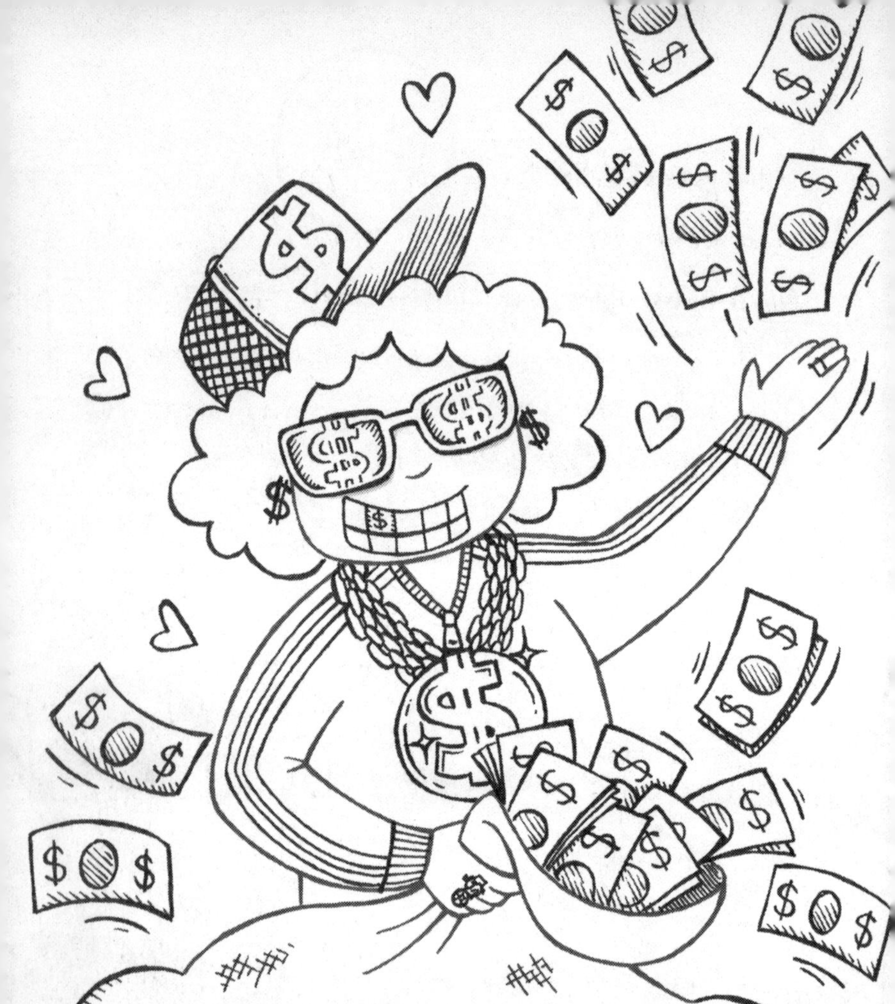

The one who loved the little revhead most of all was his elderly manager. The old lady's heart leapt for joy when she thought of all the sweet, sweet cash that he made for her! That hoodlum bike boy was a licence to print money!

The general public loved him and [redacted]he was seen absolutely everywhere! From cereal boxes to lunch boxes, there was "Little Stunt Riding Hood". In fact, wherever there was a box, he was on it! Money boxes, tissue boxes, moving boxes, bento boxes, shoe boxes, boxing bag boxes, 'The History of Boxes' DVD boxset. Kerching!

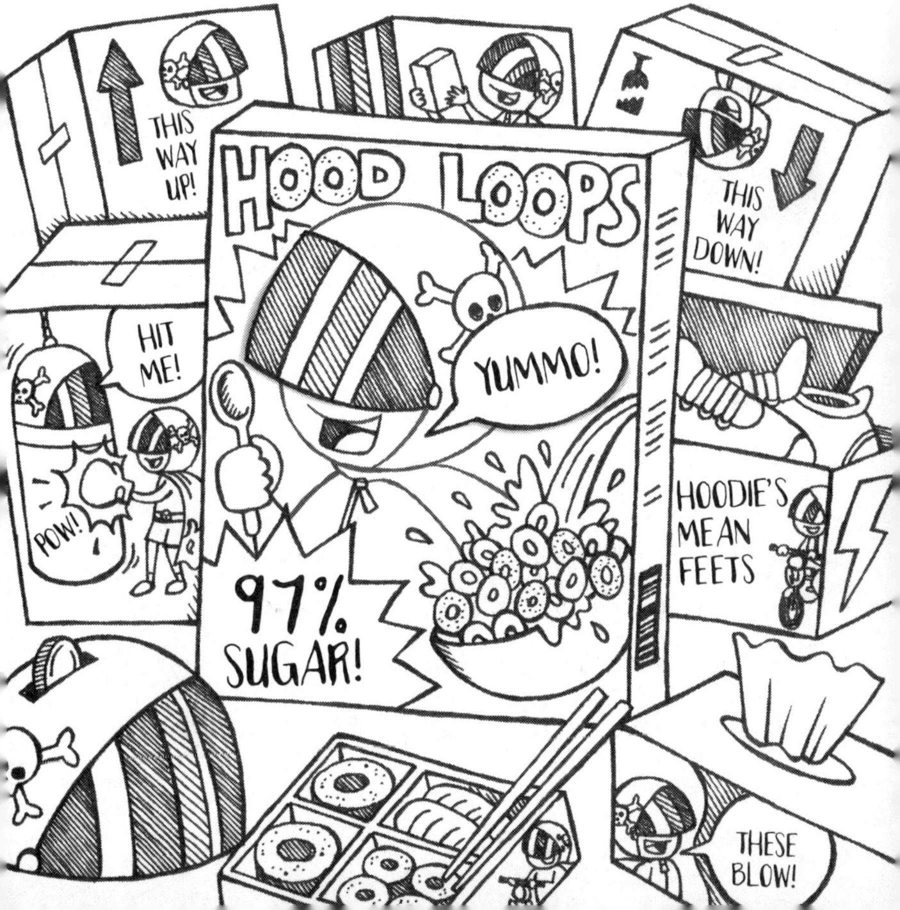
THIS WAY UP!
HOOD LOOPS
THIS WAY DOWN!
HIT ME!
YUMMO!
POW!
HOODIE'S MEAN FEETS
97% SUGAR!
THESE BLOW!

One day his manager said to him, 'Come on Little Stunt Riding Hood, you slacker! I have been thinking and I need you to win an important race for me – The Highly Utterly Dangerous Mostly Ultra Deadly (T.H.U.D.M.U.D. for short) Stunt Riding Motorcycle Grand Prix World Cup!'

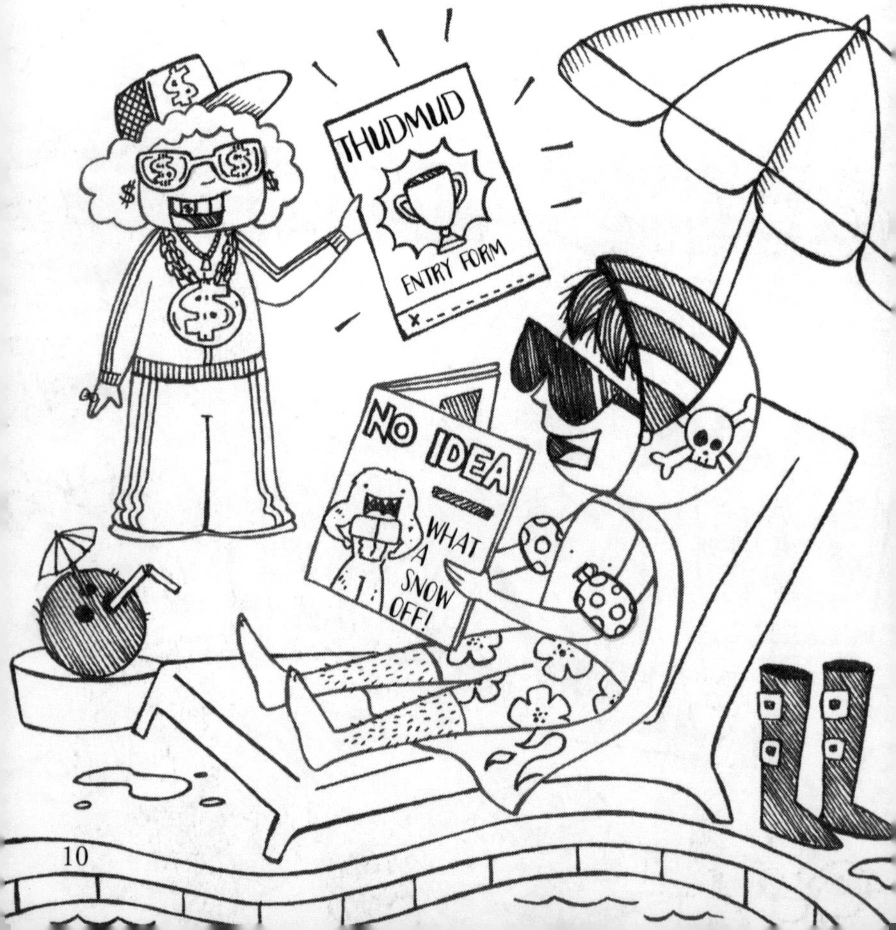
THUDMUD
ENTRY FORM
NO IDEA
WHAT A SNOW OFF!

'It will be a piece of cake. Take the title of Grand Champ for the year and it will certainly raise your appearance fee. You might even get your own reality TV show! I'm thinking "Hood Do You Think You Are?" or maybe "I'm a Stunt Driver, Get Me Outta Gear". I'm still work-shopping names.'

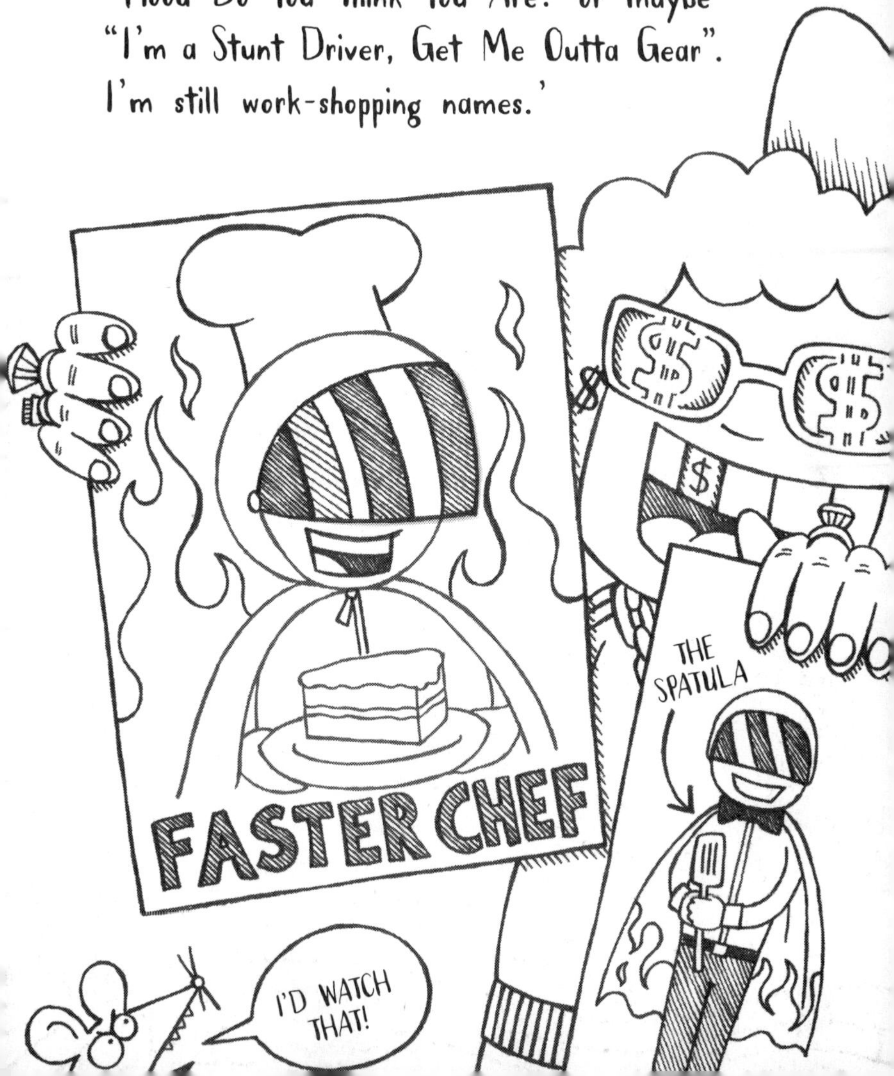
FASTER CHEF
THE SPATULA
I'D WATCH THAT!

On the morning of the big race…

Little Stunt Riding Hood took his place at the starting line and revved up his engine.

His manager called out, 'Make sure you stick to the plan, turkey! The race track can be a dangerous place, so be ready for action! Go hard and fast! Always take risks. Always take short cuts. It will make great TV. The race is being televised live around the world. Smile for the cameras! I'm thinking video games, ringtones, action figures…'

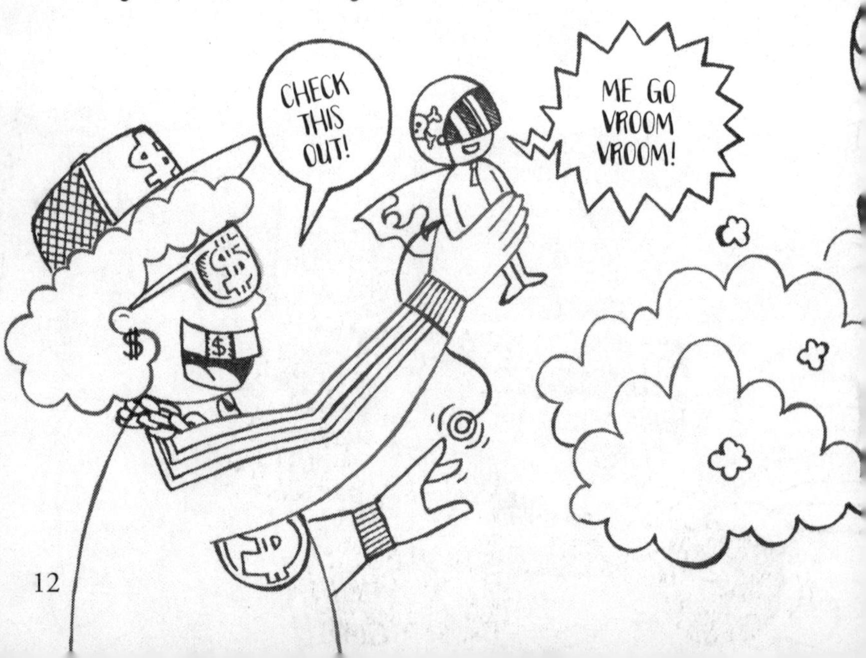
CHECK THIS OUT!
ME GO VROOM VROOM!

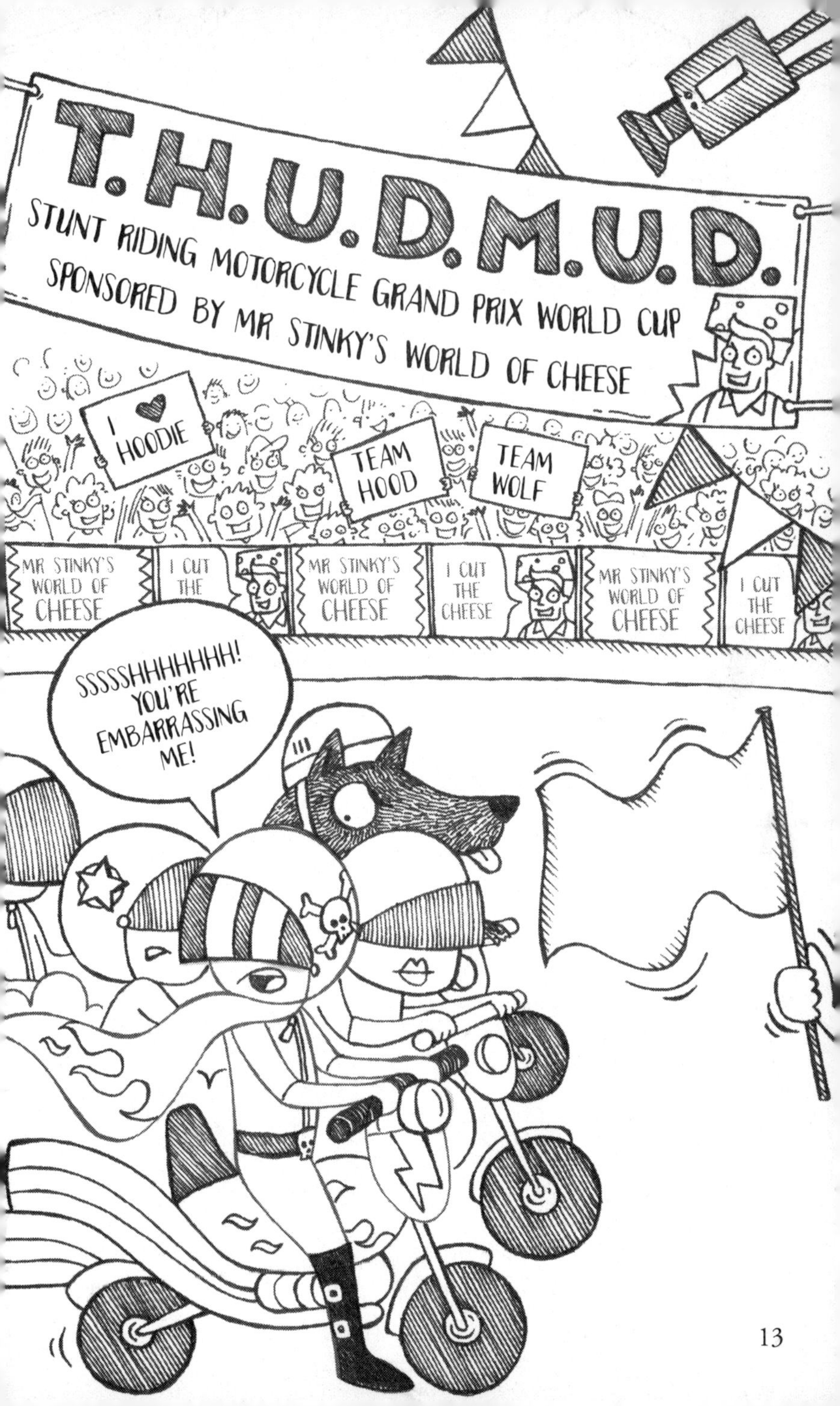
T.H.U.D.M.U.D.
STUNT RIDING MOTORCYCLE GRAND PRIX WORLD CUP
SPONSORED BY MR STINKY'S WORLD OF CHEESE
I ♥ HOODIE
TEAM HOOD
TEAM WOLF
MR STINKY'S WORLD OF CHEESE
I CUT THE
MR STINKY'S WORLD OF CHEESE
I CUT THE CHEESE
MR STINKY'S WORLD OF CHEESE
I CUT THE CHEESE
SSSSSHHHHHHH! YOU'RE EMBARRASSING ME!

'Most importantly of all, watch out for the big werewolf!' his manager shouted out after him. 'You've gotta beat that mangy mutt! He's almost as popular as you. Kick his butt, ya hear me?'

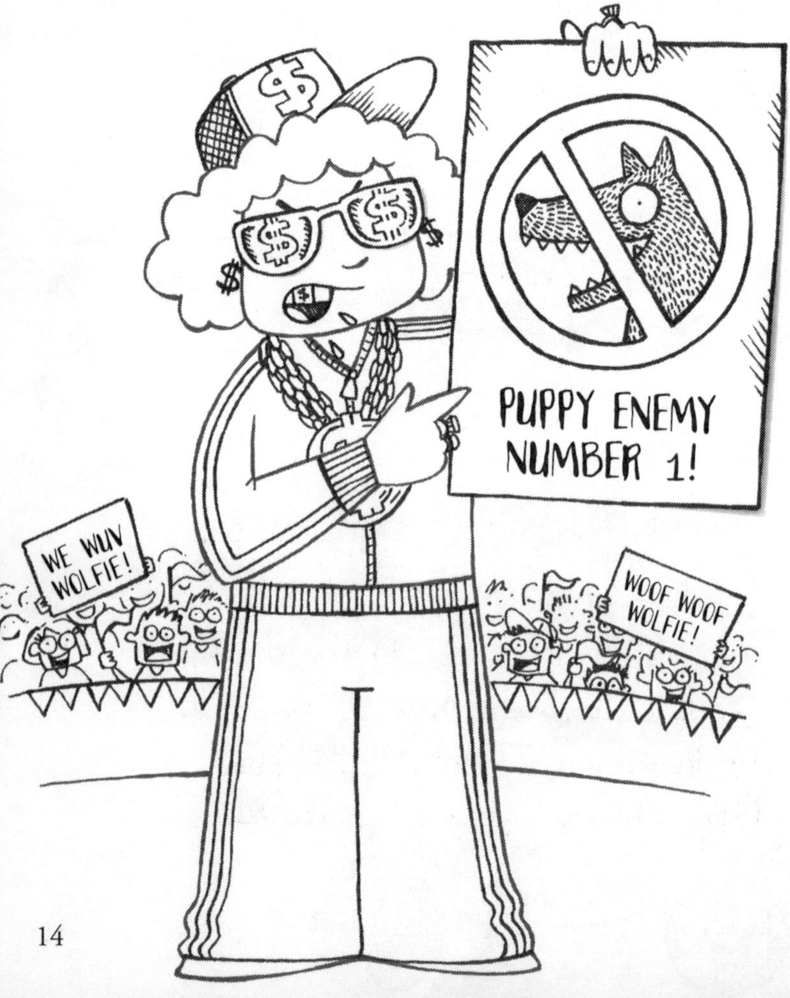
PUPPY ENEMY
NUMBER 1!
WE WUV
WOLFIE!
WOOF WOOF
WOLFIE!

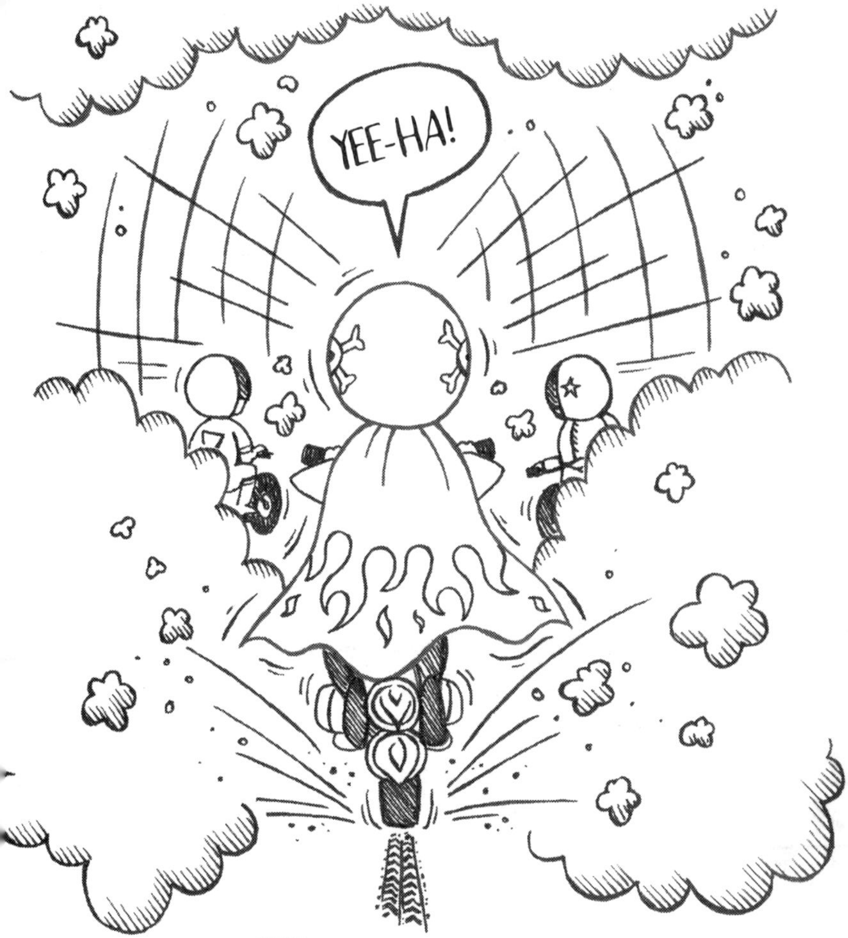
YEE-HA!

But Little Stunt Riding Hood had already disappeared into the clouds of exhaust fumes, heading for Grandmaster's Cottage Cheese Factory, which was the finish line for this year's T.H.U.D.M.U.D. Stunt Riding Motorcycle Grand Prix World Cup!

The race to Grandmaster's Cottage Cheese Factory was long and windy, with many twists and turns. There were lethal obstacles along the way, like a shark-infested tank or a deep river of acid to jump, but Little Stunt Riding Hood enjoyed the danger, and even managed a few sick stunt moves for the fans.

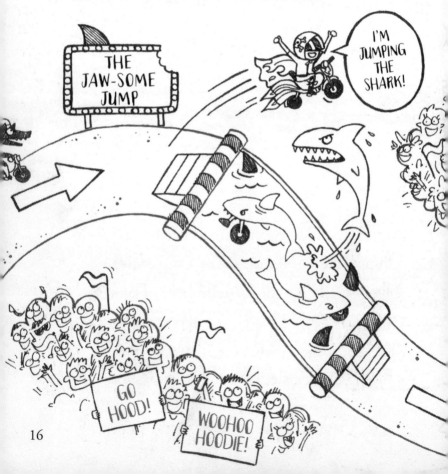

THE JAW-SOME JUMP

I'M JUMPING THE SHARK!

GO HOOD!

WOOHOO HOODIE!

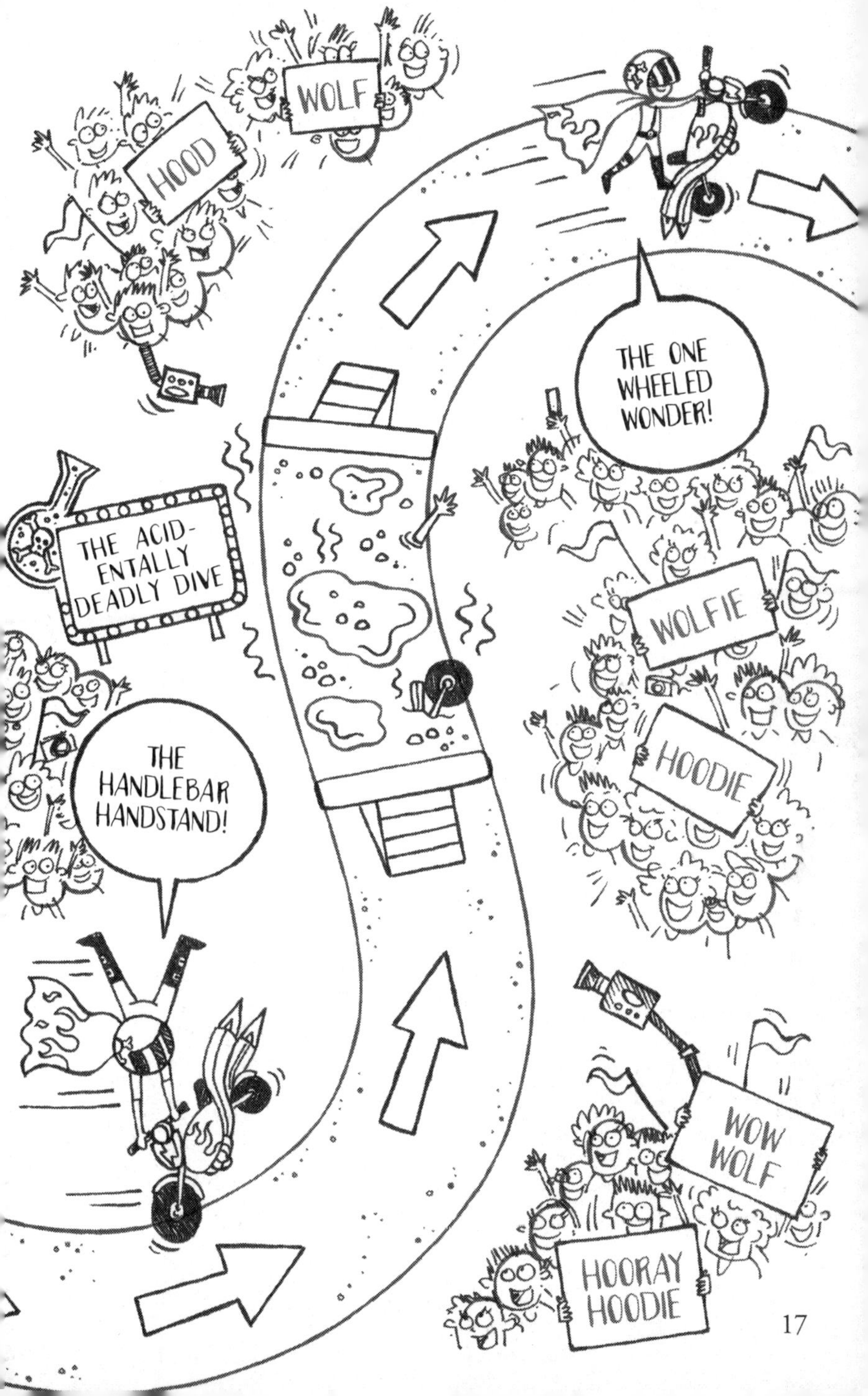
HOOD
WOLF
THE ONE WHEELED WONDER!
THE ACID-ENTALLY DEADLY DIVE
WOLFIE
HOODIE
THE HANDLEBAR HANDSTAND!
WOW WOLF
HOORAY HOODIE

At first Little Stunt Riding Hood passed a fellow rider here and there, but soon all trace of the competition fell away into the distance. He was far into the lead when suddenly the big werewolf sped out in front of him!

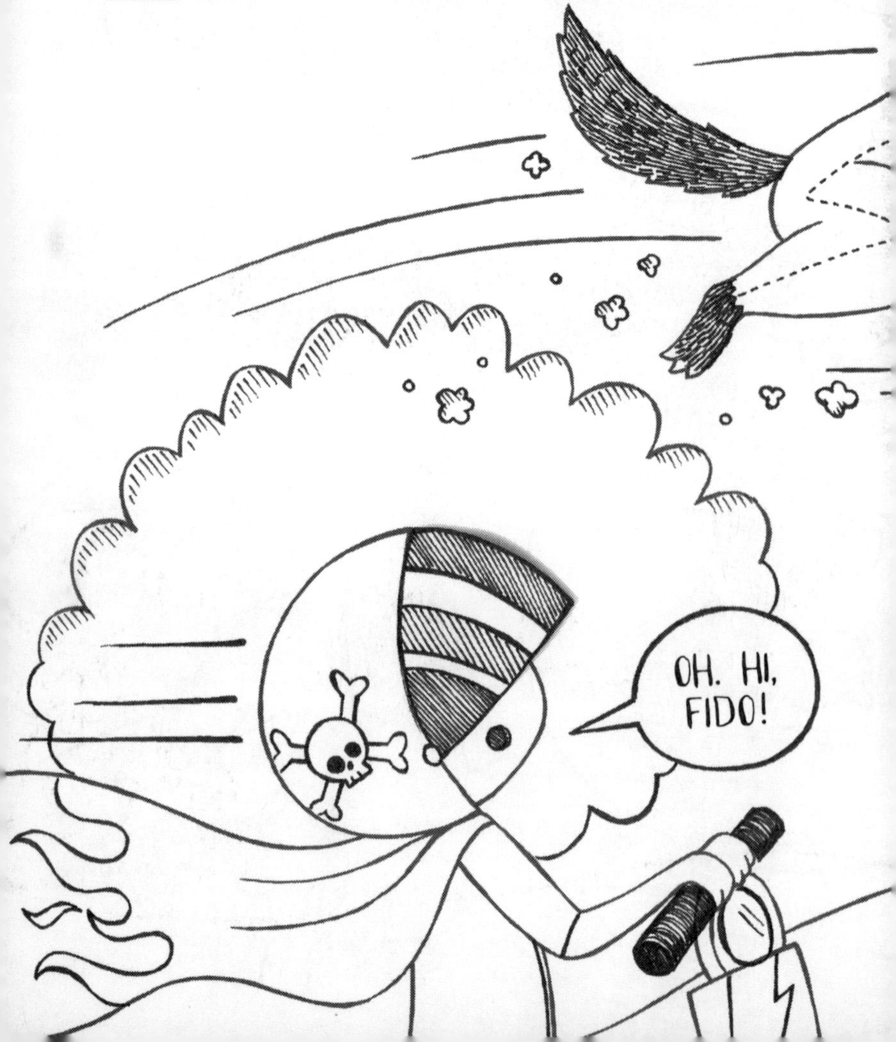
OH. HI, FIDO!

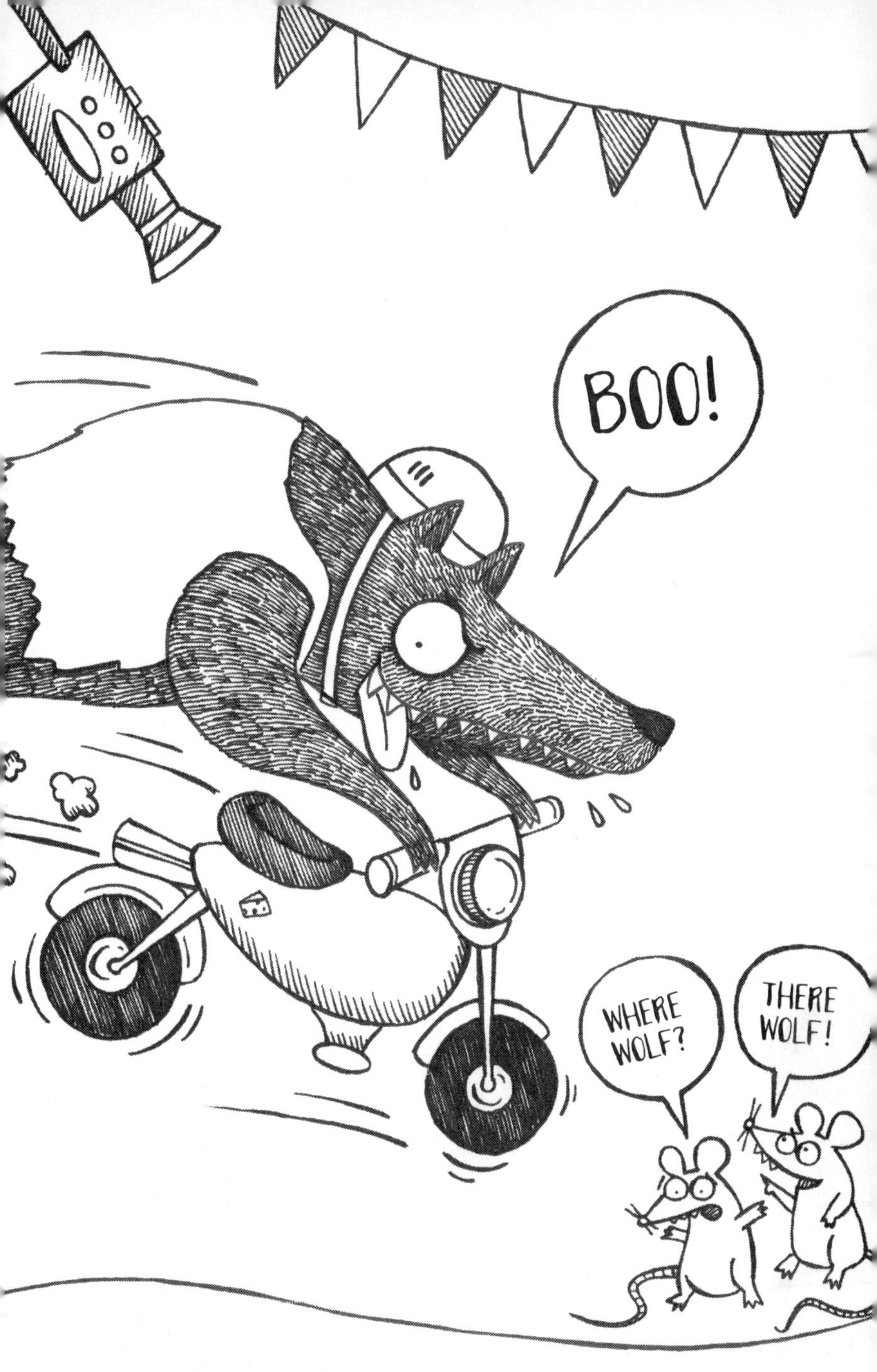
BOO!
WHERE WOLF?
THERE WOLF!

Little Stunt Riding Hood did not fear the big werewolf, as she already knew what a lousy driver he was, and was sure to beat him!

'Eat dirt, little punk!' the big werewolf said, calling out to the young rebel. 'You are so lame!'

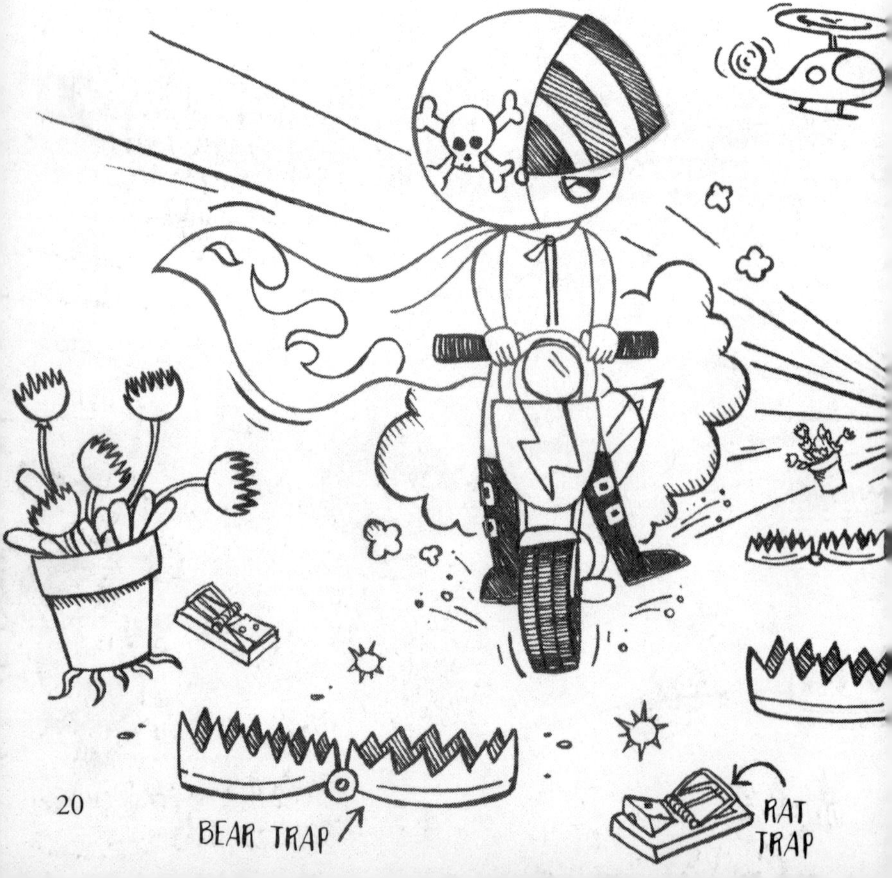
BEAR TRAP
RAT TRAP

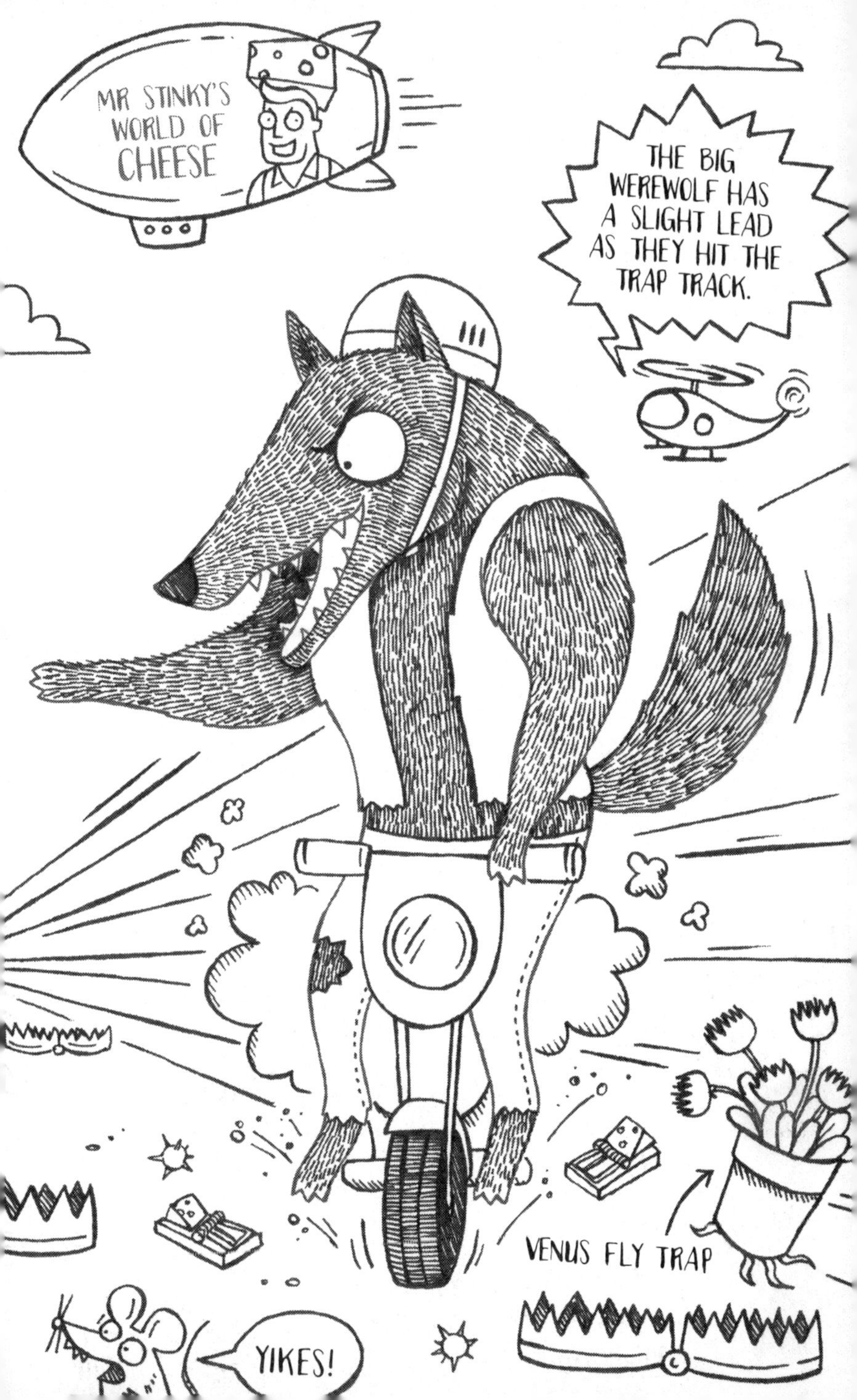
MR STINKY'S WORLD OF CHEESE
THE BIG WEREWOLF HAS A SLIGHT LEAD AS THEY HIT THE TRAP TRACK.
VENUS FLY TRAP
YIKES!

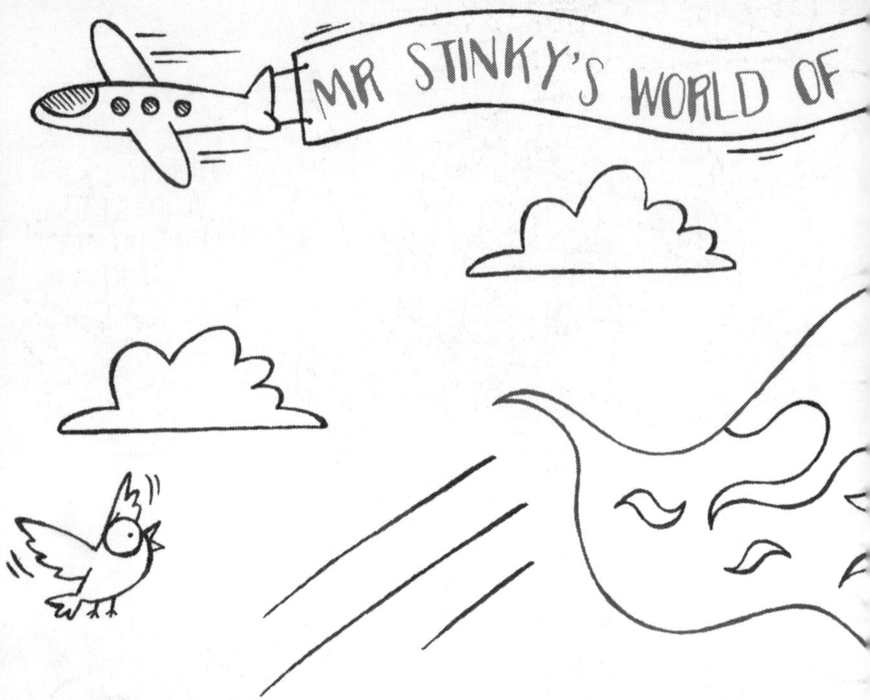
MR STINKY'S WORLD OF

'They don't call me Little Stunt Riding Hood, for nothing,' he giggled, jumping over the big werewolf.

'What a dirty show off!' the big werewolf leered at him.

'Smell you later, dog boy!' he replied, hitting the throttle and zooming off.

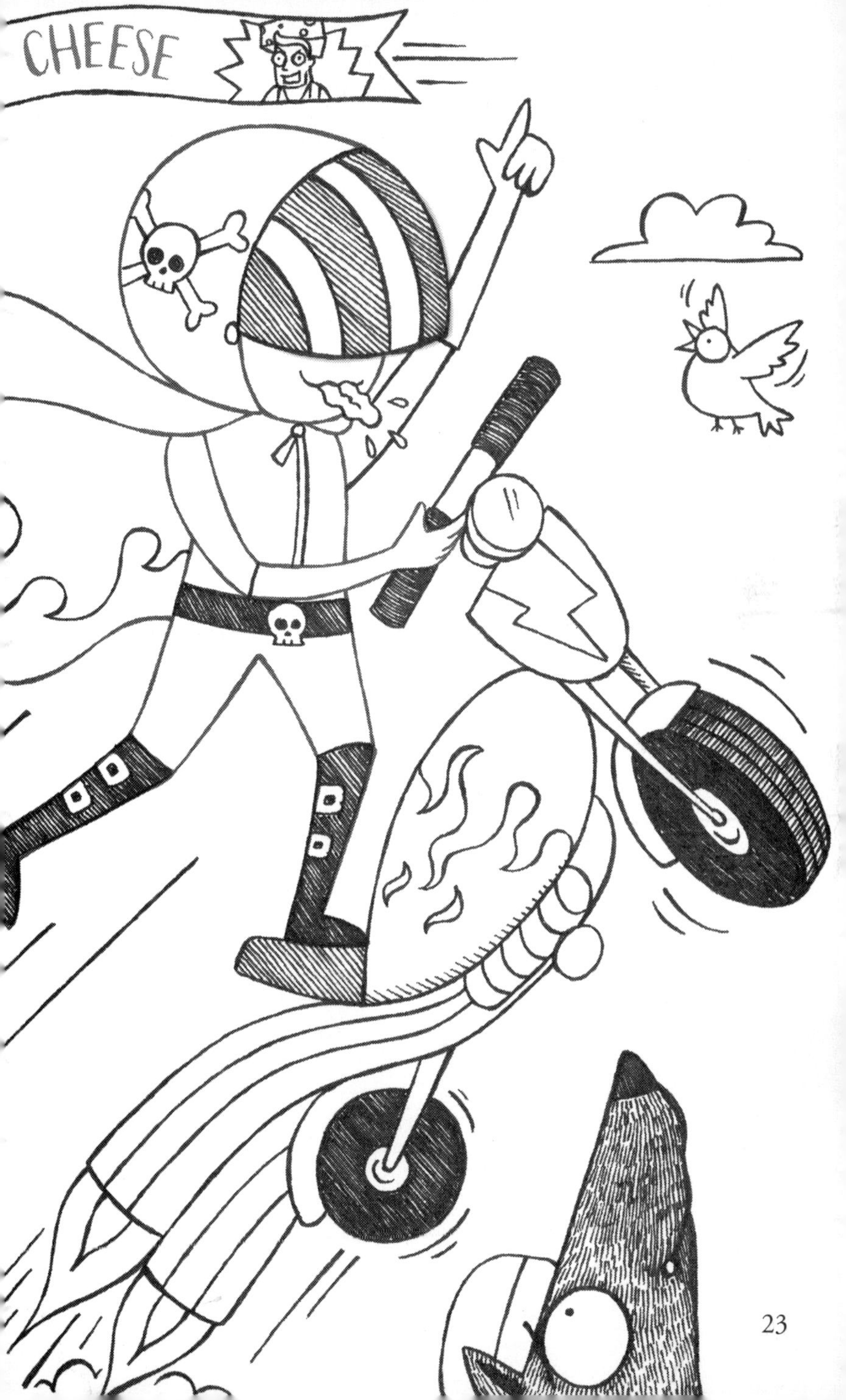
CHEESE

'Pray for mercy kid! I am so going to beat you this time!' the big werewolf yelled angrily.

'Pretty sure that I'm getting to Grandmaster's Cottage Cheese Factory first!' Little Stunt Riding Hood replied.

'You are truly out of your mind!' the big werewolf declared, all the while revving his turbo engine as much as it would take.

He would have rammed the hoodlum off the cliff, but he dared not in case any of the television cameras along the race track were filming. Instead, the conniving big werewolf resolved to wait for the perfect moment to cheat Little Stunt Riding Hood out of first place.

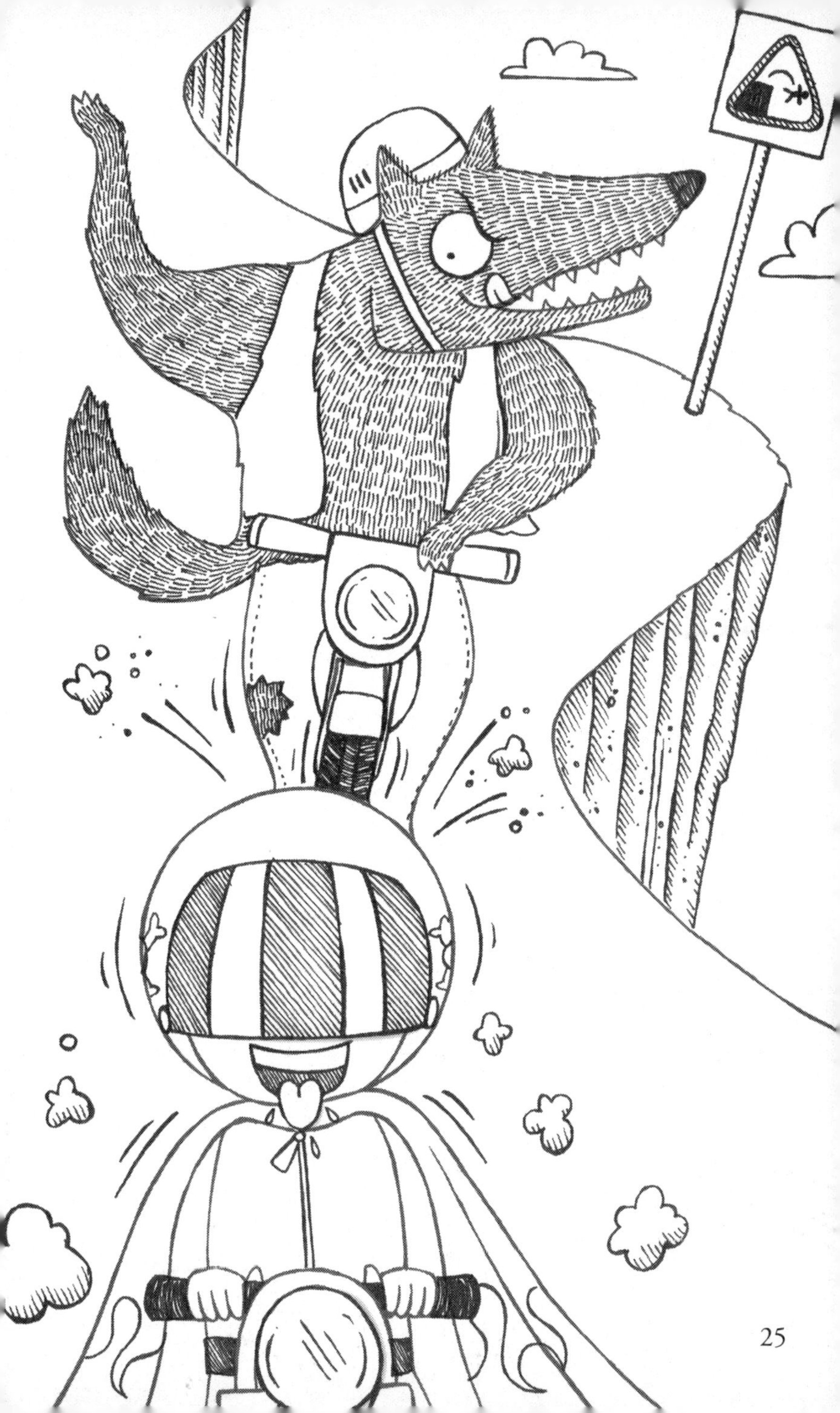

They continued speeding up the winding racetrack, the big werewolf following closely behind Little Stunt Riding Hood, as they jumped higher over the fiery volcanoes, through the billowing smoke and molten lava that left them melting in their boots.

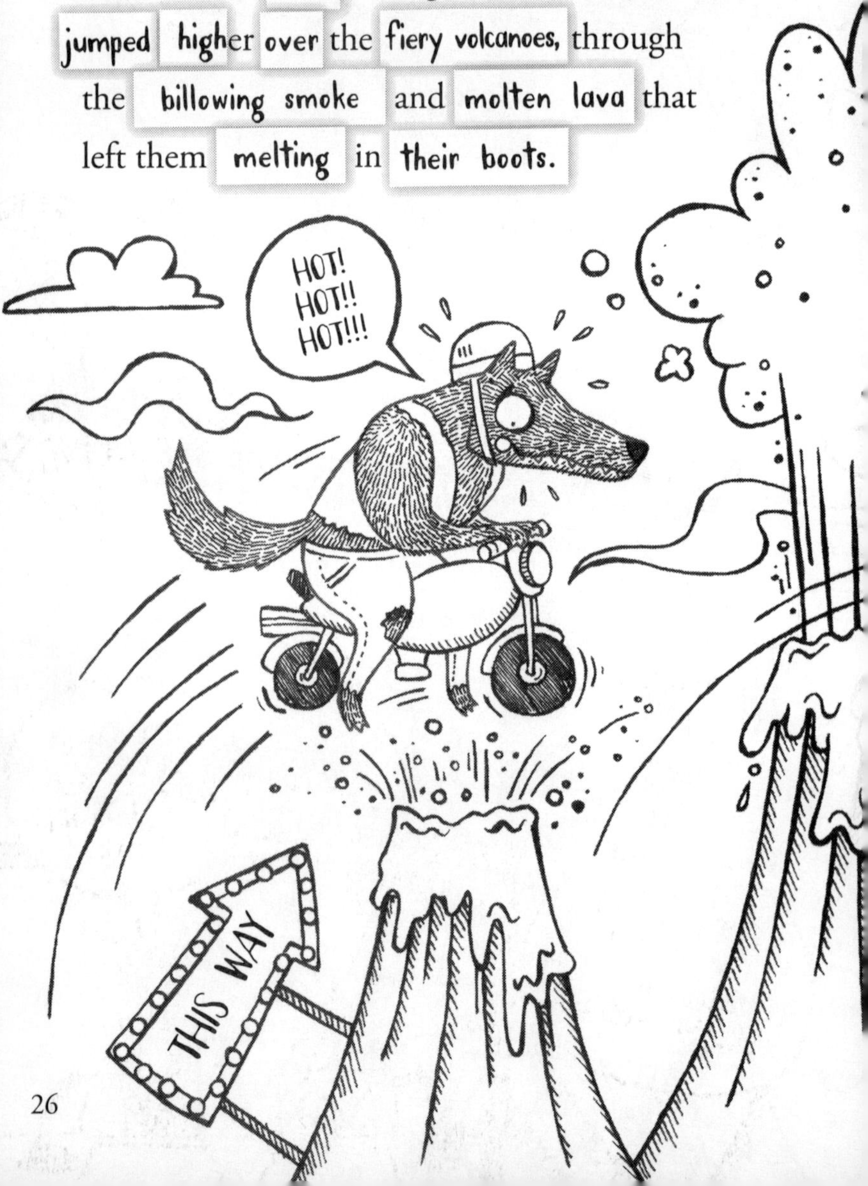
HOT!
HOT!!
HOT!!!
THIS WAY

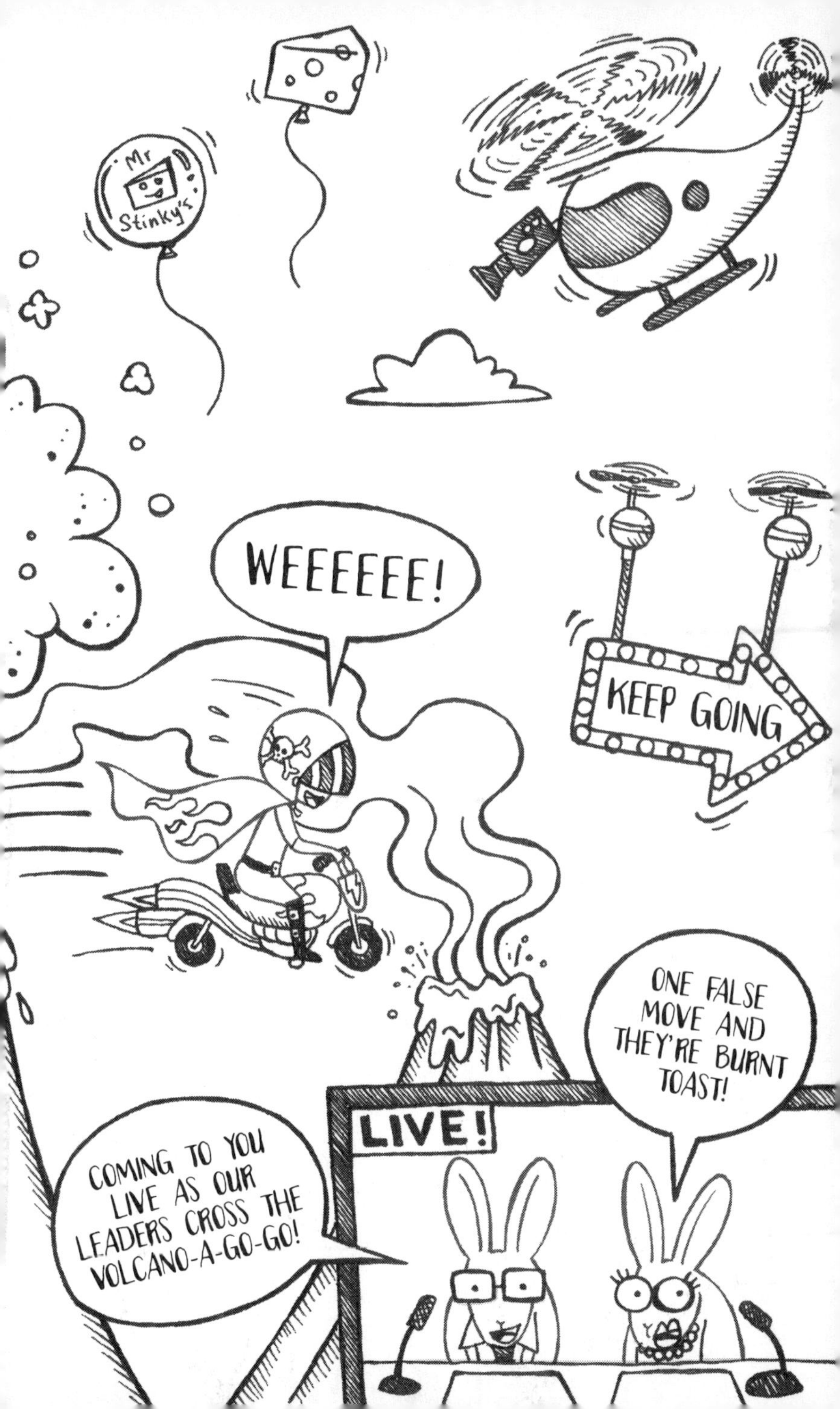
Mr Stinky's
WEEEEEE!
KEEP GOING
LIVE!
COMING TO YOU LIVE AS OUR LEADERS CROSS THE VOLCANO-A-GO-GO!
ONE FALSE MOVE AND THEY'RE BURNT TOAST!

They continued zooming along the bumpy racetrack, the big werewolf following closely behind Little Stunt Riding Hood, as they went deeper into the dark sewers, through the festering muck and stinky pipes that left them smeared in gross goop.

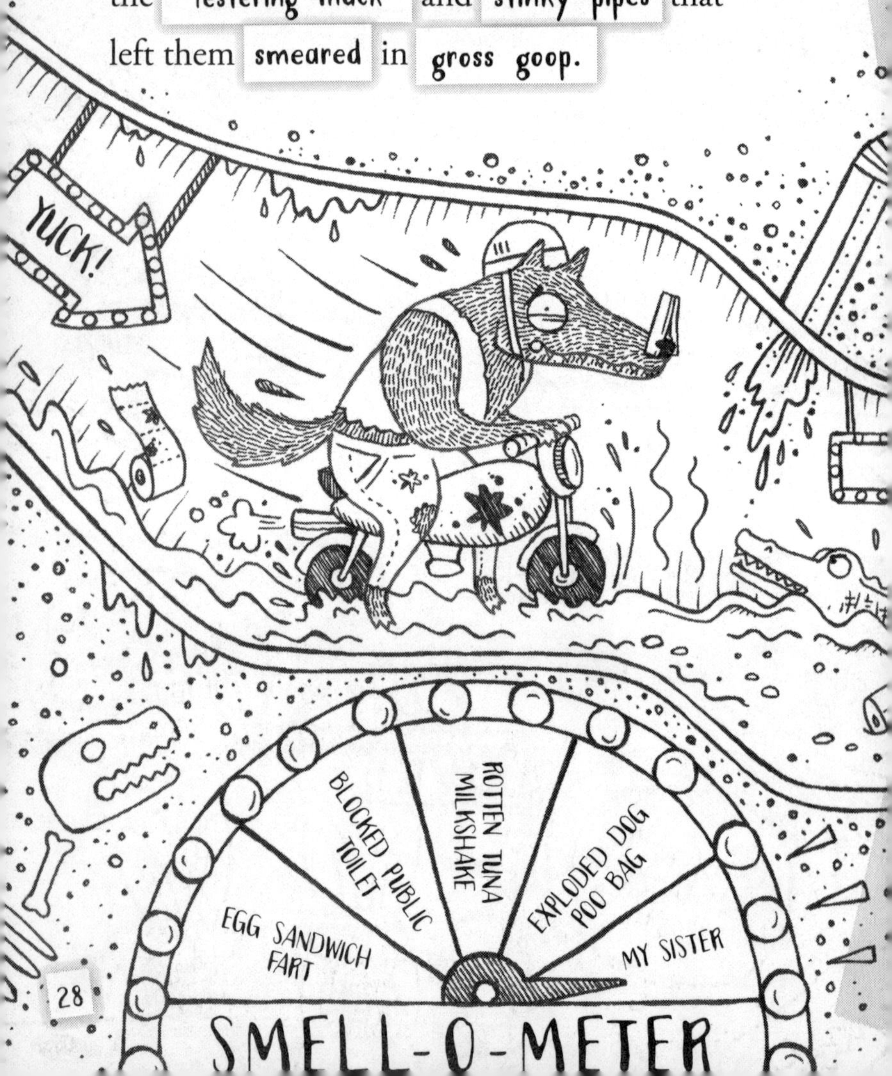
YUCK!
BLOCKED PUBLIC TOILET
ROTTEN TUNA MILKSHAKE
EXPLODED DOG POO BAG
EGG SANDWICH FART
MY SISTER
SMELL-O-METER

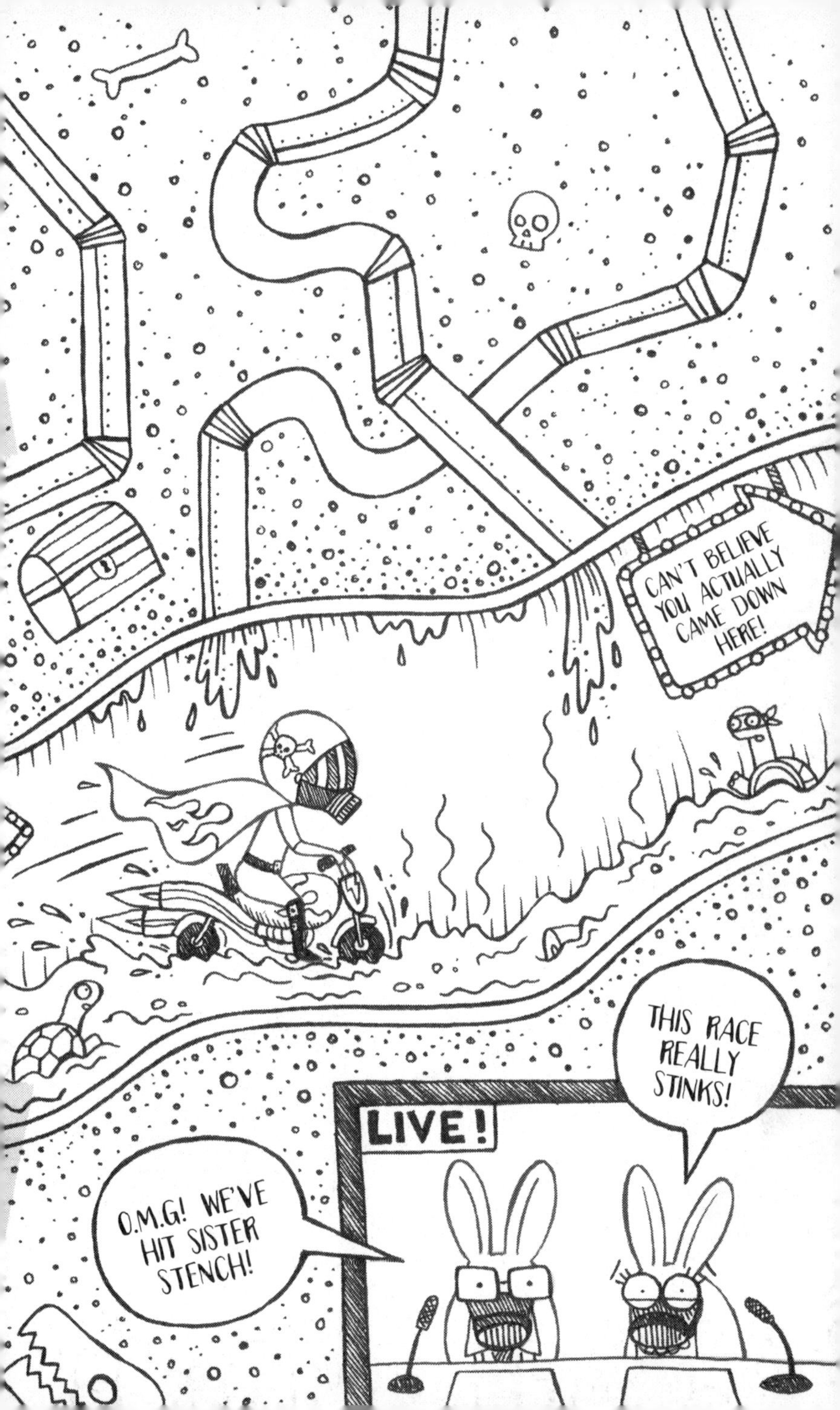
CAN'T BELIEVE YOU ACTUALLY CAME DOWN HERE!
O.M.G! WE'VE HIT SISTER STENCH!
THIS RACE REALLY STINKS!
LIVE!

They continued swerving along the slippery race track, the big werewolf skidding closely behind Little Stunt Riding Hood, as they drifted wildly into the banana peel factory, the coconut oil store and sunscreen plant that left them sliding in slooshy slickness.

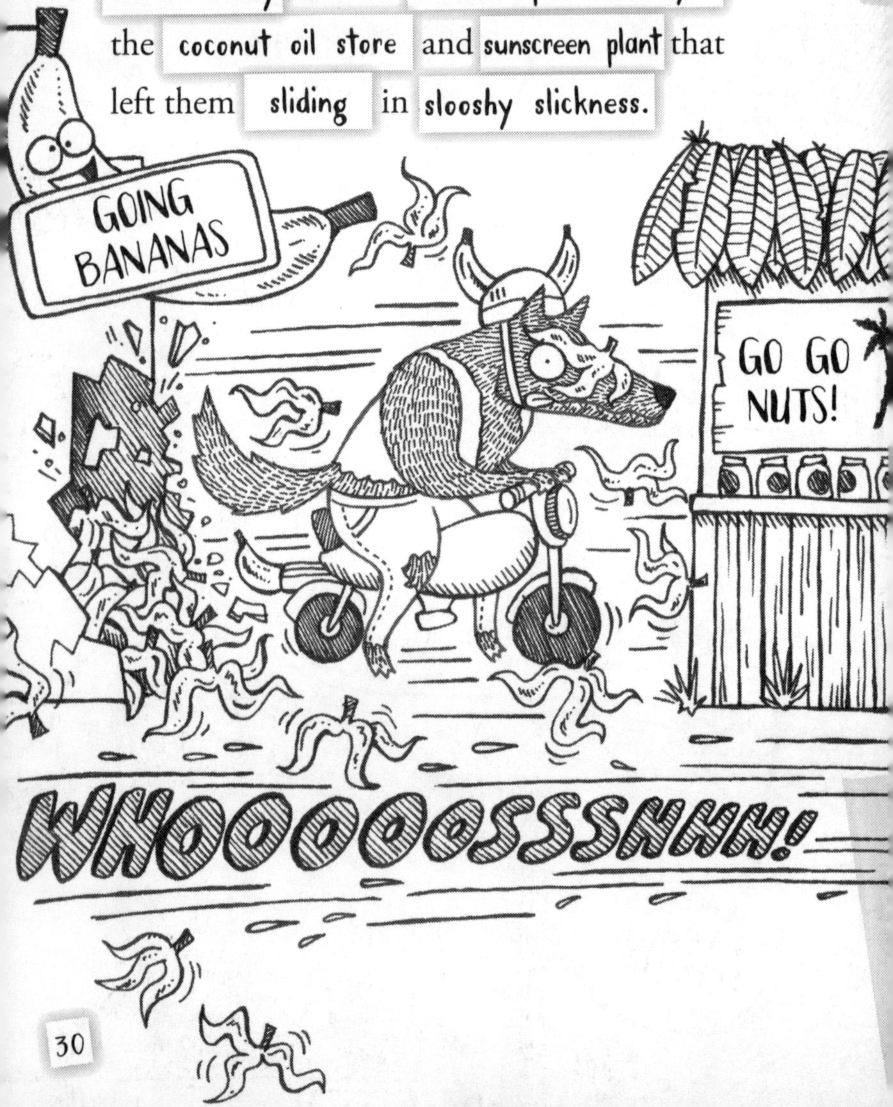
GOING BANANAS
GO GO NUTS!
WHOOOOOSSSHHH!

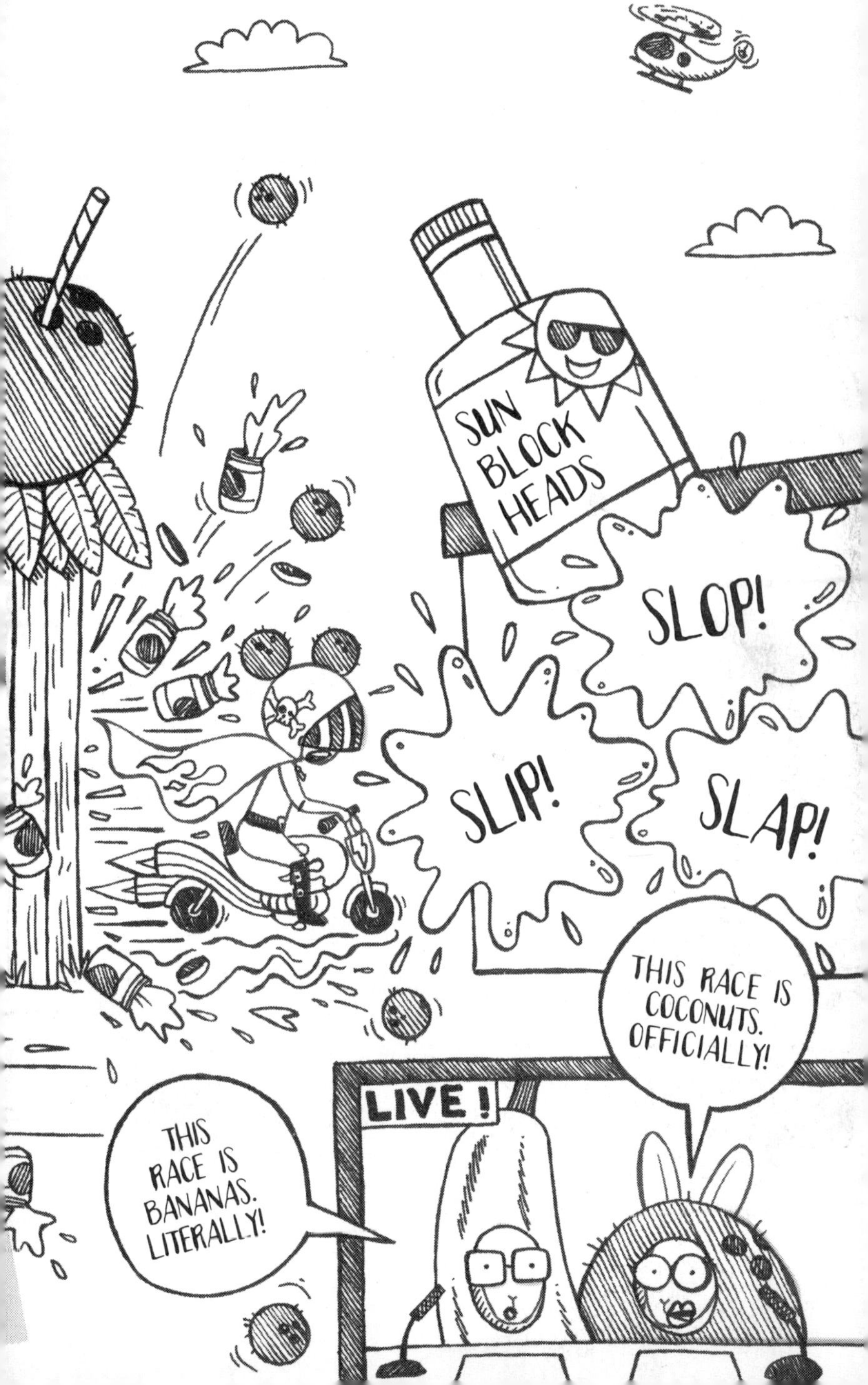
SUN BLOCK HEADS
SLOP!
SLIP!
SLAP!
THIS RACE IS COCONUTS. OFFICIALLY!
LIVE!
THIS RACE IS BANANAS. LITERALLY!

They continued whizzing along the scary racetrack, the big werewolf yelping closely behind Little Stunt Riding Hood, as they went howling into the chainsaw testing facility, the shaver supermarket and scissors shop that gave them radical new haircuts.

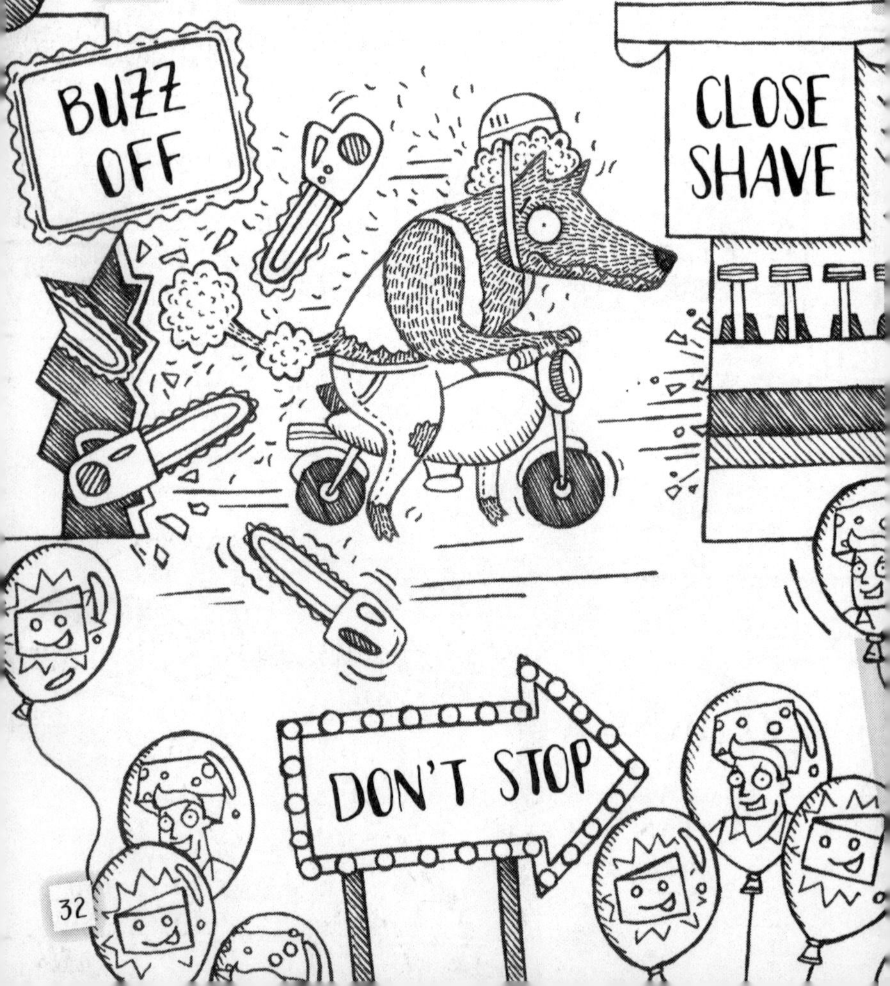
BUZZ OFF
CLOSE SHAVE
DON'T STOP

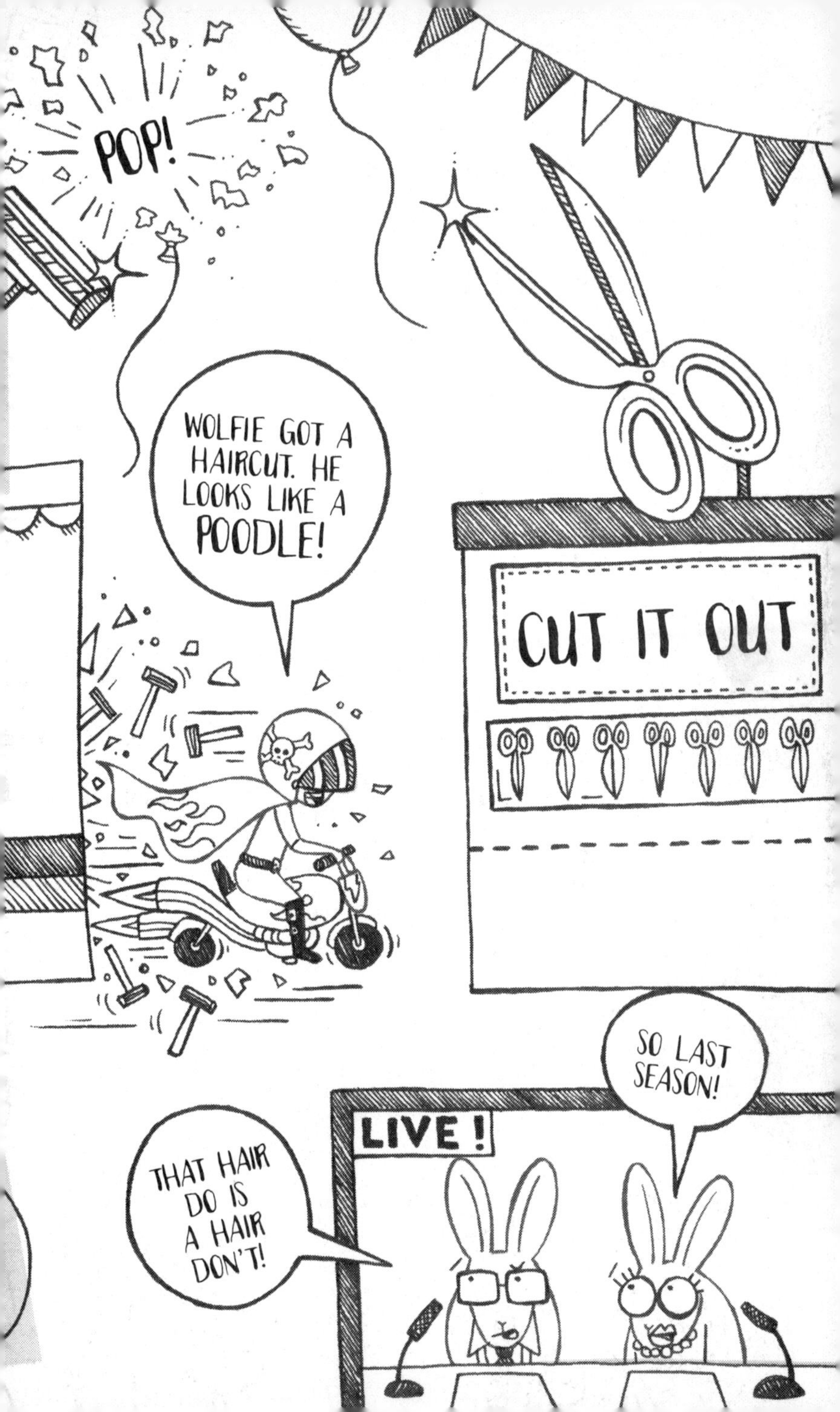
POP!
WOLFIE GOT A HAIRCUT. HE LOOKS LIKE A POODLE!
CUT IT OUT
SO LAST SEASON!
LIVE!
THAT HAIR DO IS A HAIR DON'T!

They continued screaming along the freaky race track, the big werewolf wailing closely behind Little Stunt Riding Hood, as they went deeper into the cursed cemetery, through a zombie apocalypse and a clown school that left them mentally scarred and unable to attend a circus ever again.

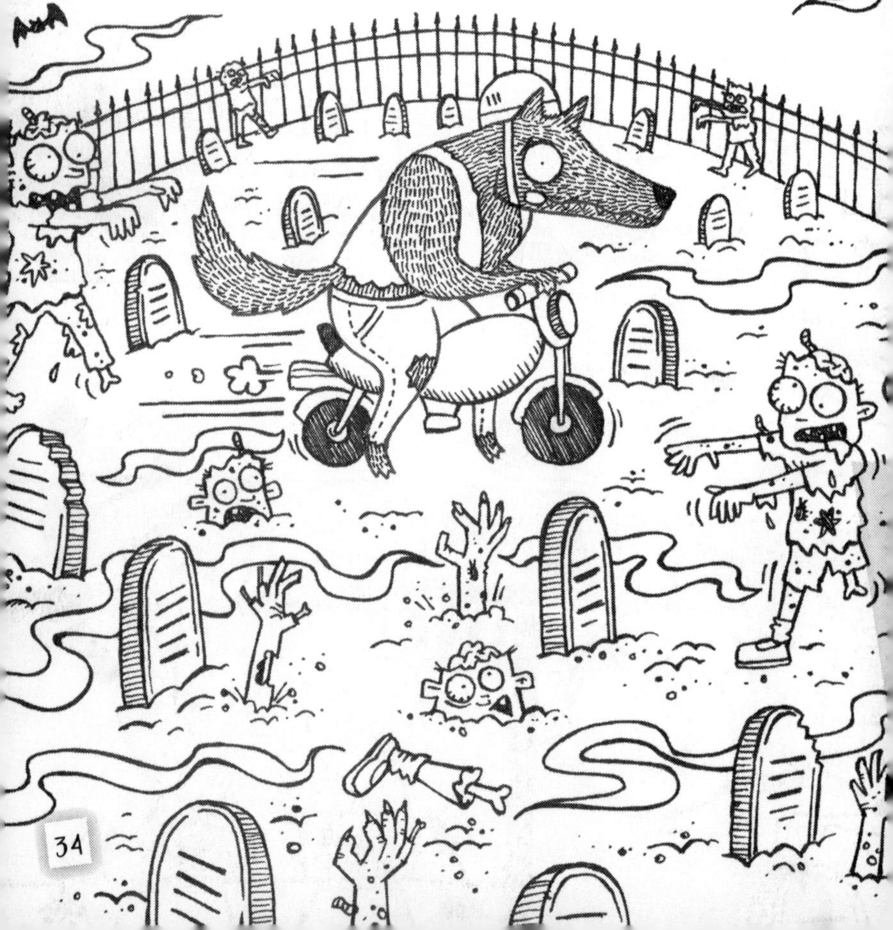

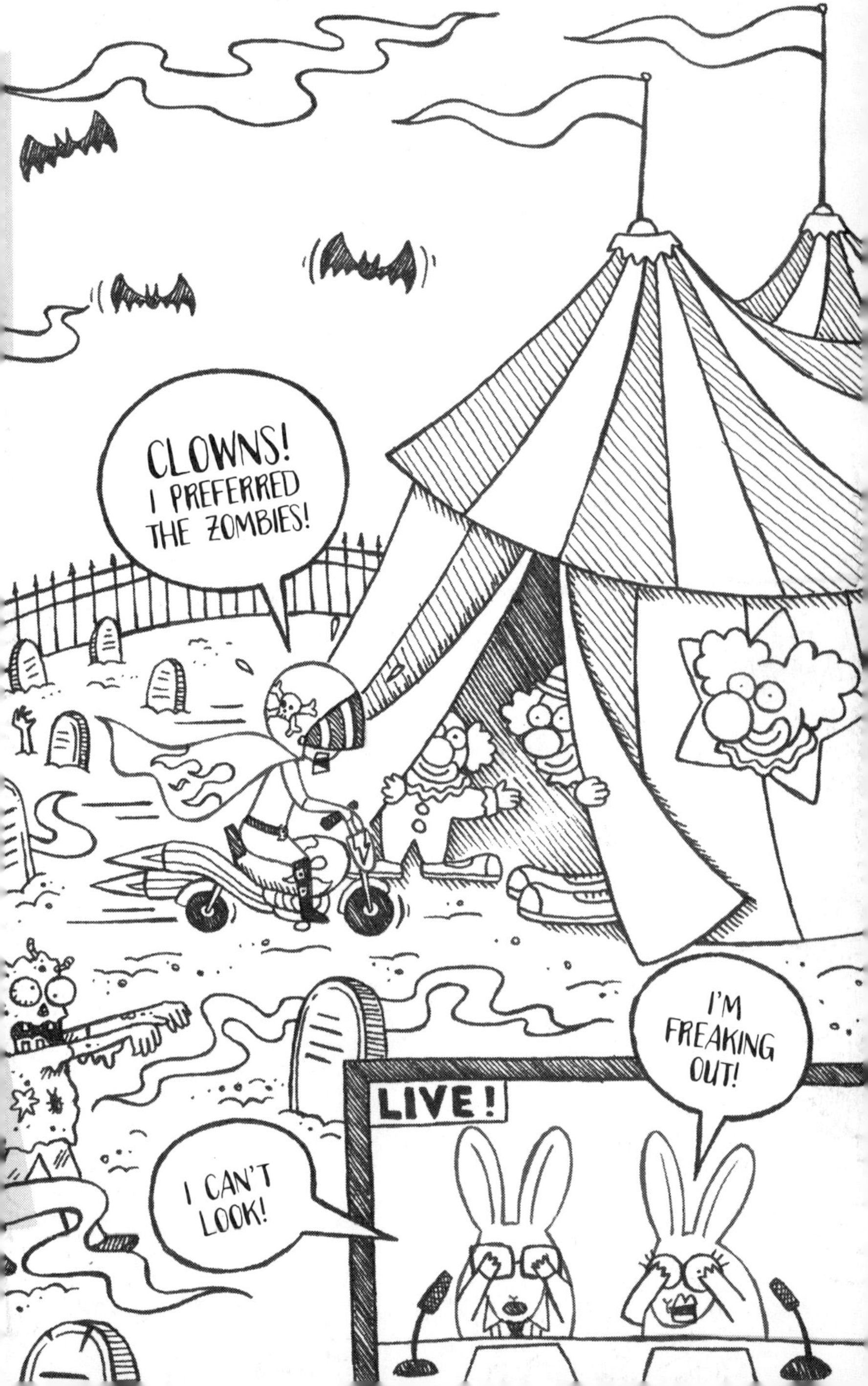
CLOWNS! I PREFERRED THE ZOMBIES!
I'M FREAKING OUT!
LIVE!
I CAN'T LOOK!

They continued barrelling along the whacky racetrack, the big werewolf following closely behind Little Stunt Riding Hood, as they went around and around in circles through the flaming, oversized hamster wheels that left them seared with scorch marks.

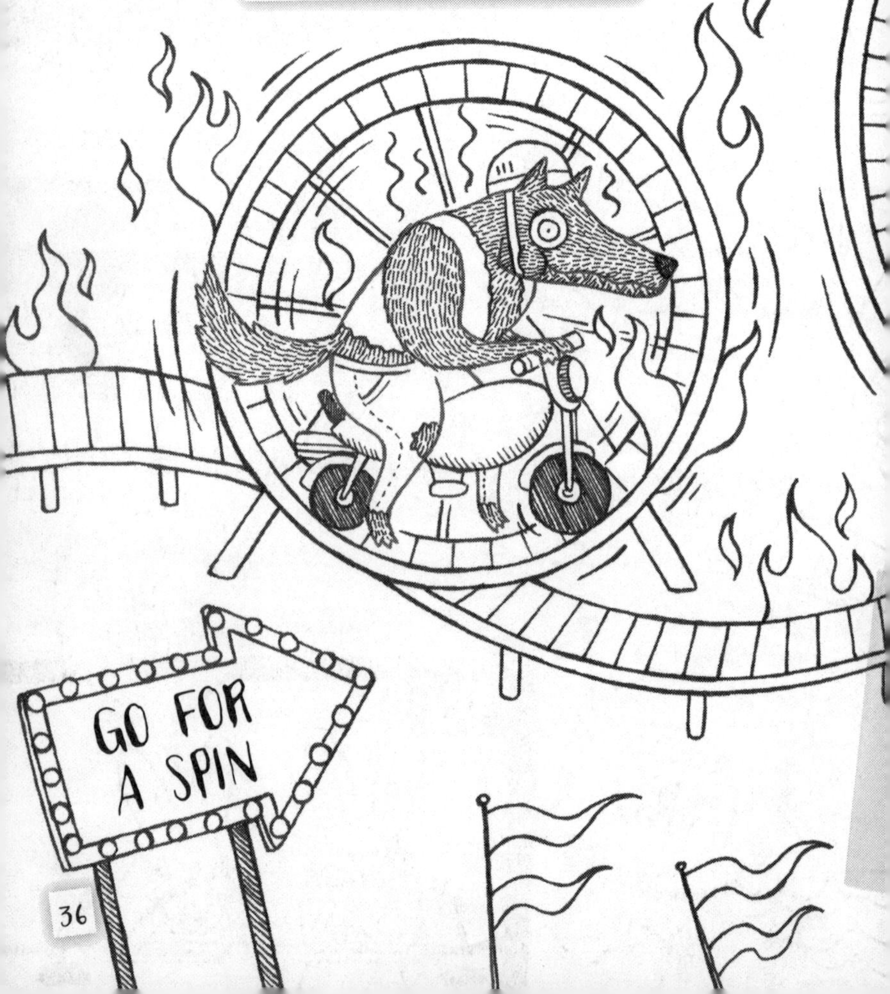
GO FOR A SPIN

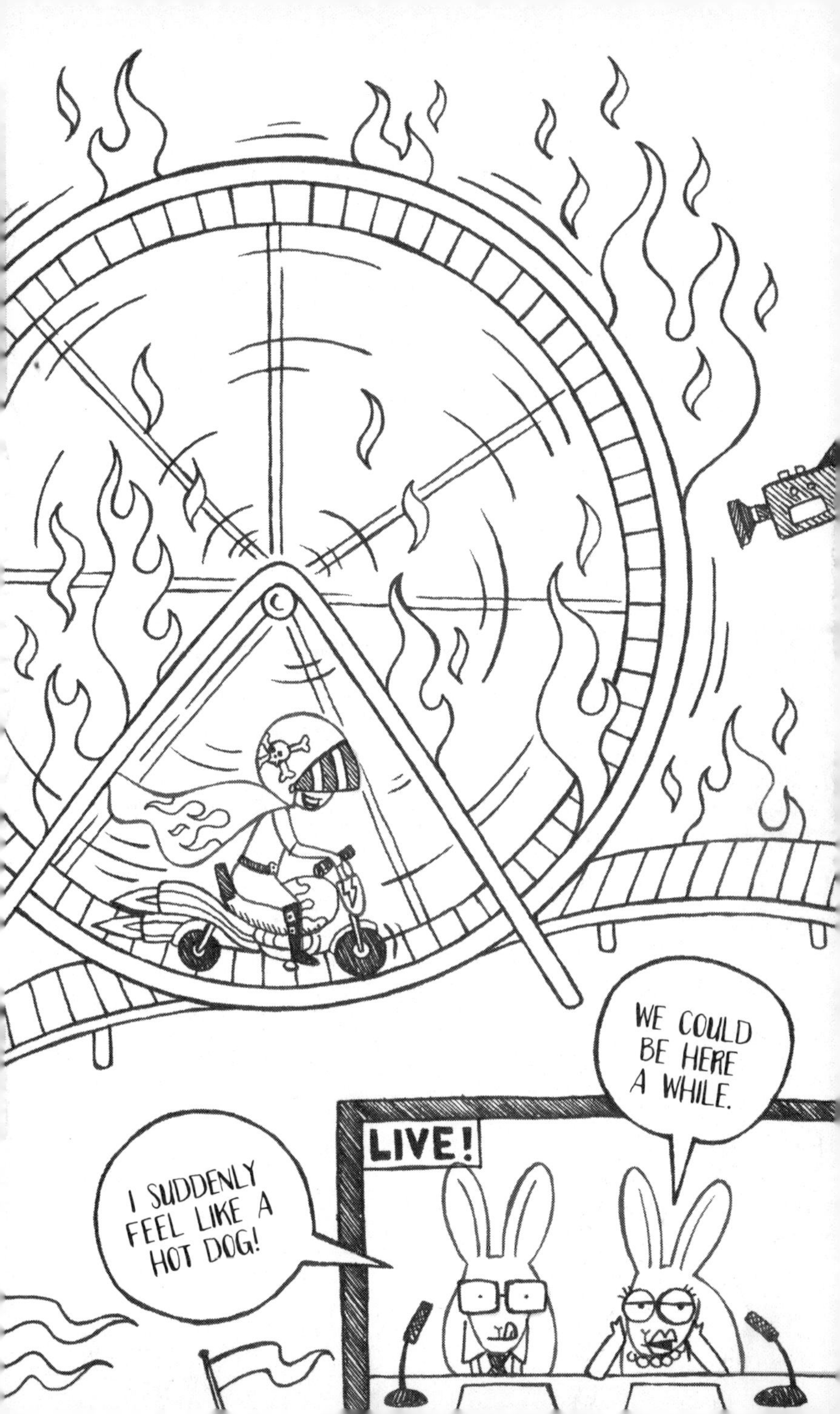
LIVE!
I SUDDENLY FEEL LIKE A HOT DOG!
WE COULD BE HERE A WHILE.

They continued tearing along the deadly racetrack, the big werewolf following closely behind Little Stunt Riding Hood, as they sped faster into the next stage, through the echidna petting zoo and cactus farm that left them covered in painful prickles.

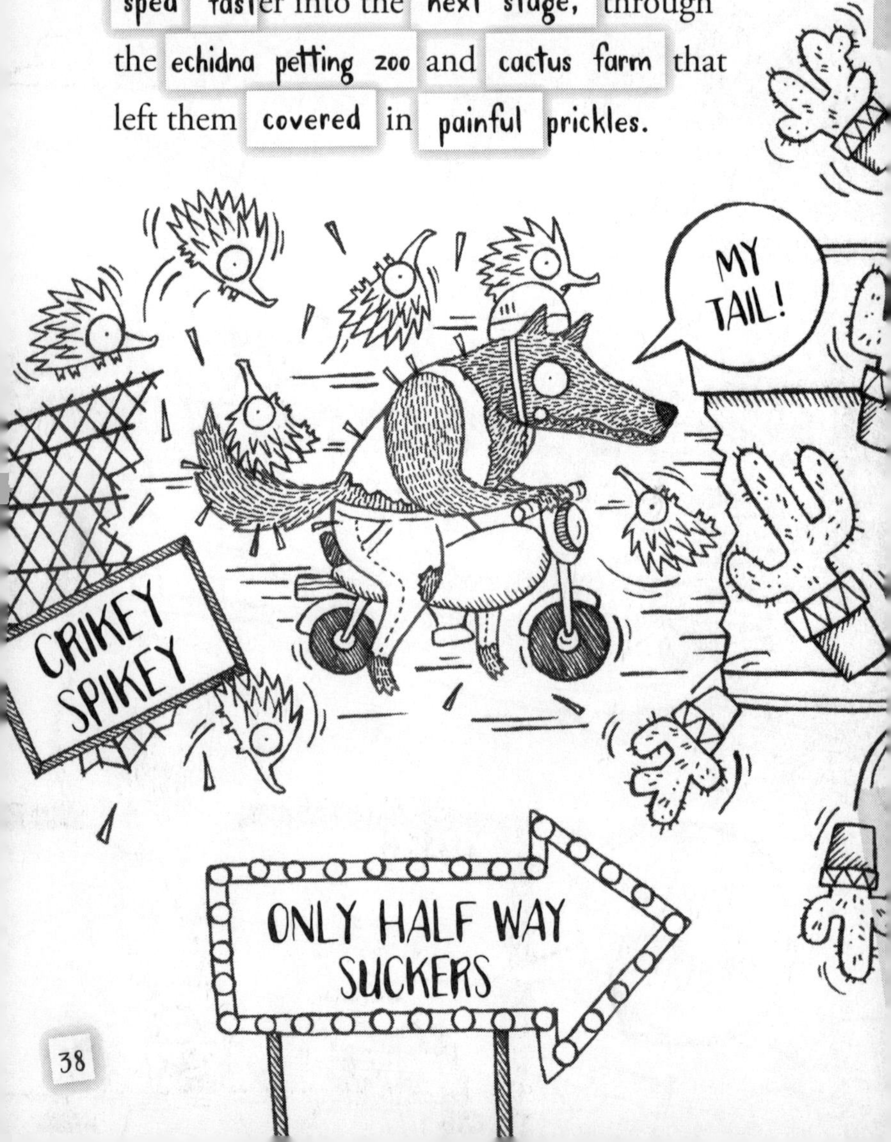
MY TAIL!
CRIKEY SPIKEY
ONLY HALF WAY SUCKERS

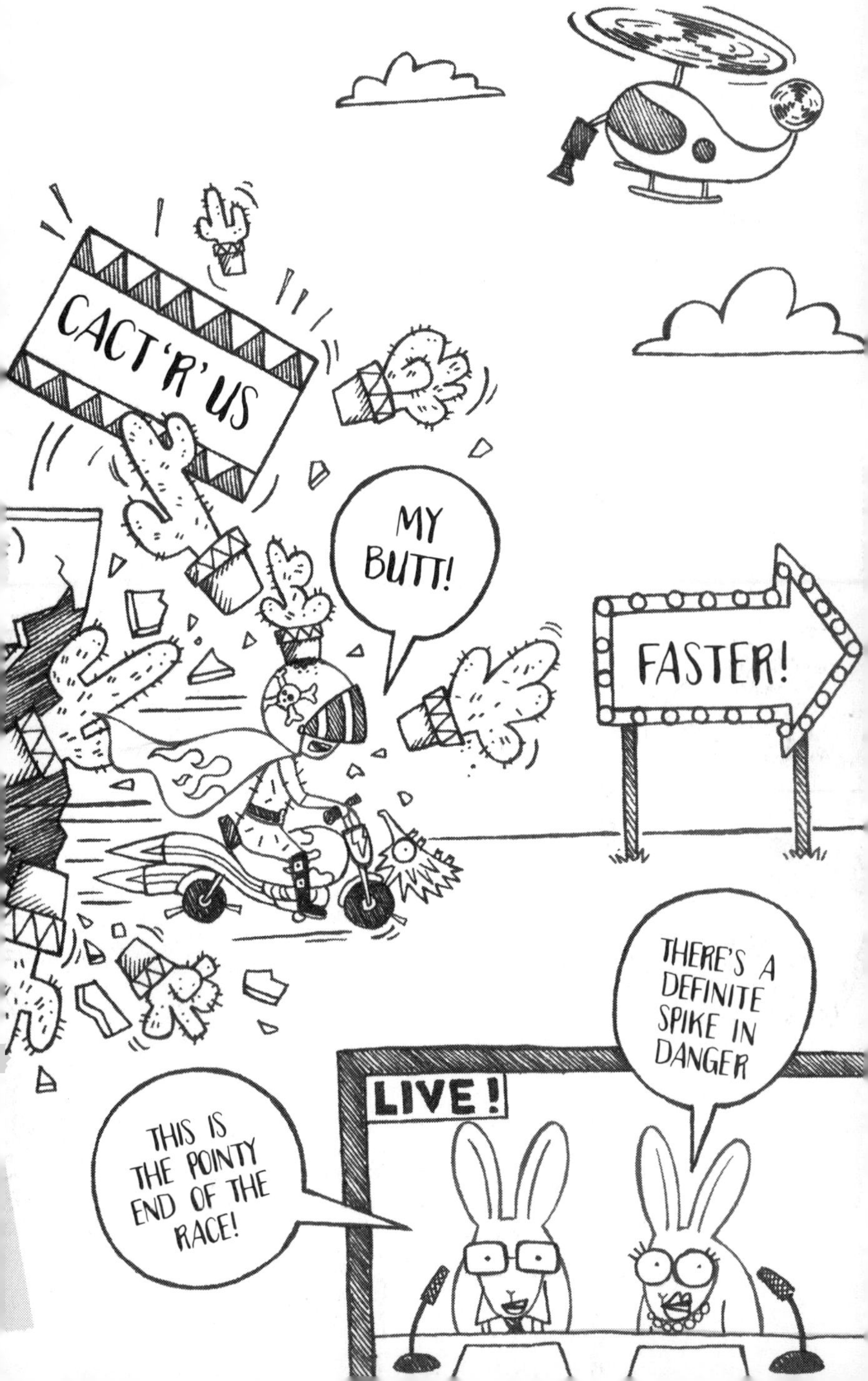
CACT'R'US
MY BUTT!
FASTER!
THERE'S A DEFINITE SPIKE IN DANGER
LIVE!
THIS IS THE POINTY END OF THE RACE!

'See Little Stunt Riding Hood,' the big werewolf said. 'You haven't beaten me yet! I can almost hear the crowd singing, "Hoodie is a has-been! Hoodie is a has-been!"

'Why don't you give up now, you loser! Enjoy second place and enjoy the flat tyre, punk!' the big werewolf said, pointing to the echidna spikes poking out of the back wheel.

'Dang!' yelled Little Stunt Riding Hood, and she stopped to pluck the spikes from the tyre.

With the young kid preoccupied with patching his flat tyre, the big werewolf quickly sped off ahead, for he knew a secret short cut to Grandmaster's Cottage Cheese Factory.

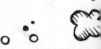

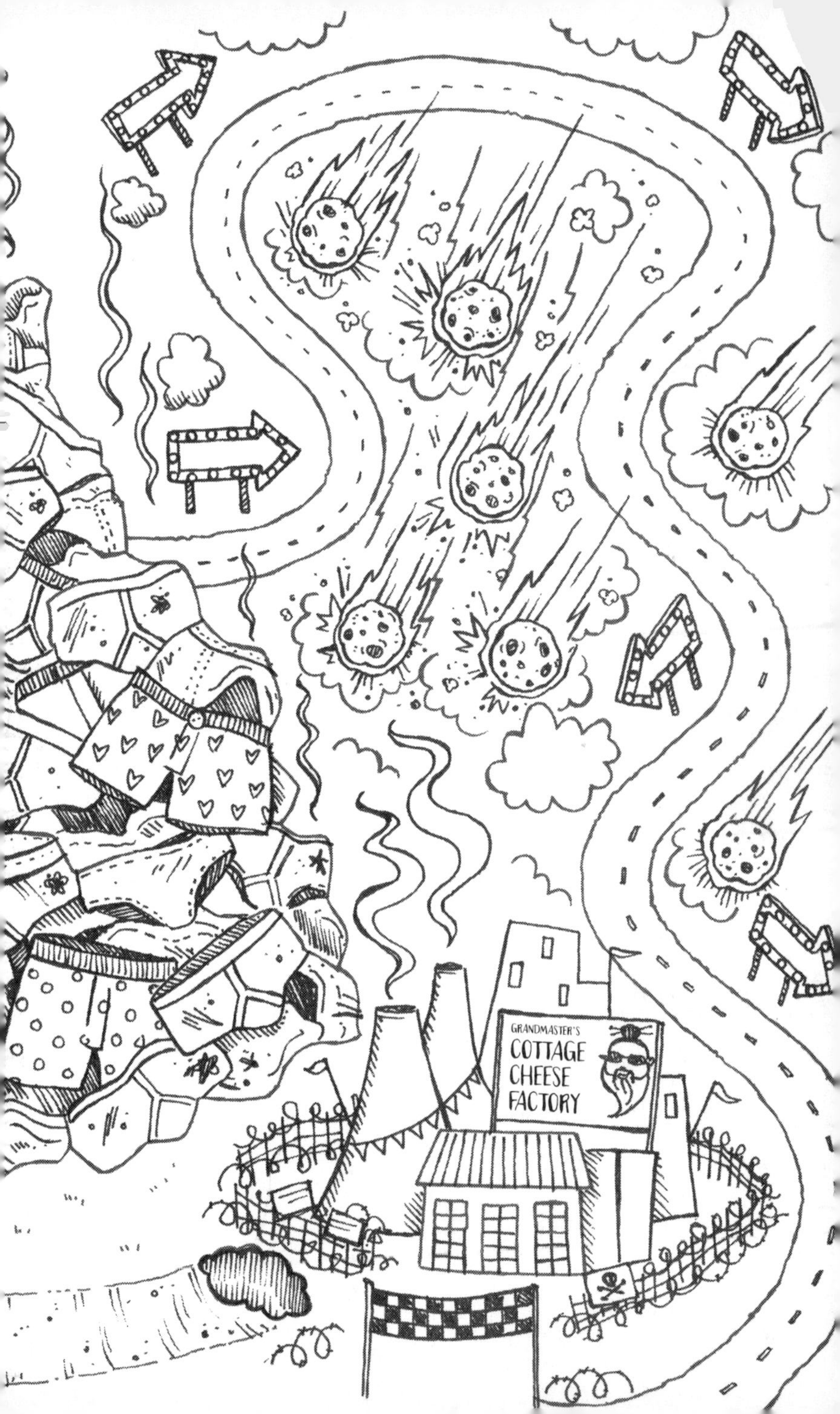
GRANDMASTER'S
COTTAGE
CHEESE
FACTORY

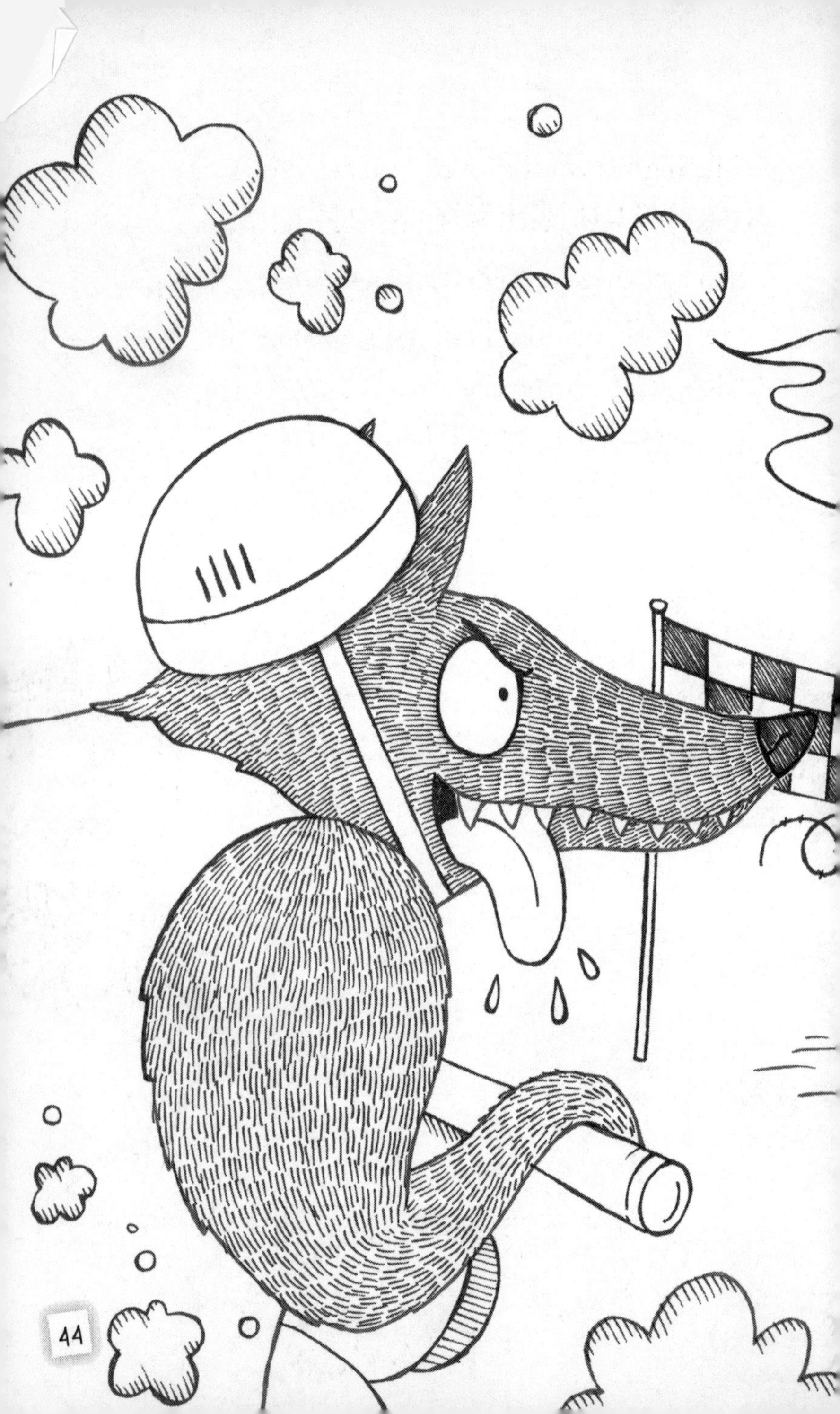

The big we[...] arrived at Grandmaster's Cottage Ch[...]ctory before the television crew had a cha[...] get there and start filming. He park[...]he finish line, waiting for his triumpha[...]-up.

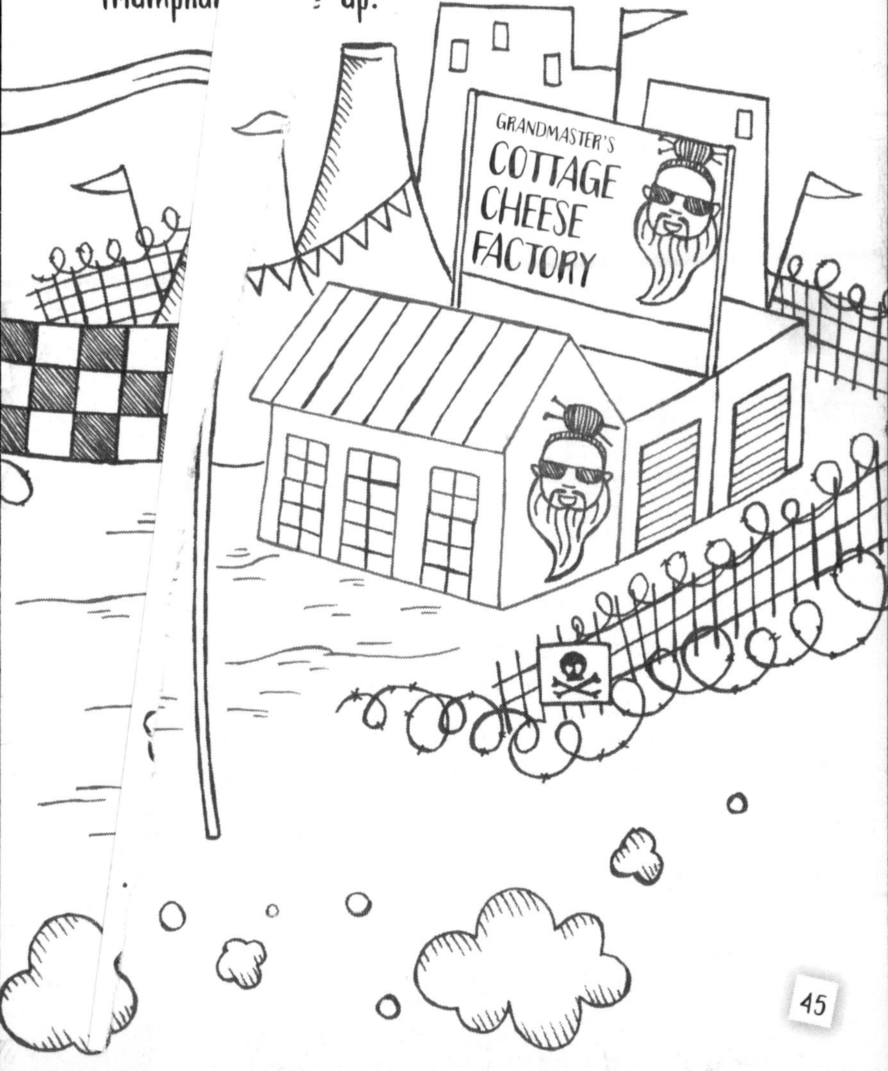
GRANDMASTER'S
COTTAGE
CHEESE
FACTORY

'Who's there?' called the raspy voice of an old man from inside the Cottage Cheese Factory.

'Not Little Stunt Riding Hood,' replied the big werewolf. 'That's for sure. He's way behind. I'm the big werewolf, by the way. But you can call me Wolfie! I'm a big fan of yours!'

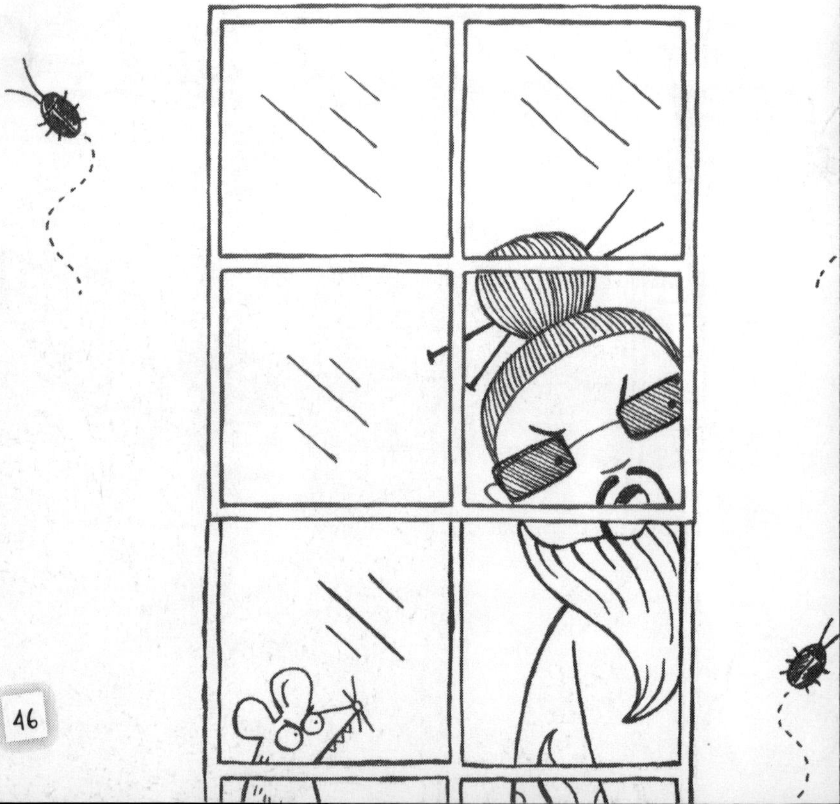

'May I come in to your Cottage Cheese Factory, Grandmaster? I'm desperate to pee! It's been too long since I last went to the toilet. I'm busting! And the TV crew are going to take ages to get ready. I'm rambling I know. I'm just so excited to meet you and to be here and I seriously can't hold it much longer!'

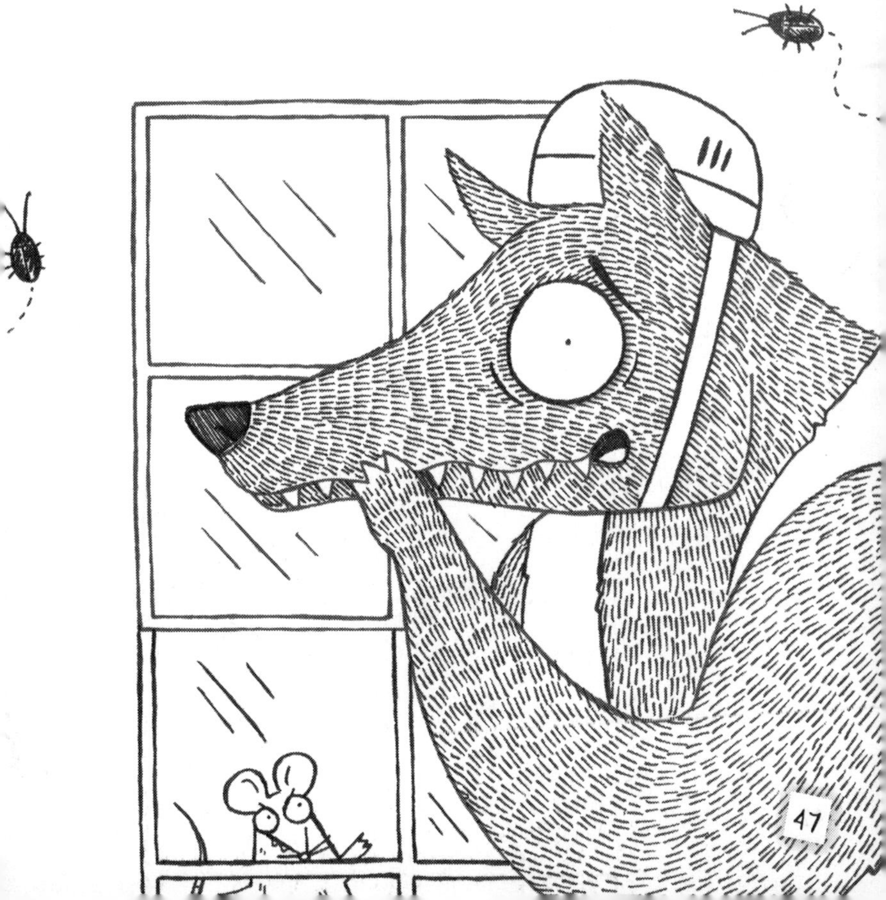

'Of course,' the Grandmaster replied. 'Just down the hallway and the loo is on the left. It's a bit smelly in there though, sorry!'

The big werewolf followed the directions, almost springing a leak. He raced past the Grandmaster, who only had the chance to cry, 'What a weirdo!' before the big werewolf disappeared to do his business.

The Grandmaster then climbed into his king-sized waterbed for a quick power nap, awaiting the other riders and TV crew.

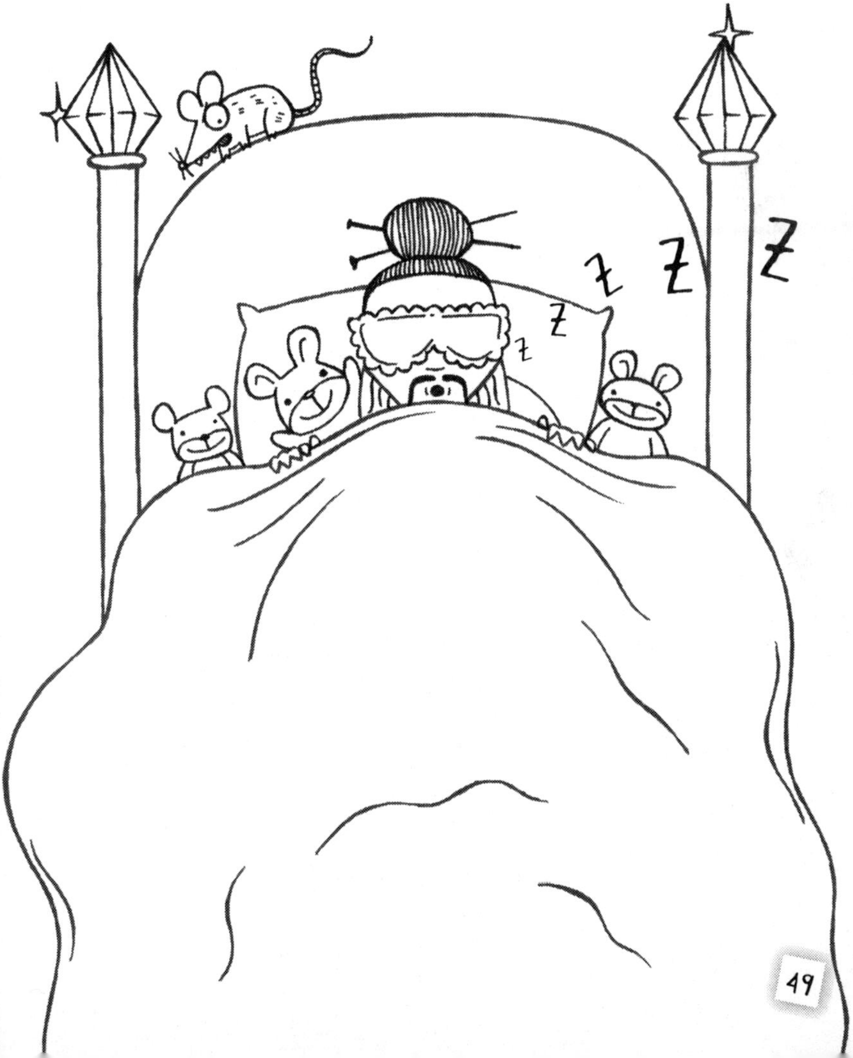
Z
Z
Z
Z
Z

Meanwhile, Little Stunt Riding Hood had patched more holes than he could count. He remembered what his manager had said about coming first and he set off again on the racetrack, riding as fast as he could.

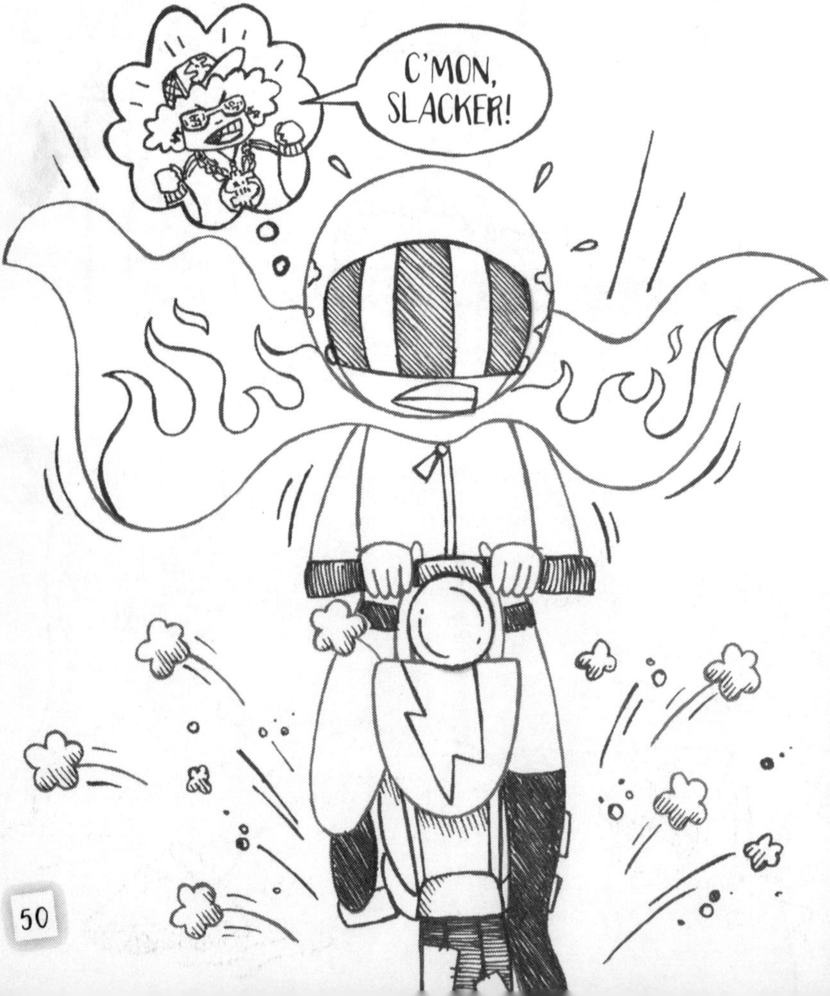
C'MON, SLACKER!

First, [redacted]he crossed the river of toxic waste on a rickety bridge, the slime shimmering beneath him. A mutant piranha popped its head out of the ooze to take a quick bite.

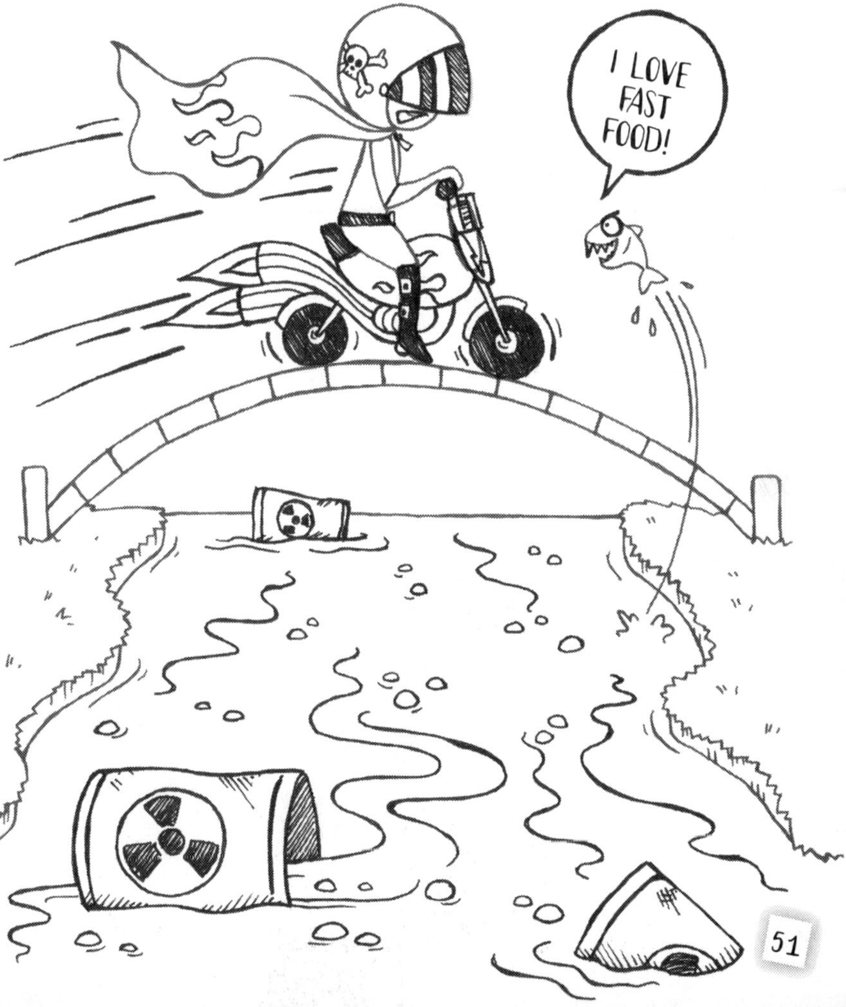
I LOVE FAST FOOD!

Next, he continued on the road around the base of the towering mountain of dirty undies. It was a smell to behold, filled with stains and skidmarks that made his eyes water in terror.

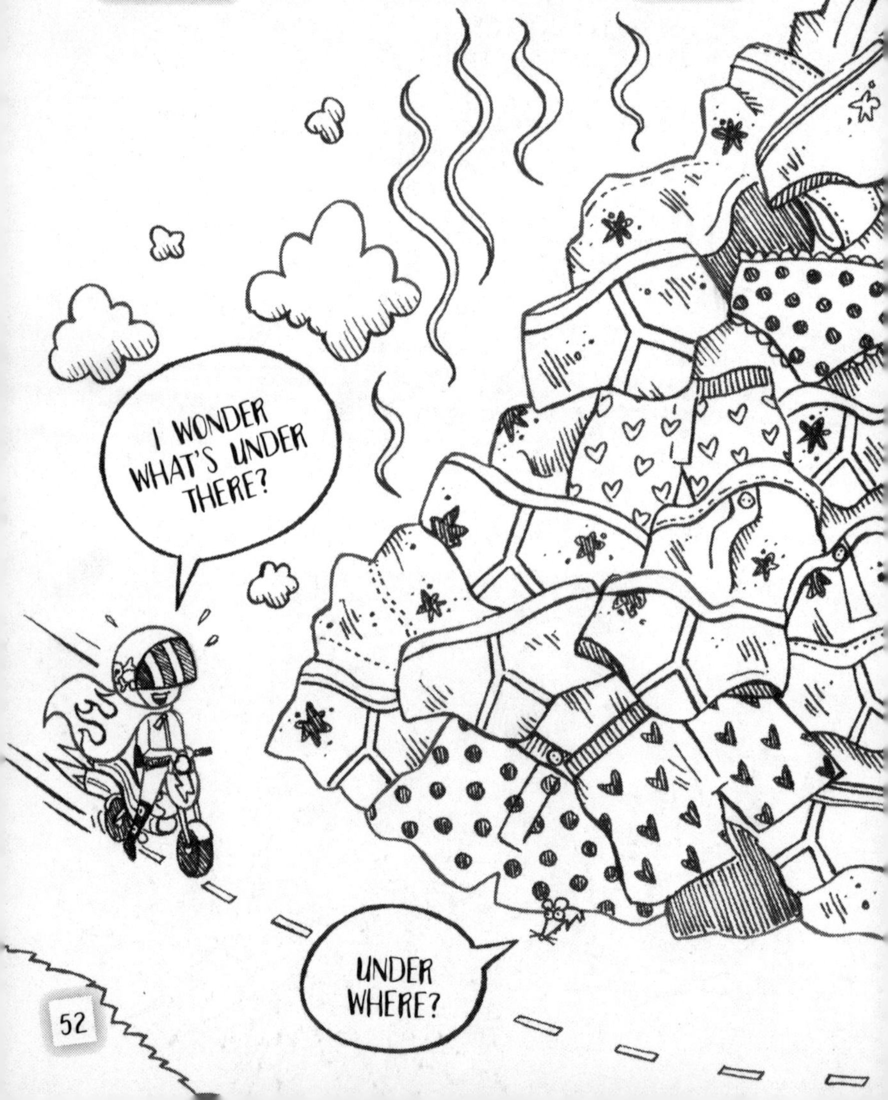
I WONDER WHAT'S UNDER THERE?
UNDER WHERE?

Then she travelled through the deadly shower of random meteorites. He weaved through the explosions, shouting rude words at the top of his voice.

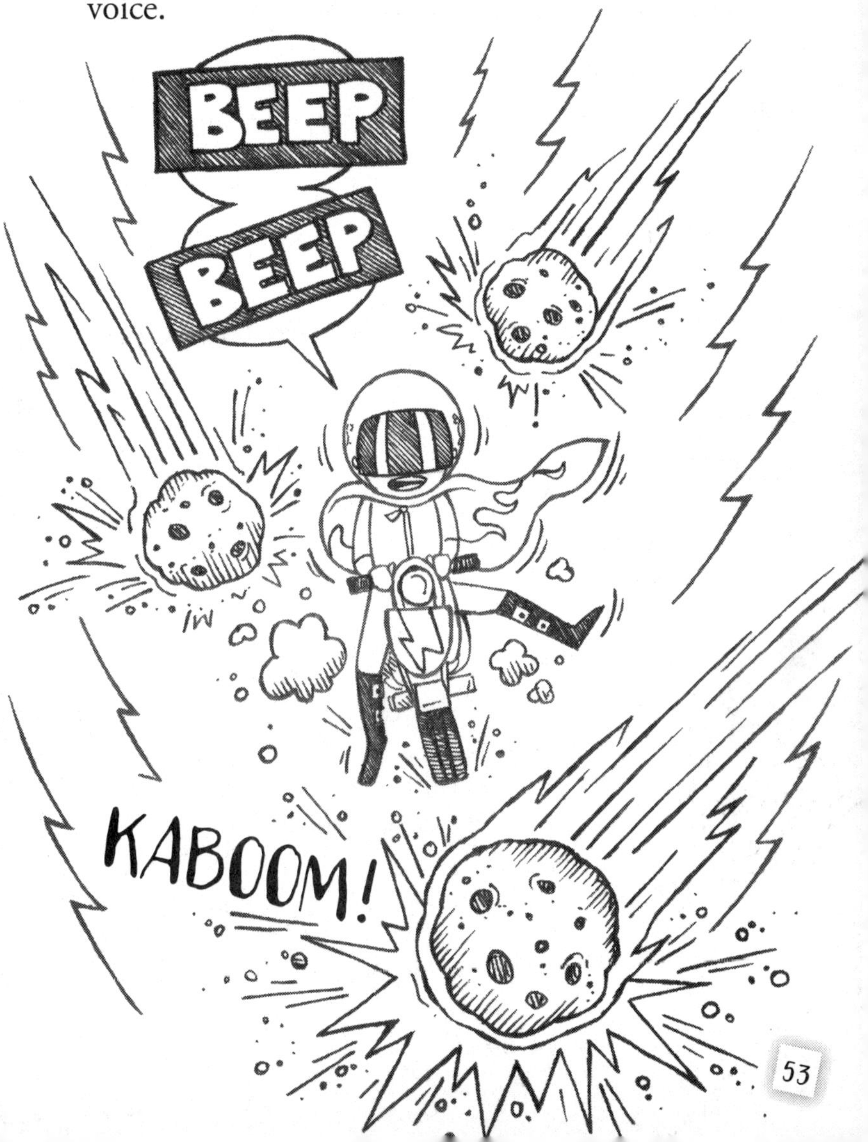
BEEP
BEEP
KABOOM!

And then, in the distance, Little Stunt Riding Hood saw the finish line – Grandmaster's Cottage Cheese Factory! It was a huge building surrounded by barbed wire and warning signs, but there was no trace of any people, anywhere. No crowds. No TV crew. Nobody at all. Something was fishier than All You Can Eat Fish Finger Fridays at Fishy McFishalicious' Seafood Family Restaurant!

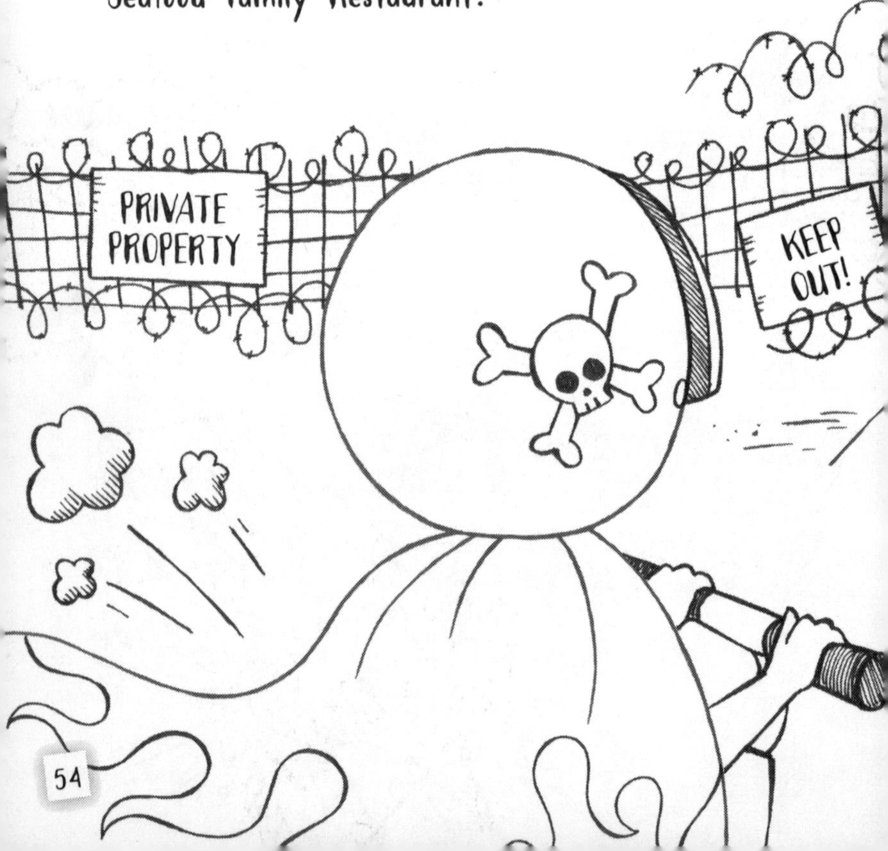
PRIVATE PROPERTY
KEEP OUT!

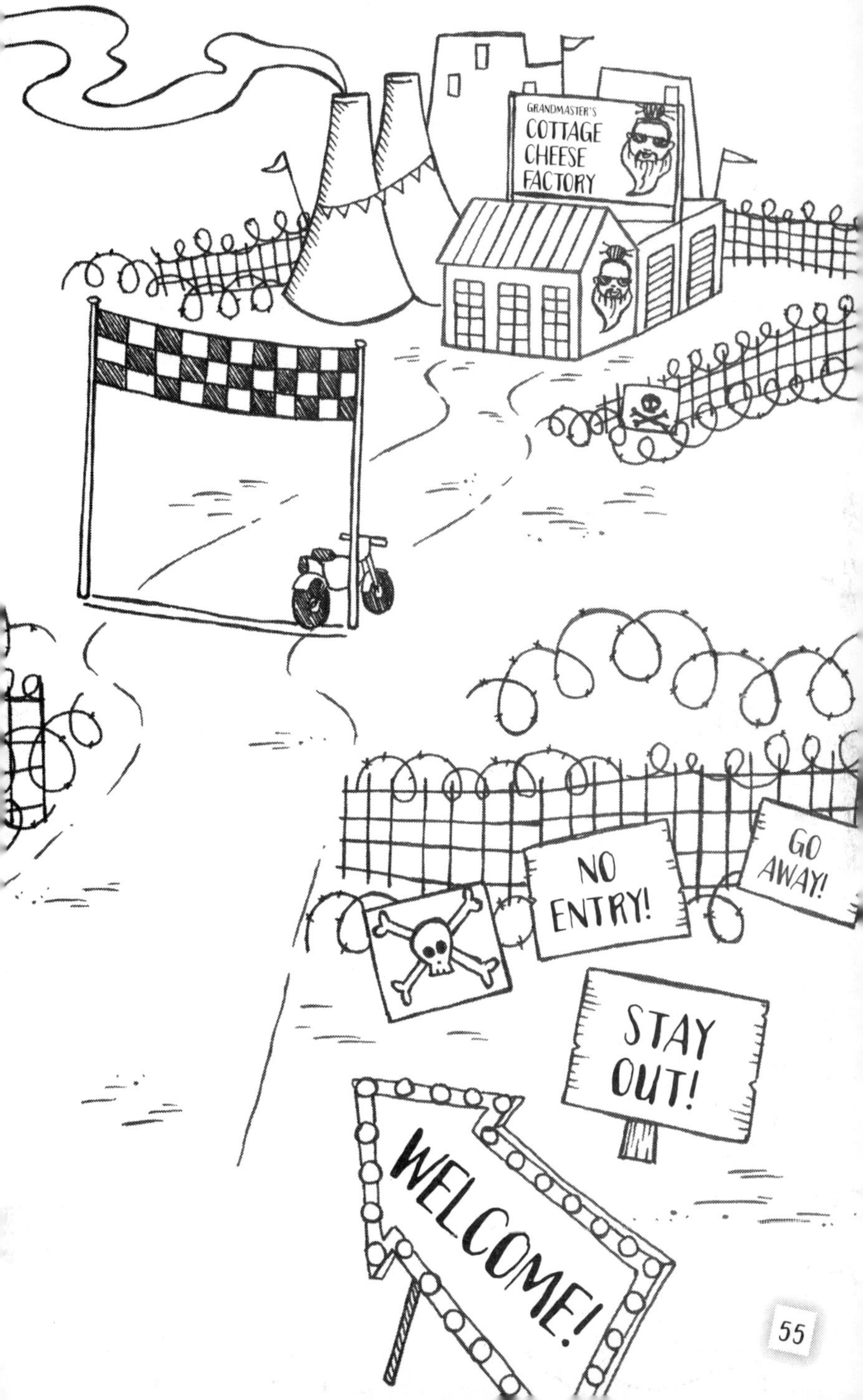
GRANDMASTER'S
COTTAGE CHEESE FACTORY
NO ENTRY!
GO AWAY!
STAY OUT!
WELCOME!

He zoomed up the racetrack to the finish line and was surprised to find the werewolf's bike abandoned. Sensing something wasn't quite right, he paused before walking cautiously over to the front door of the Cottage Cheese Factory.

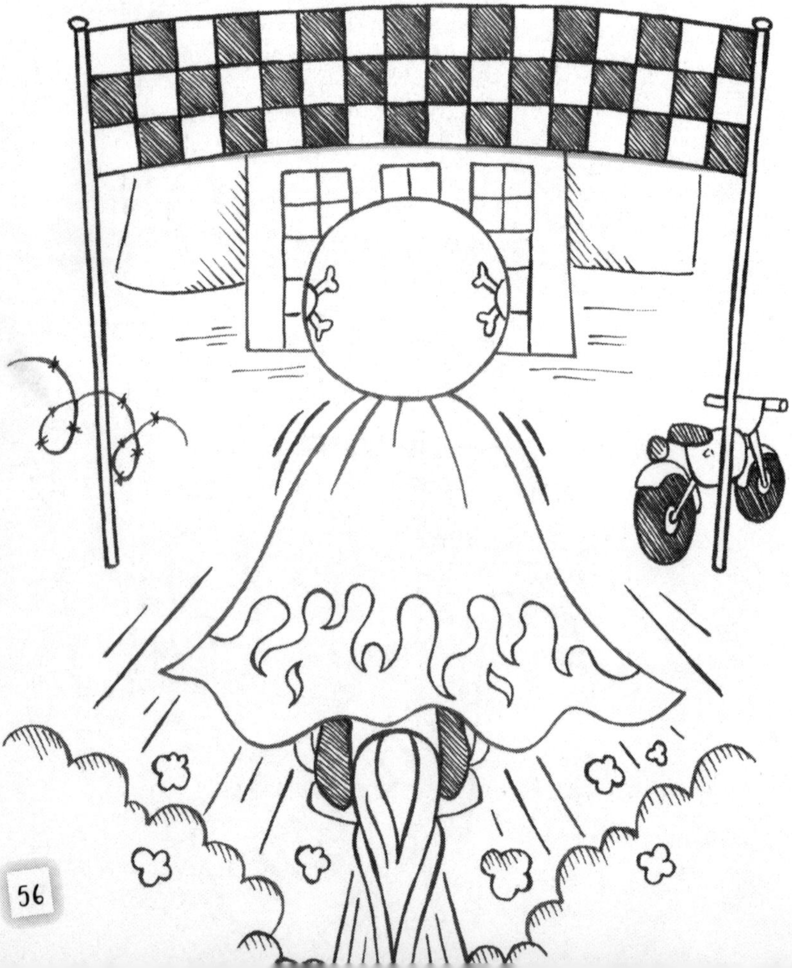

'Hello!' Little Stunt Riding Hood called out. 'Are you there, Grandmaster? Dog Boy? Anyone? Where did everybody go? This is starting to creep me out!'

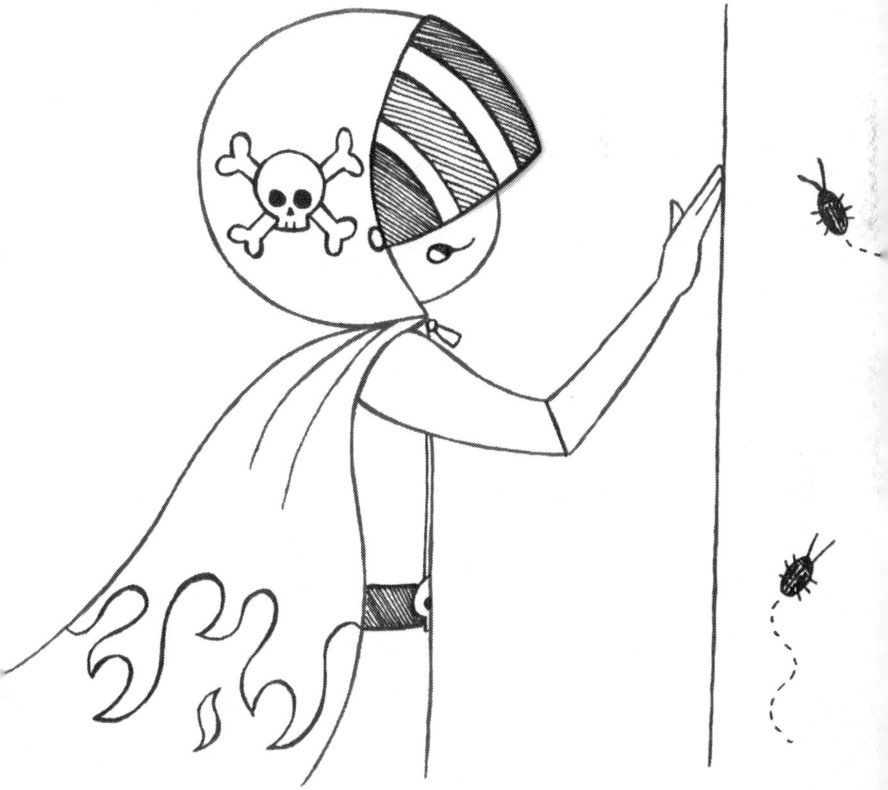

'Come in, you loser!' came a voice from inside.

Little Stunt Riding Hood tiptoed across the factory to the cool games room in the corner. Hiding behind the curtains was the famous Grandmaster, although [redacted]he looked quite different from how [redacted]he usually did in his promotional posters.

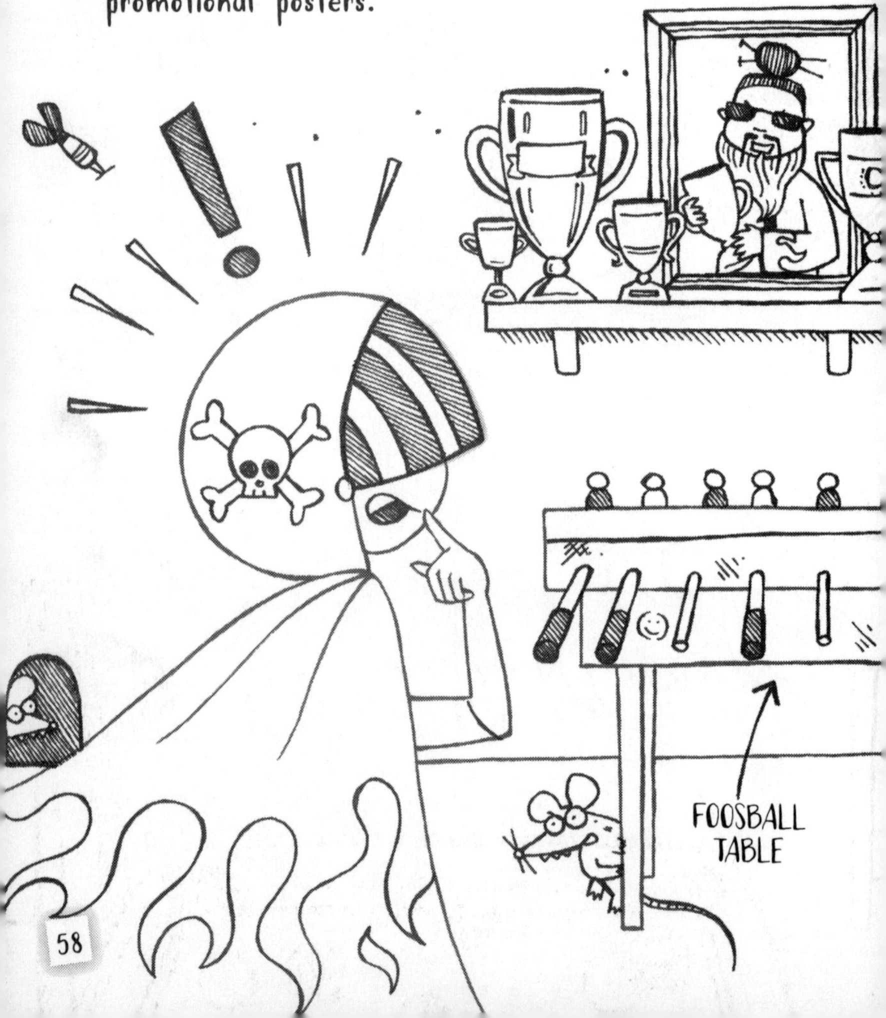
FOOSBALL
TABLE

It was obviously the big werewolf dressed in the Grandmaster's clothes, but Little Stunt Riding Hood was kind of intrigued, so he didn't say anything.

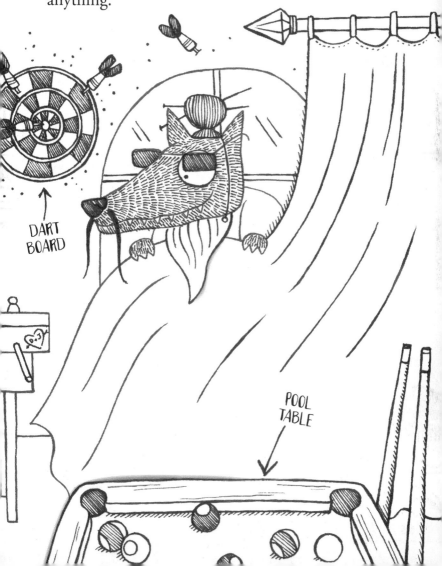

DART
BOARD

POOL
TABLE

'Come closer,' the "Grandmaster" said.

Little Stunt Riding Hood approached the hairy dude and commented, 'You've really let yourself go, Grandmaster! Better lay off the cheeseburgers. And maybe think about shaving... YOUR WHOLE BODY!'

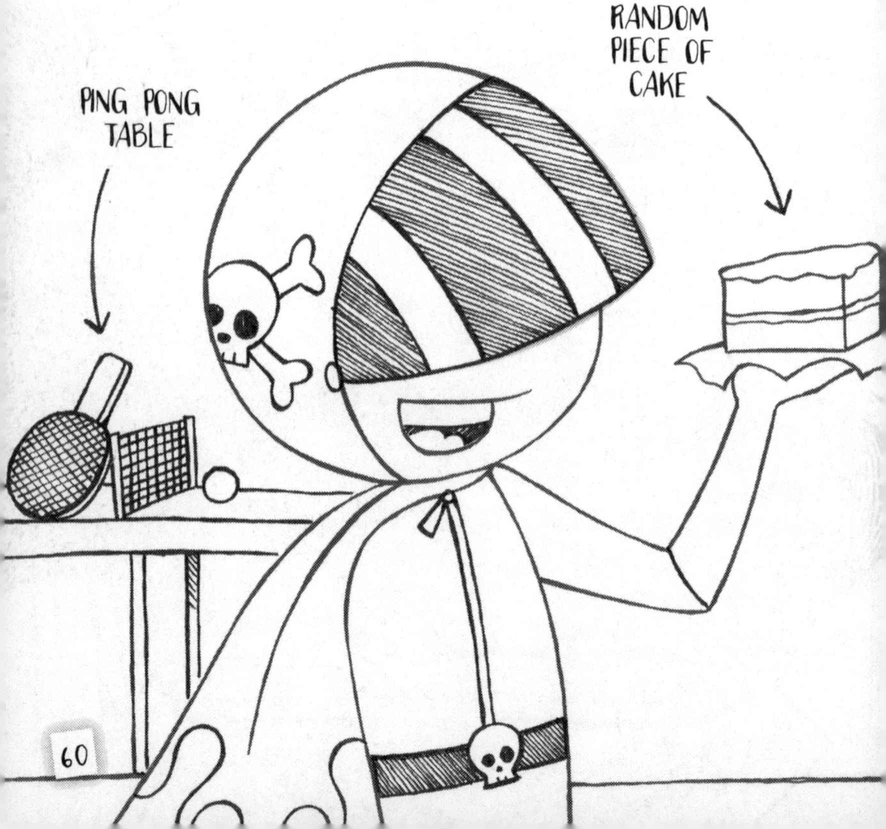
RANDOM PIECE OF CAKE
PING PONG TABLE

The "Grandmaster" sneered and motioned for Little Stunt Riding Hood to come closer still.

'Your place looks fully sick! Why don't you give me the grand tour?' Hoodie said.

'Very well,' the "Grandmaster" replied, taking the hoodlum around the games room.

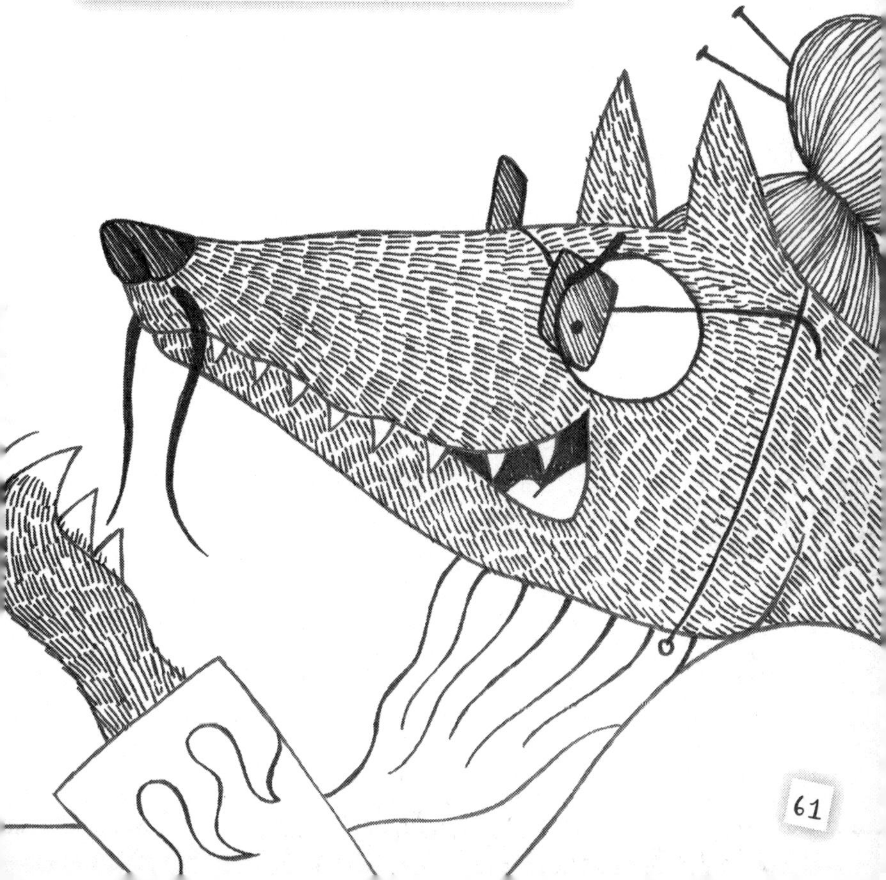

'Oh, Grandmaster,' Little Stunt Riding Hood said. 'What big speakers you have,' pointing at the huge stack of subwoofers and amps.

'All the better to blast music at the neighbours!' was the reply. 'I crank it to eleven and then bust moves like nobody's business. All night long! Wanna see me do the robot?'

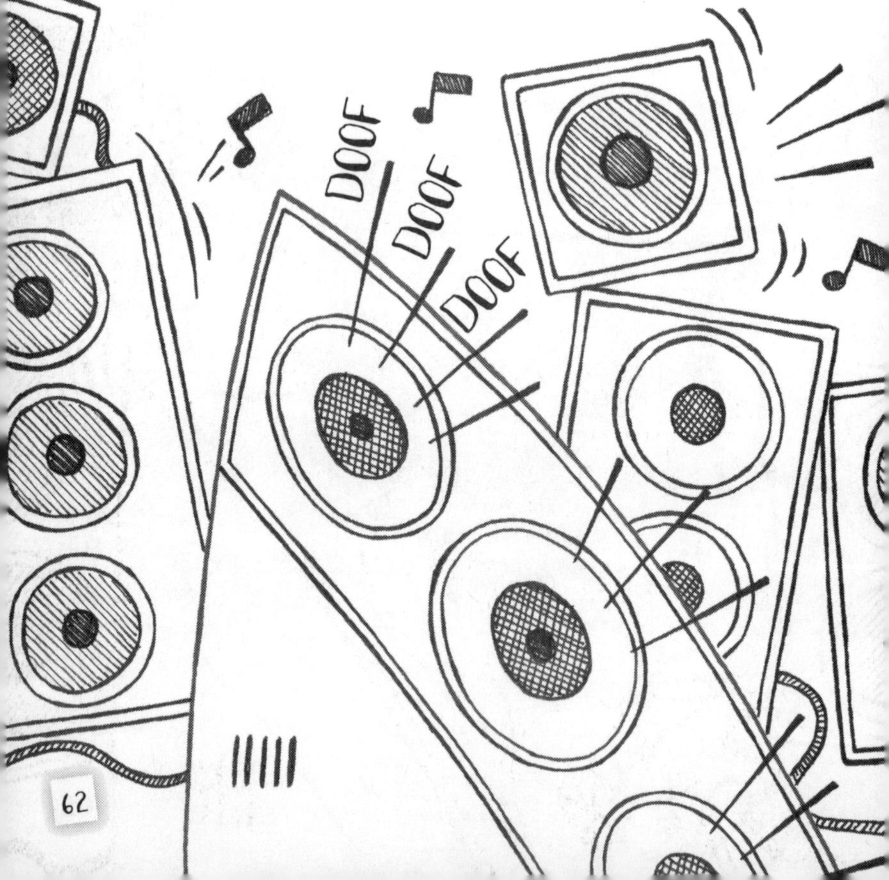
DOOF
DOOF
DOOF

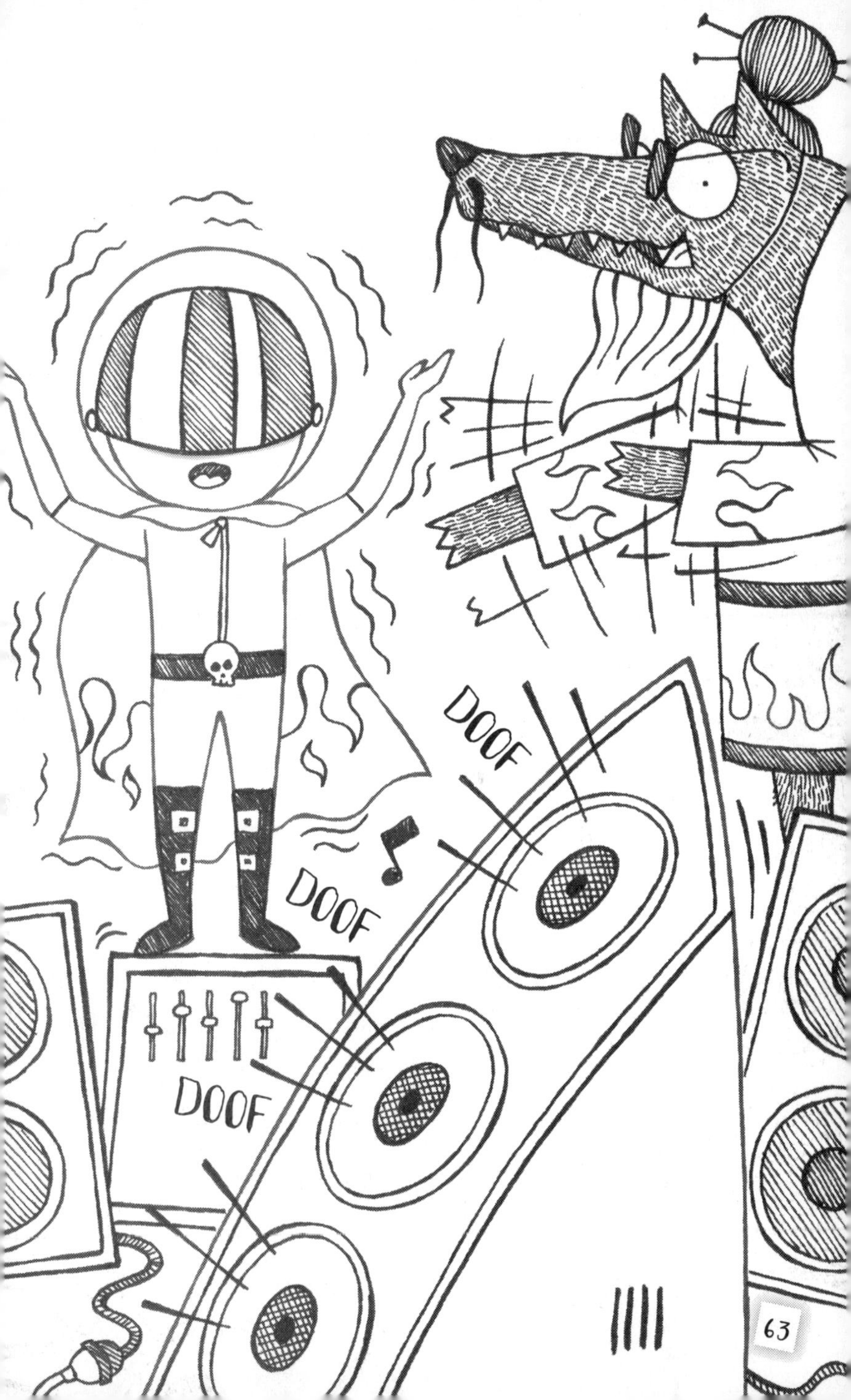
DOOF
DOOF
DOOF

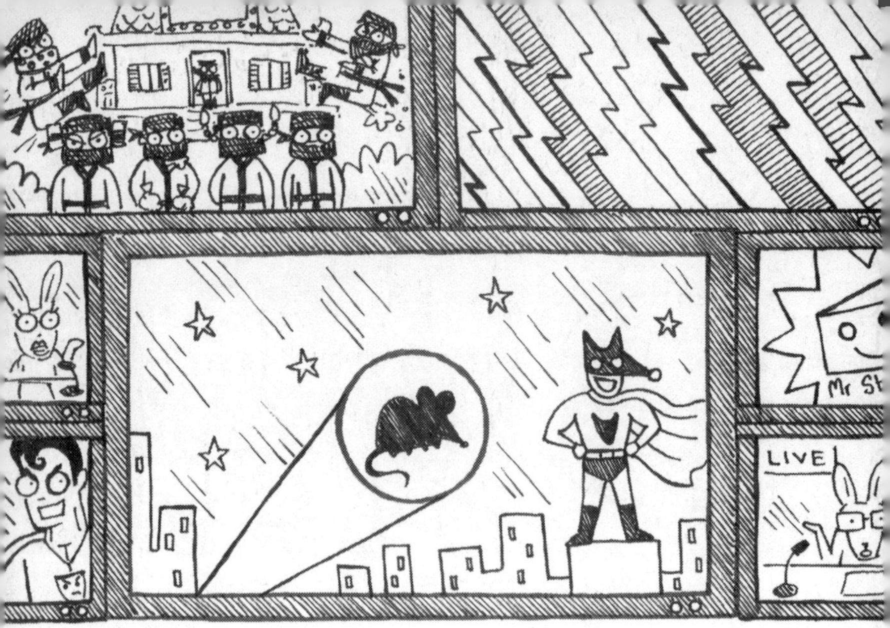
Mr St
LIVE

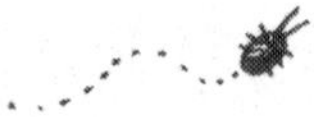

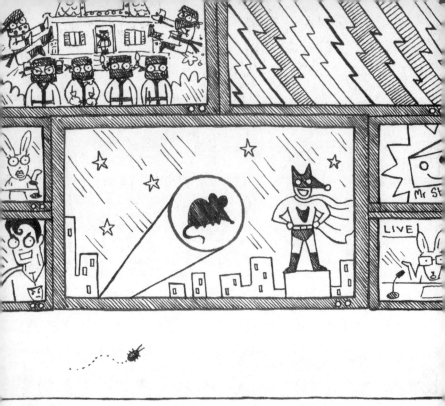

'But, Grandmaster, what big TV screens you have!' the little guy exclaimed, staring at the large flat screen televisions lining all the walls.

'All the better to see the latest action blockbusters on. It's like you're at the movies! And I can binge watch all the must-see new shows at the same time. It's totally sweet!'

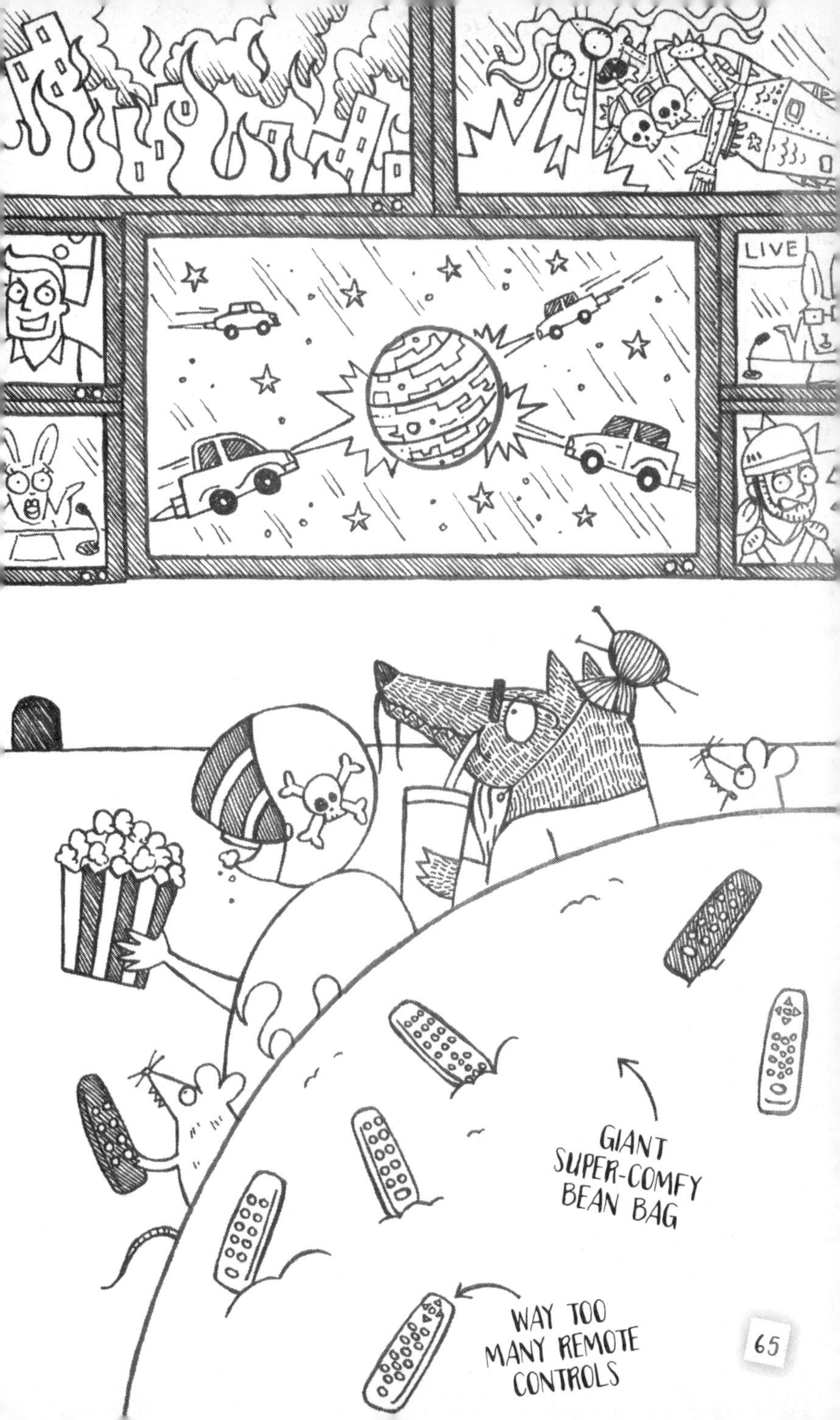
LIVE
GIANT SUPER-COMFY BEAN BAG
WAY TOO MANY REMOTE CONTROLS

Little Stunt Riding Hood then noticed the Grandmaster's large collection of video game consoles and asked, 'What games do you have?'

'All the better ones, Hoodie! And all in 5D, holographic, fully immersive, interactive virtual reality!'

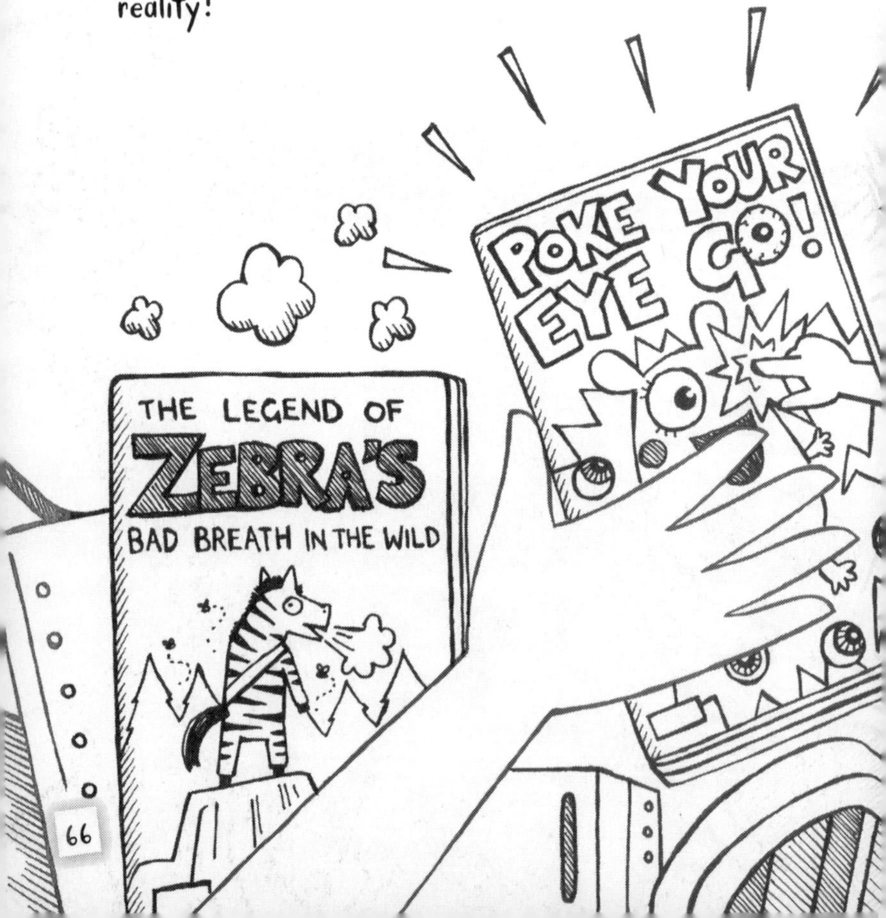
POKE YOUR EYE GO!
THE LEGEND OF ZEBRA'S BAD BREATH IN THE WILD

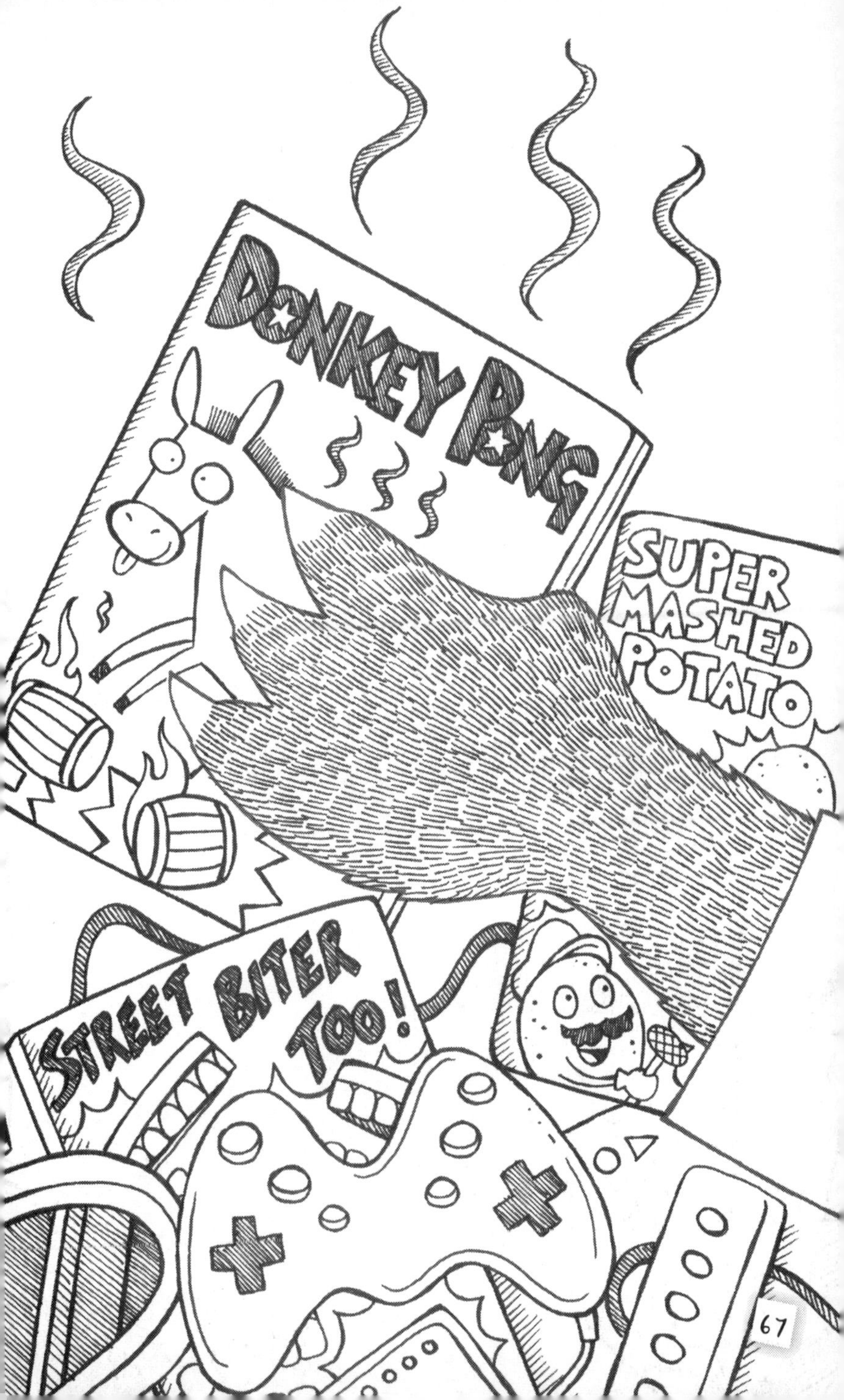
DONKEY PONG
SUPER MASHED POTATO
STREET BITER TOO!

'What cool, retro arcade games you have too, Grandmaster!' Little Stunt Riding Hood declared.

'All the top scores are mine! I am the champ!'

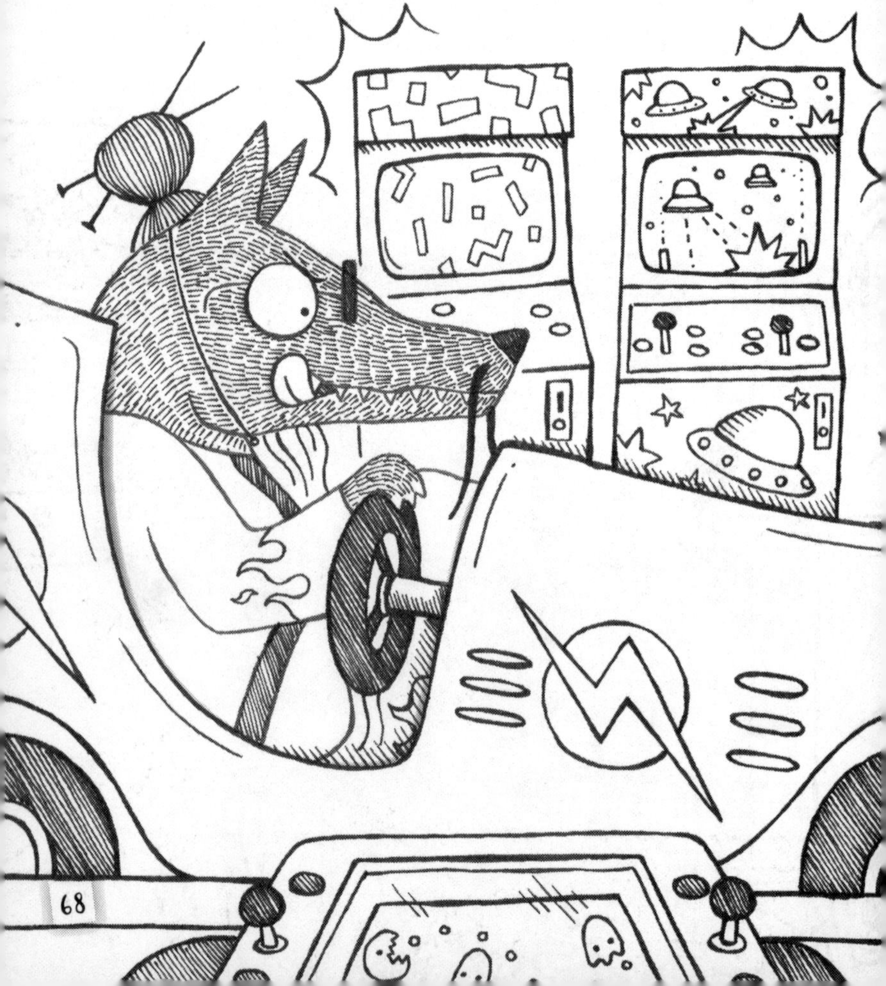

'Oh, boy Grandmaster, what big, stinking lies you have been telling!' the punk exclaimed.

'All the top scores ARE mine!'

'I'm not talking about that. EVERYONE exaggerates their top score. I mean your whole, weird "I'm the Grandmaster" act!'

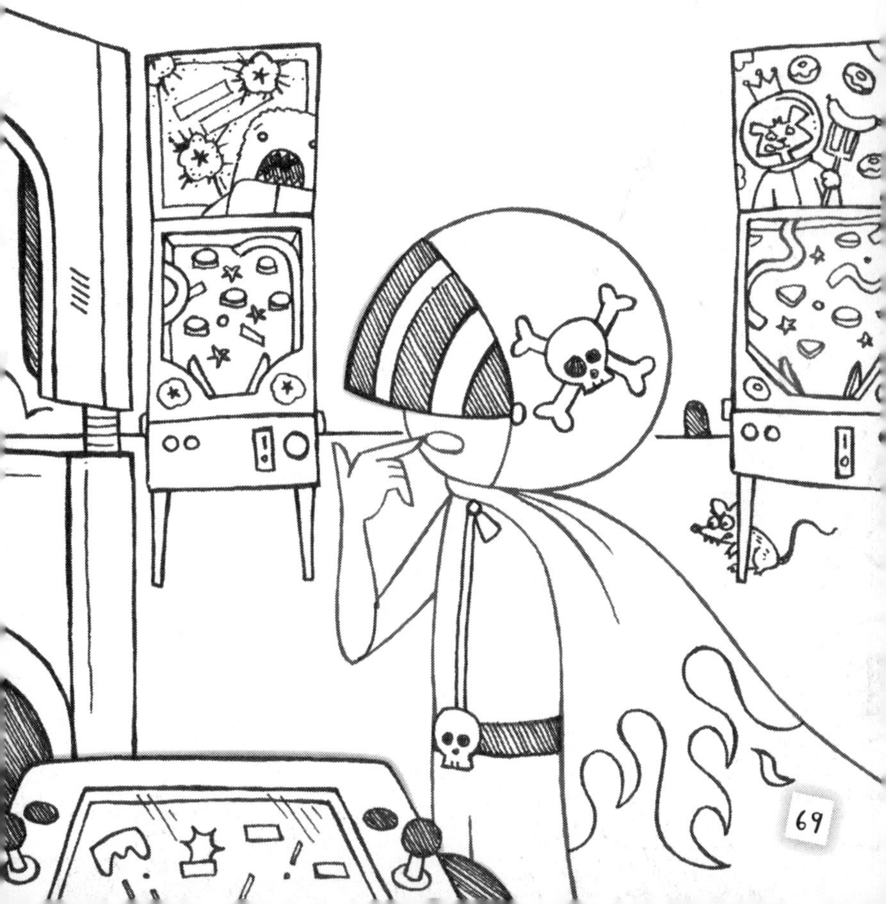

And with that, the big werewolf threw off the disguise.

'It is I, the big werewolf!'

'No joke!' laughed Little Stunt Riding Hood. 'I'm not an idiot! Who would be fooled by a wolf dressed up in clothes? Seriously?!'

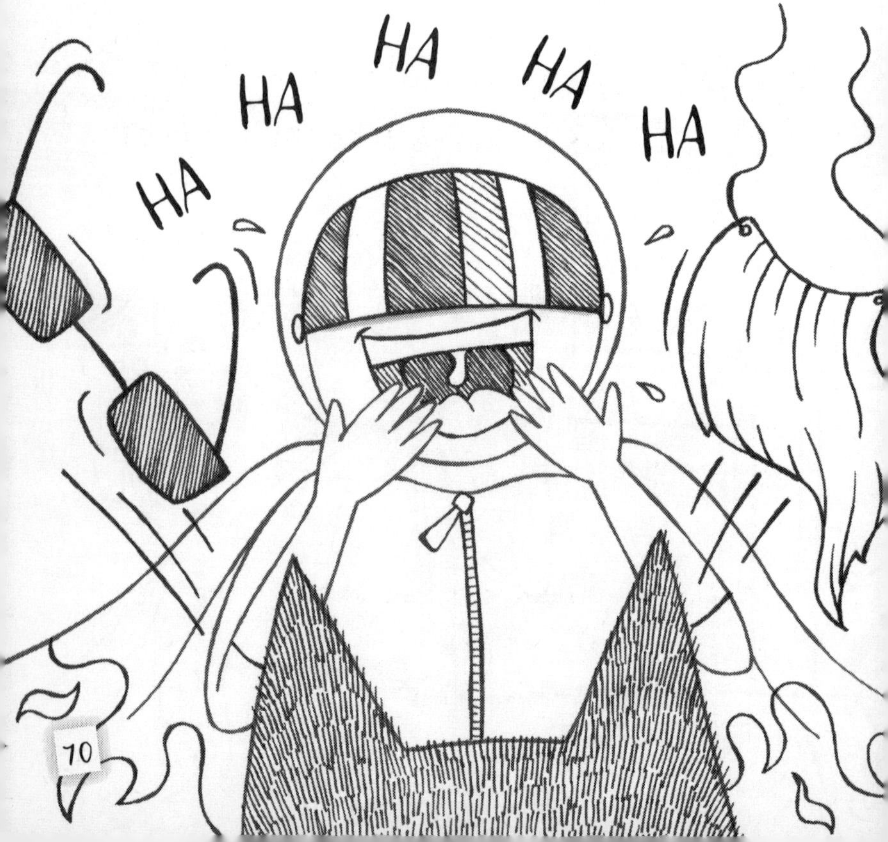
HA
HA
HA
HA
HA

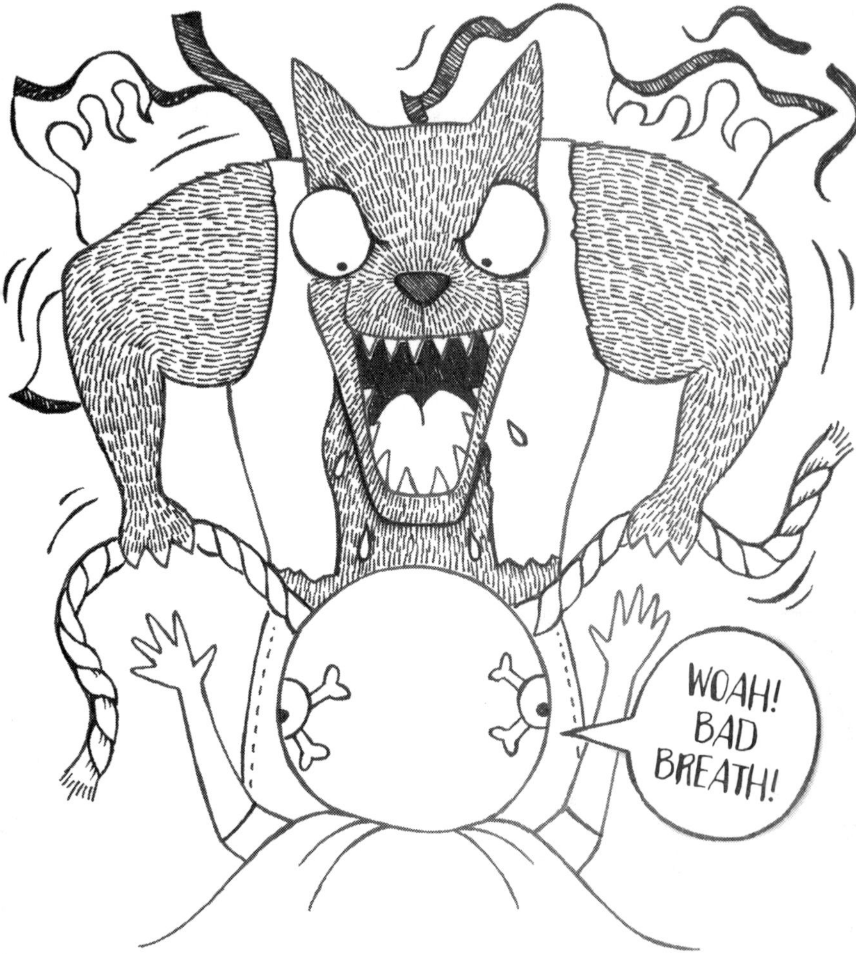
WOAH! BAD BREATH!

The big werewolf leapt angrily upon Little Stunt Riding Hood.

'I tied up the Grandmaster and now I'm going to TIE... UP... YOU!'

'Please explain! I beg you!' the little dude implored.

But the big werewolf didn't explain and in one second he tied up Little Stunt Riding Hood tightly.

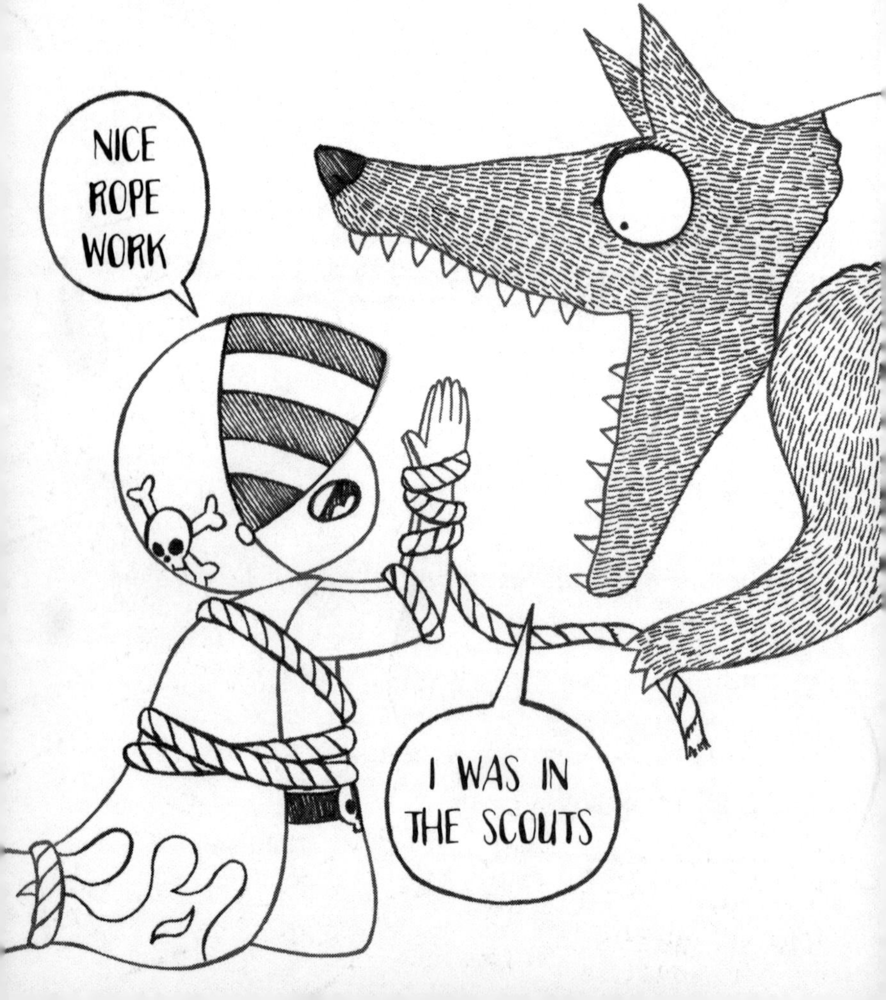
NICE ROPE WORK
I WAS IN THE SCOUTS

With the young kid detained, the big werewolf began to search everywhere... for a safe.

He looked downstairs, upstairs, under the bed and sink. He was searching the large factory from top to bottom.

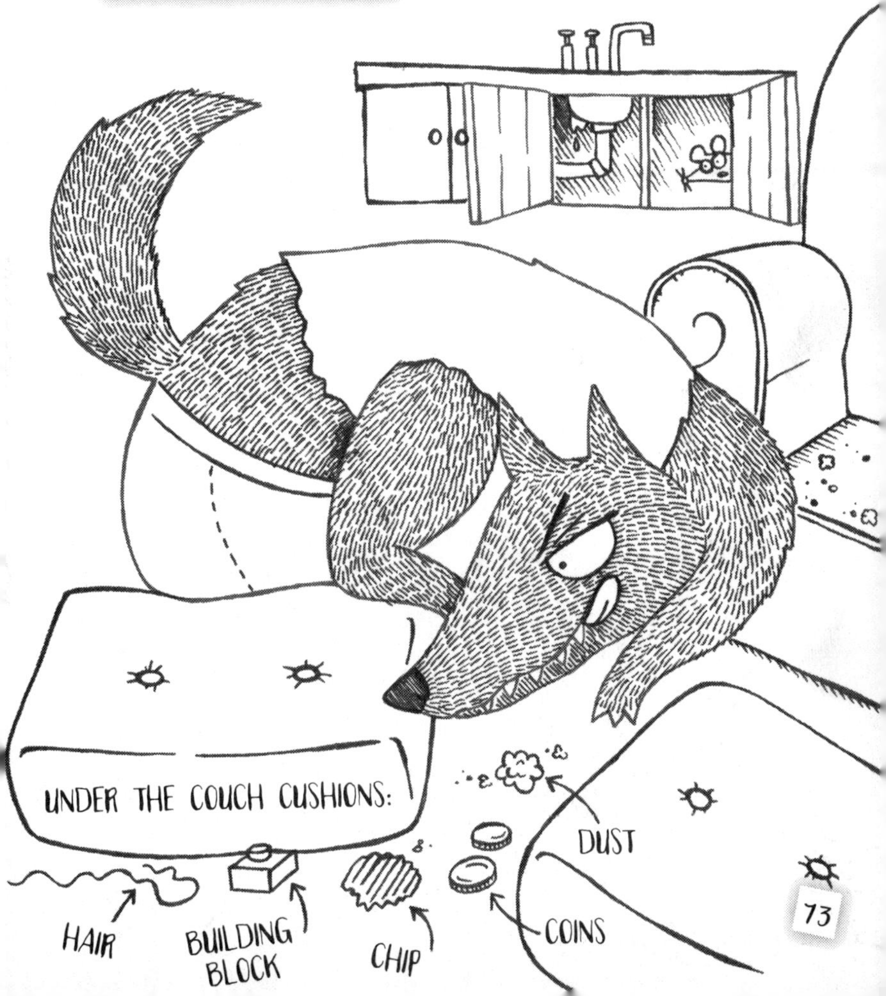
UNDER THE COUCH CUSHIONS:
DUST
HAIR
BUILDING BLOCK
CHIP
COINS

Meanwhile, deep down inside the factory's storage room, Little Stunt Riding Hood found himself face to face with the real Grandmaster, who had also been tied up.

'Hey Grandmaster! What's the deal with dogboy?' Little Stunt Riding Hood sighed.

'That creepy old werewolf is actually a rare reverse werewolf.'

'Whatchu talkin' about Grandmaster?!'

'Unless I'm mistaken, that furball is a reverse werewolf and turns into a human when the full moon is out! It's a bit random, I know, but when you get to my age, you've seen everything, kiddo!'

THERE GOES THE NEIGHBOURHOOD!

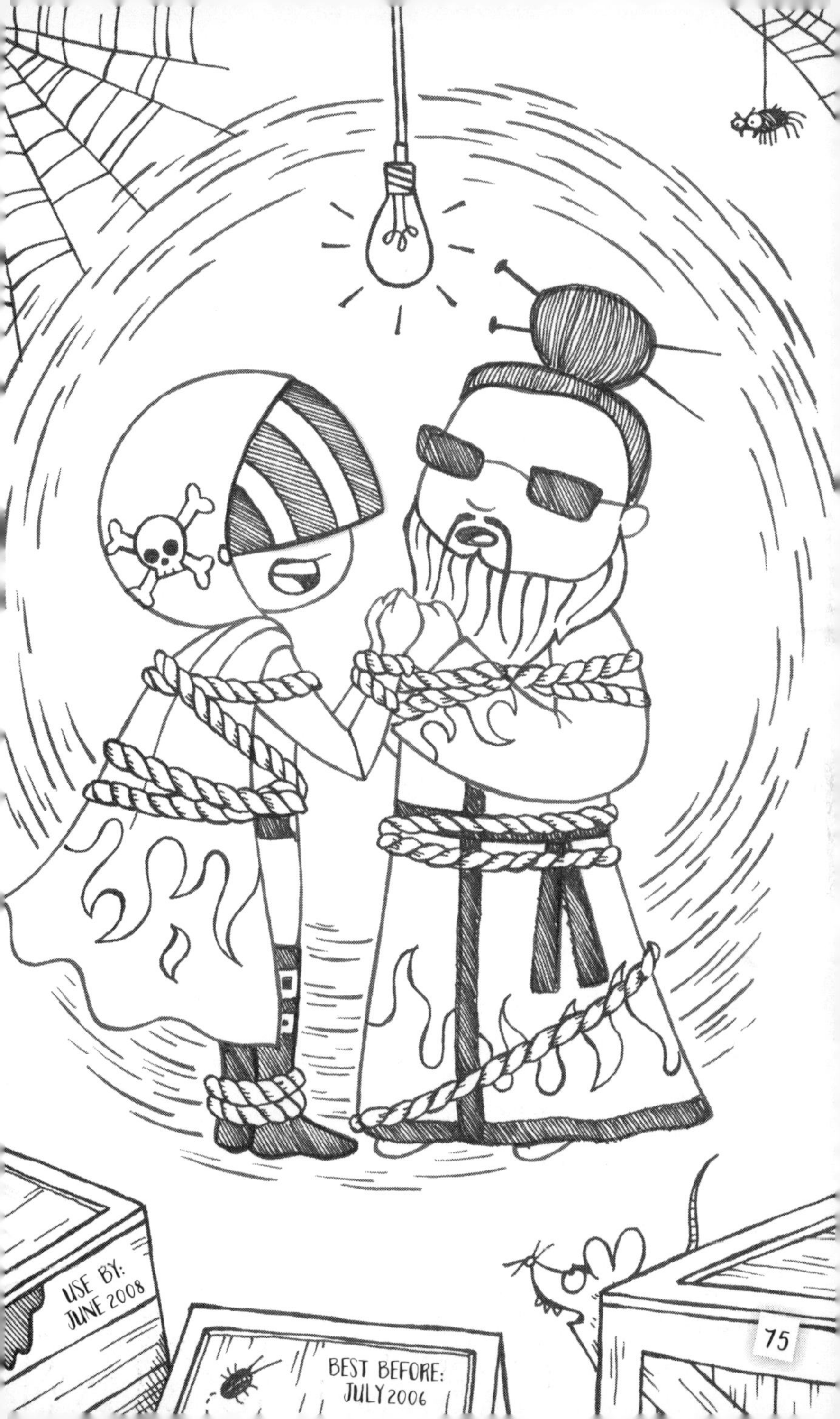
USE BY:
JUNE 2008
BEST BEFORE:
JULY 2006
75

Little Stunt Riding Hood and the Grandmaster plotted together in the darkness of the storage room, hatching their escape plan.

One thing they knew, there was no full moon on the way…

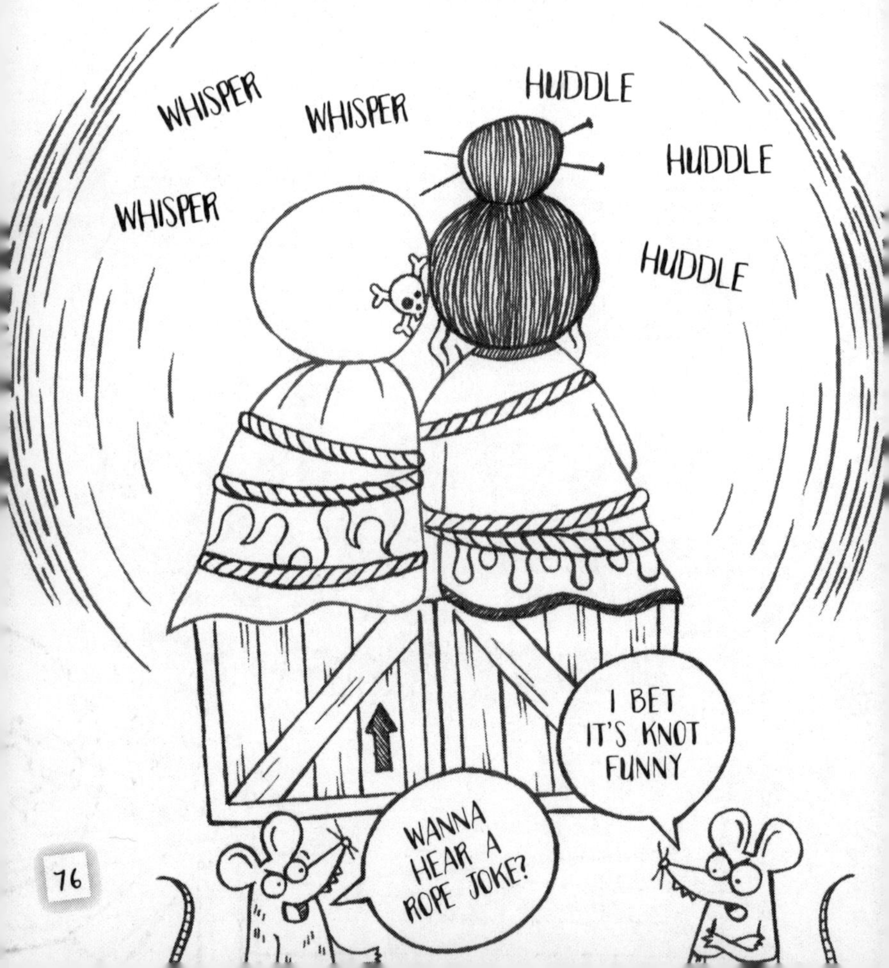
WHISPER
WHISPER
WHISPER
HUDDLE
HUDDLE
HUDDLE
WANNA HEAR A ROPE JOKE?
I BET IT'S KNOT FUNNY

…so they would have to make their own! They heard the big werewolf coming back from upstairs. As he was passing by, an idea came to Hoodie!

'I hope the Grandmaster is right,' he said as he wiggled out of his ropes.

When he saw the reverse werewolf looking under the rug, the young hoodlum knew it was time to unveil his plan.

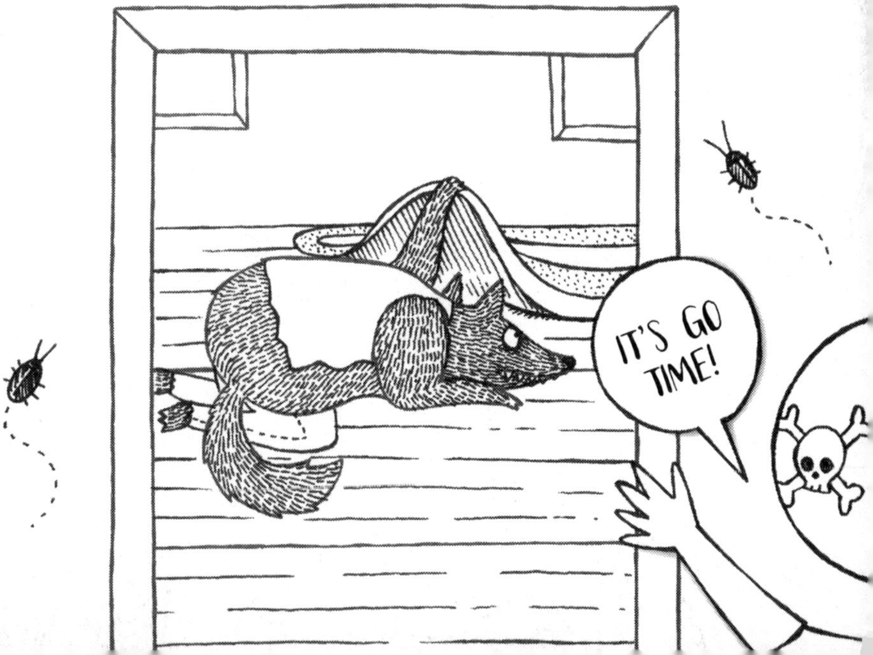
IT'S GO TIME!

He crept up behind the searching big werewolf.

'Check out this!' he said, brandishing his shiny buttocks!

The big werewolf covered his eyes in horror, but it was too late. The light bounced off the cheeks of Little Stunt Riding Hood's bum.

The reverse werewolf had seen his full moon!

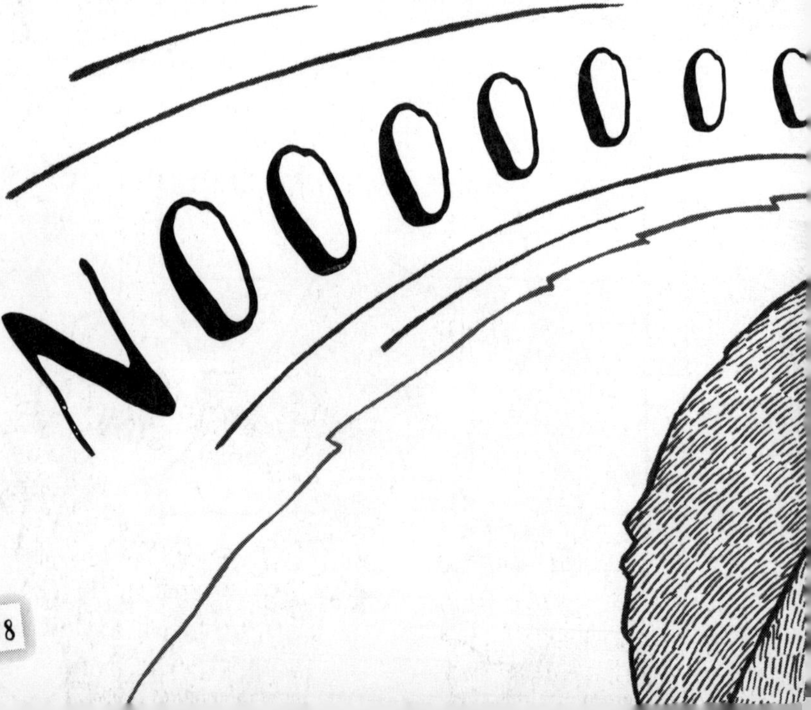
NOOOOOOOO

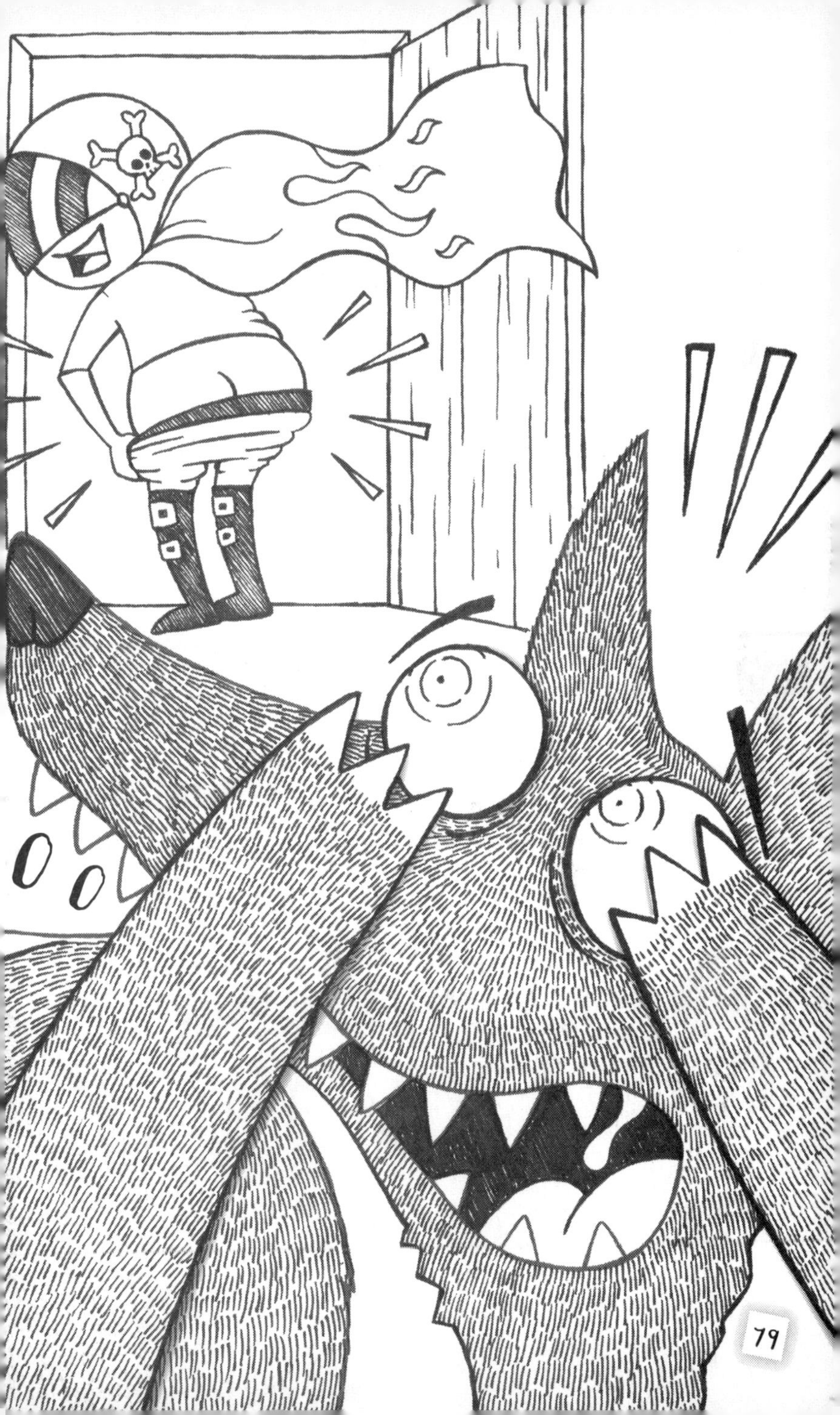

The big werewolf shrieked like a little baby!

He twisted and turned, writhing in pain, but however hairy and scary he may have been, he was slowly transforming back into a man.

The stinky cheesecutter was eventually revealed!

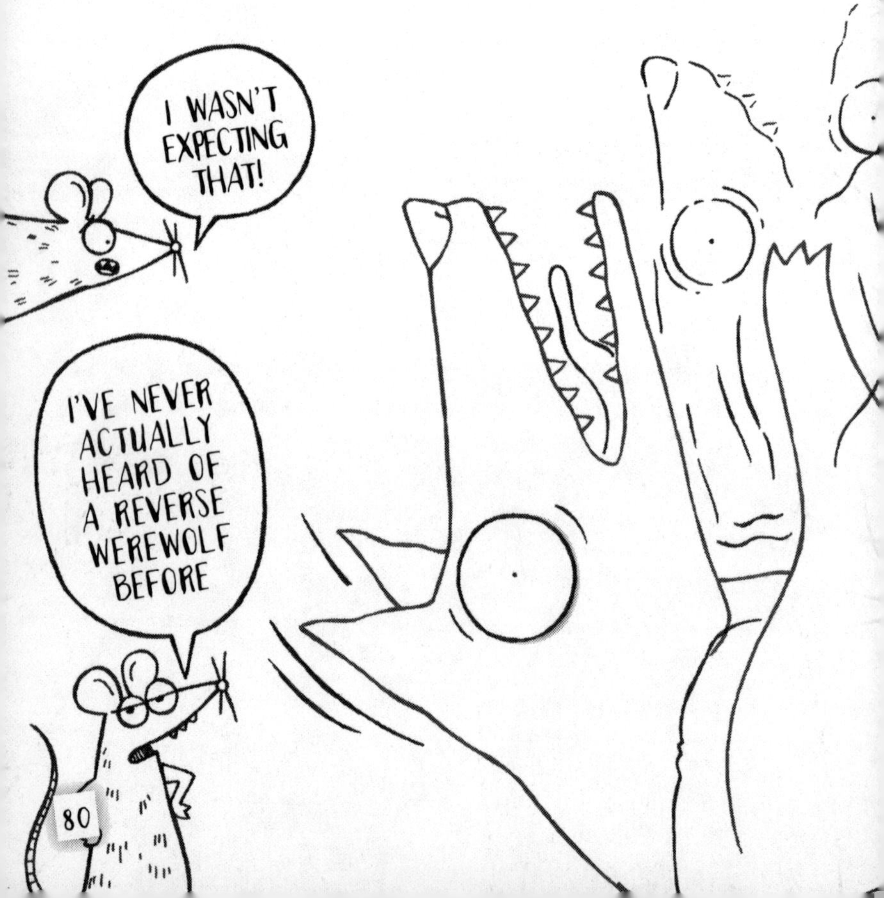
I WASN'T EXPECTING THAT!
I'VE NEVER ACTUALLY HEARD OF A REVERSE WEREWOLF BEFORE

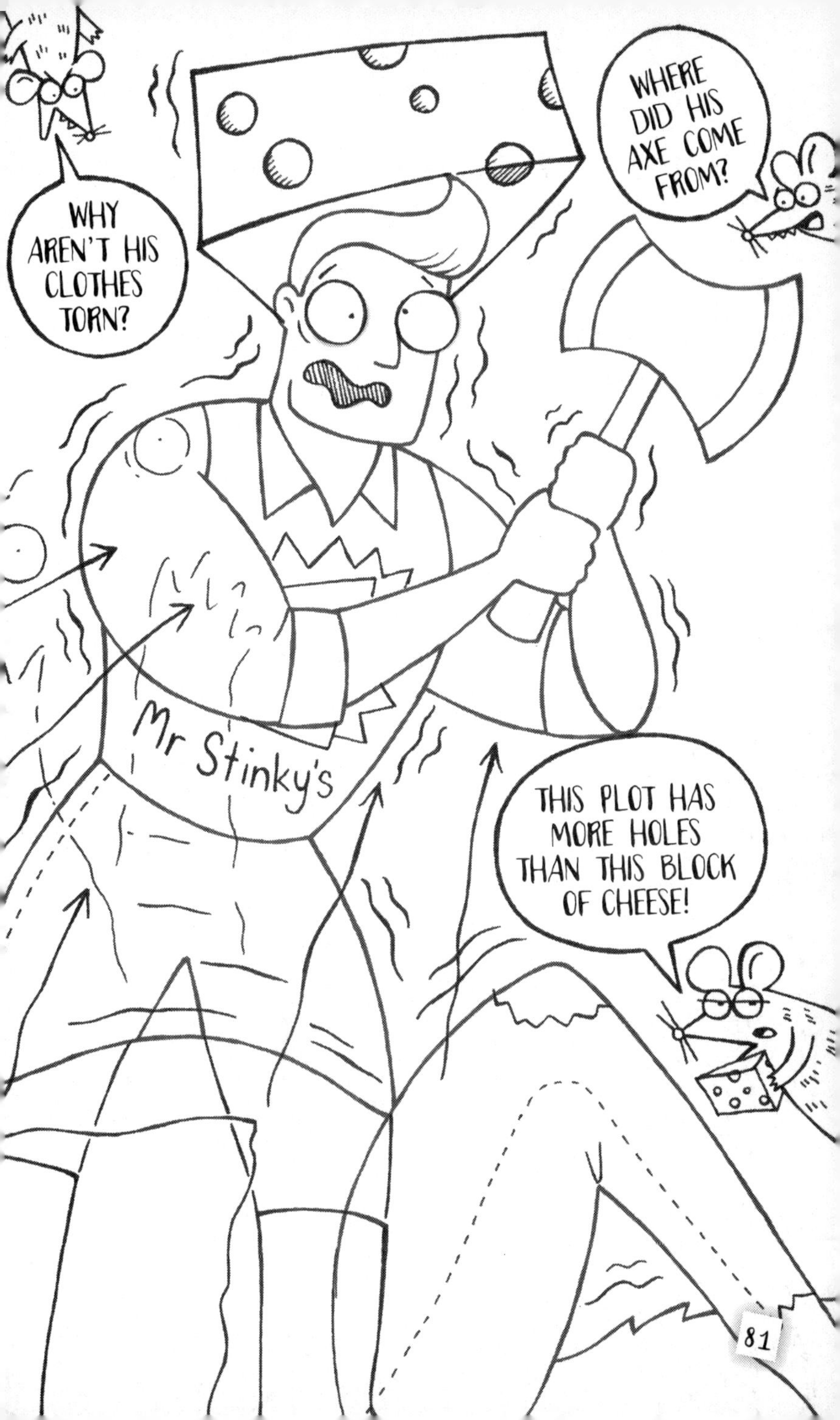
WHY AREN'T HIS CLOTHES TORN?
WHERE DID HIS AXE COME FROM?
Mr Stinky's
THIS PLOT HAS MORE HOLES THAN THIS BLOCK OF CHEESE!

The cheesecutter, owner of Mr Stinky's World of Cheese, had been the big werewolf all along! Little Stunt Riding Hood and the Grandmaster's eyes popped out, looking shocked but remarkably unimpressed.

'O.K. cheesecutter. What's up, bozo?' the Grandmaster demanded. 'You cheat at the race. You tie us up. You snoop around my factory. And worst of all, you use my toilet and don't flush! What gives?!'

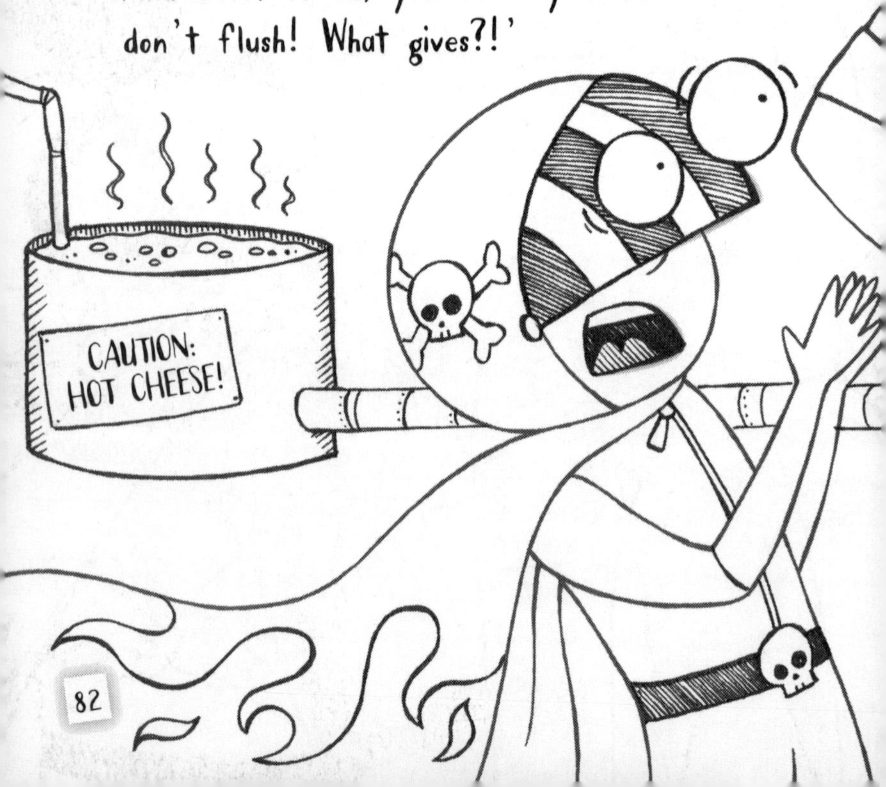
CAUTION:
HOT CHEESE!

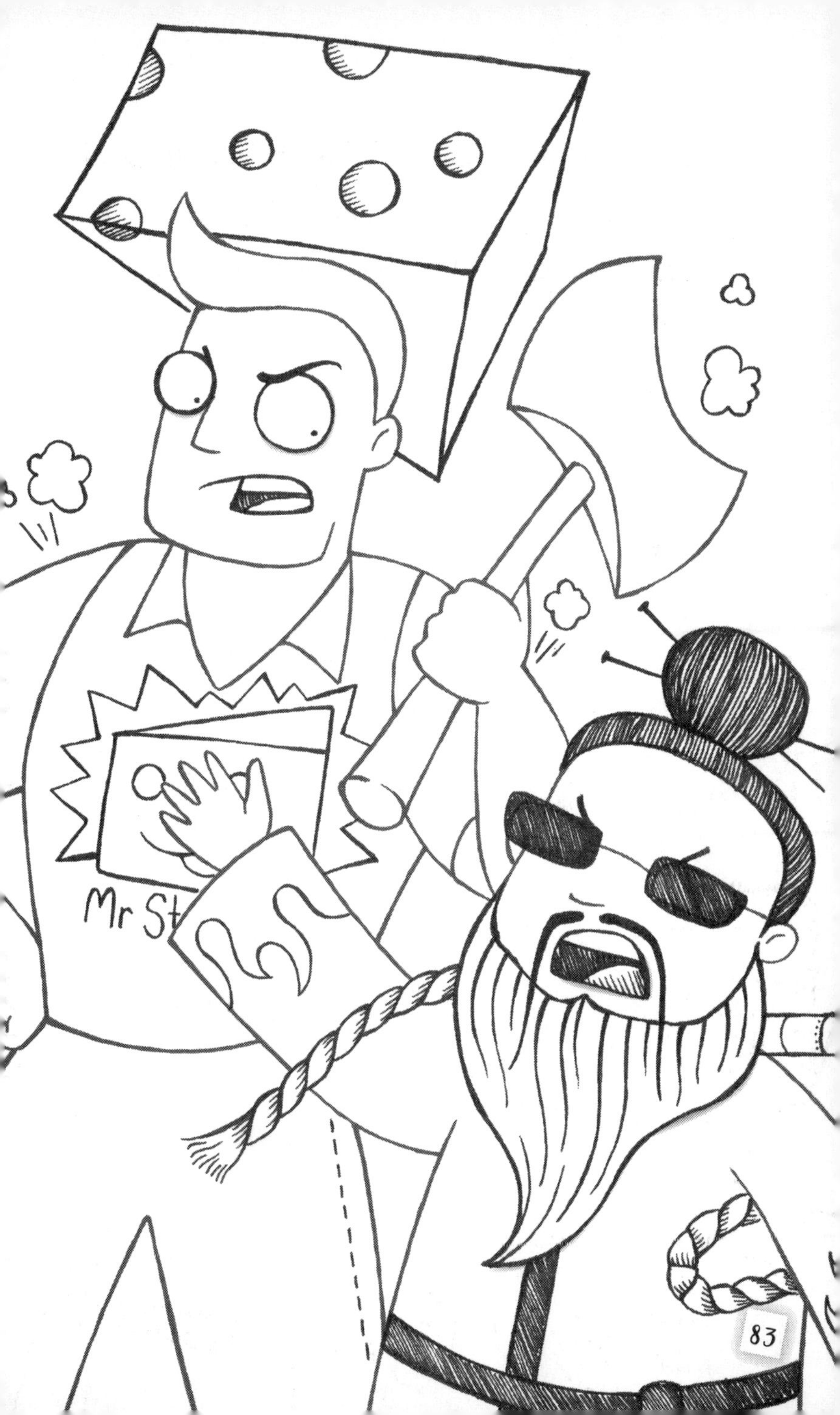
Mr St

'Why I only did what anyone who owns the world's largest cheese company would do, Grandmaster. I have been posing as that big werewolf for years, getting closer and closer to the one thing that has always eluded me. Today is the day I get what I deserve – Your top secret cottage cheese recipe! That's right! I sponsored this race and made your factory the finish point to get past your airtight security and sneak in and steal the recipe passed down in your family for generations. It's gonna make me even richer than I already am!'

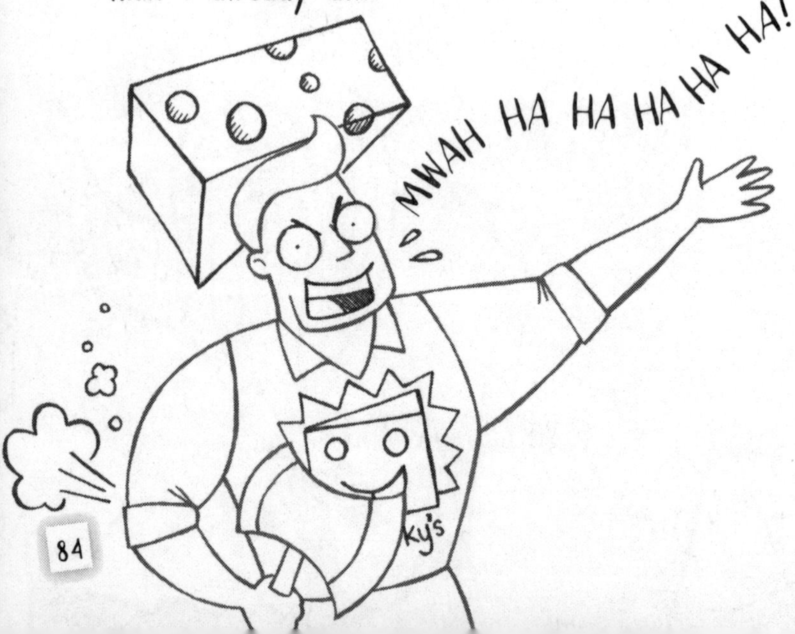
MWAH HA HA HA HA HA!
KYJ'S

'You STINK, cheesecutter,' cried Little Stunt Riding Hood. 'Really, you are the dumbest dude ever! I mean, talk about pointless, ridiculous, over-the-top, evil genius plans! Yours is THE WORST! No-one even likes cottage cheese!! No offence Grandmaster.'

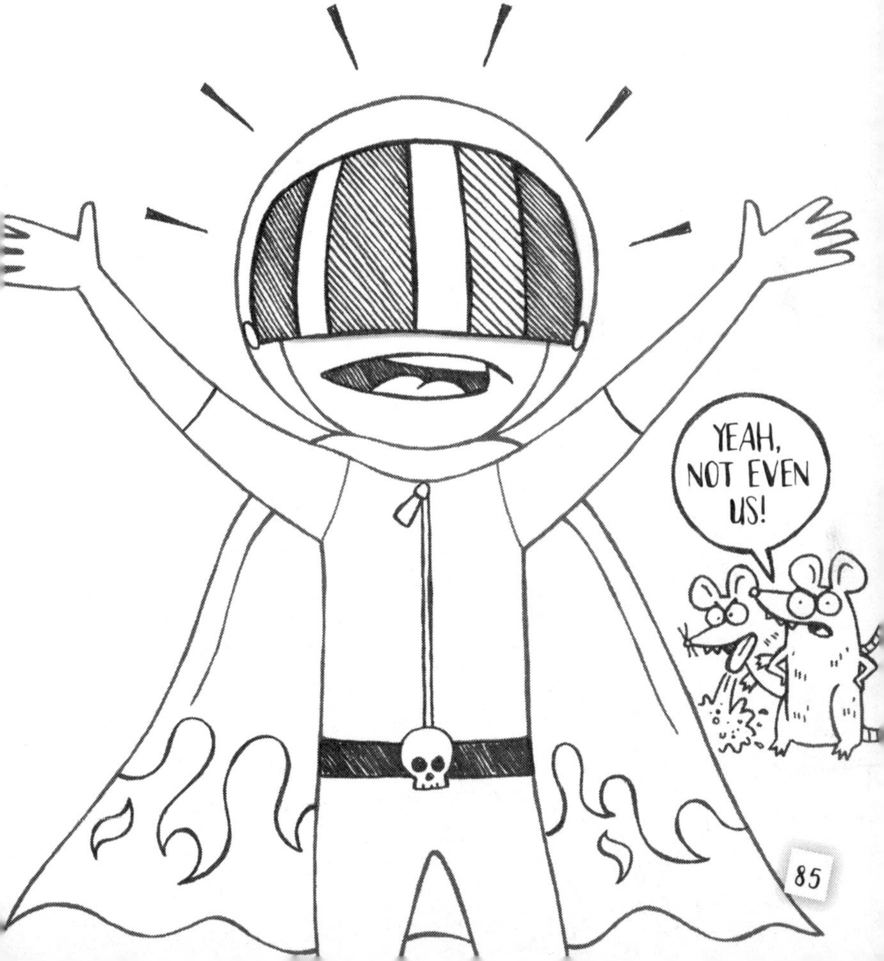
YEAH, NOT EVEN US!

Little Stunt Riding Hood leaned over and flicked the cheesecutter right on his forehead.

'OUCH! No-one talks about cottage cheese like that!' he yelled, brandishing his oversized cheese cutter. 'Now tell me old man, where is your recipe, so that I may steal it from you.'

'No thank you, Cheese Boy.'

'All right, we're going to do this the hard way! Get in that vat of melted cheese. Both of you!'

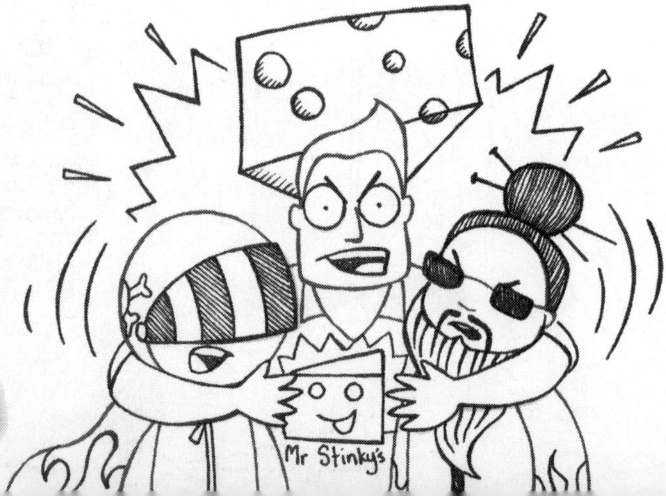
Mr Stinky's

And so it came to be that Little Stunt Riding Hood and the Grandmaster found themselves slowly cooking in a pot of melted cheese, being stirred around by the cheesecutter.

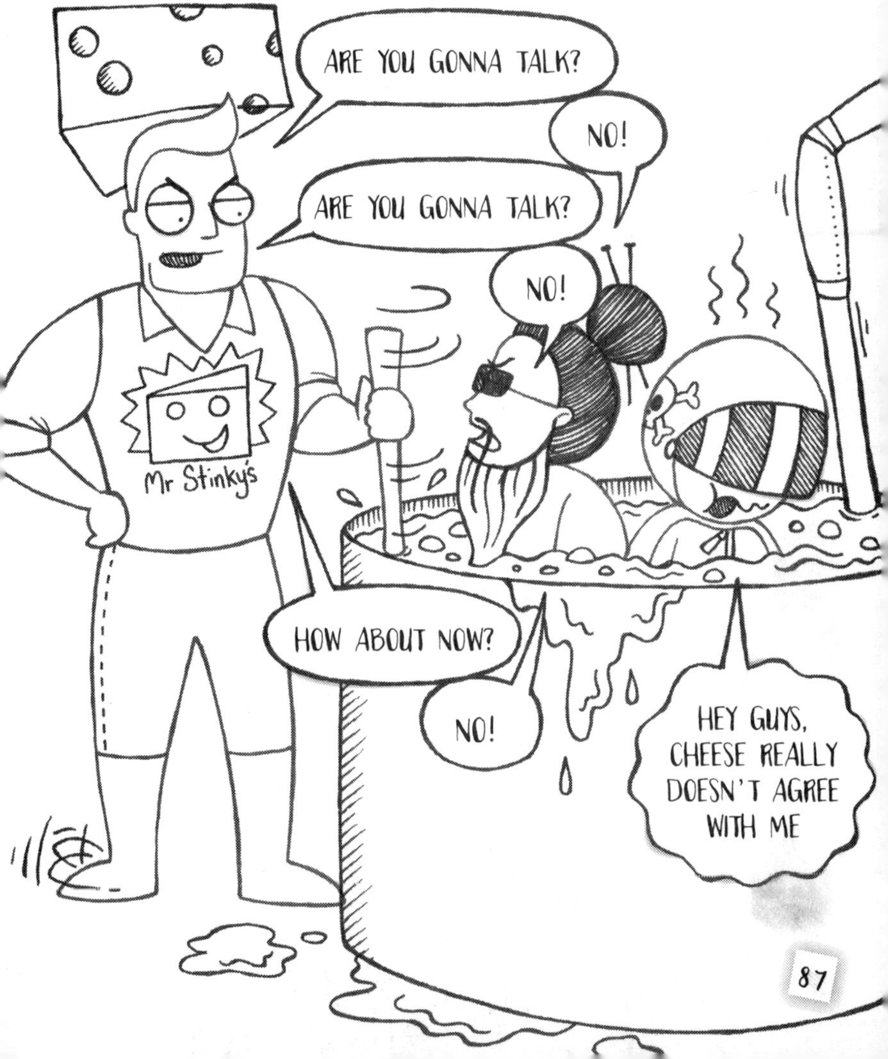
ARE YOU GONNA TALK?
NO!
ARE YOU GONNA TALK?
NO!
Mr Stinky's
HOW ABOUT NOW?
NO!
HEY GUYS, CHEESE REALLY DOESN'T AGREE WITH ME

When Little Stunt Riding Hood's manager heard what had happened, she rushed to the Cottage Cheese Factory and yelled at the camera crew for being so lazy. 'Why are you just sitting outside? Get in there and start filming! This is ratings gold!'

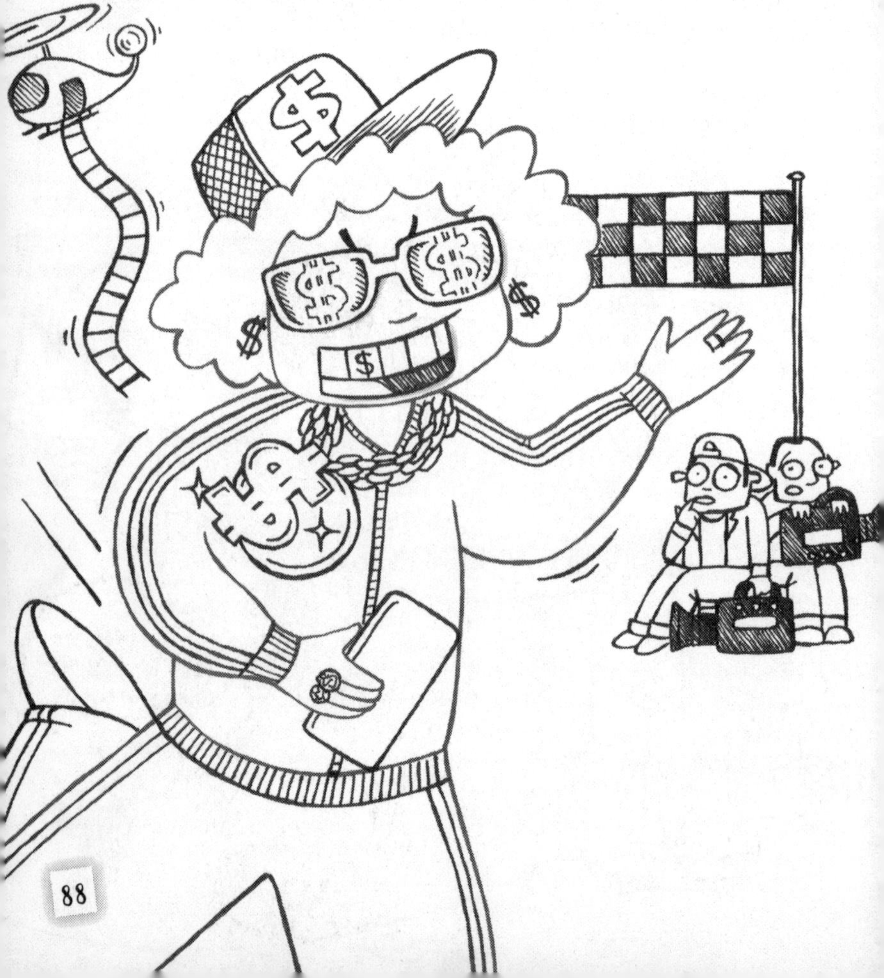

But Little Stunt Riding Hood had less to smile about as he was lactose intolerant and swirling around in a giant pot of melted cheese.

'You have been warned,' he said gravely. 'I have accidentally swallowed some runny cheese, so now you're about to see the power of my upset intestines.'

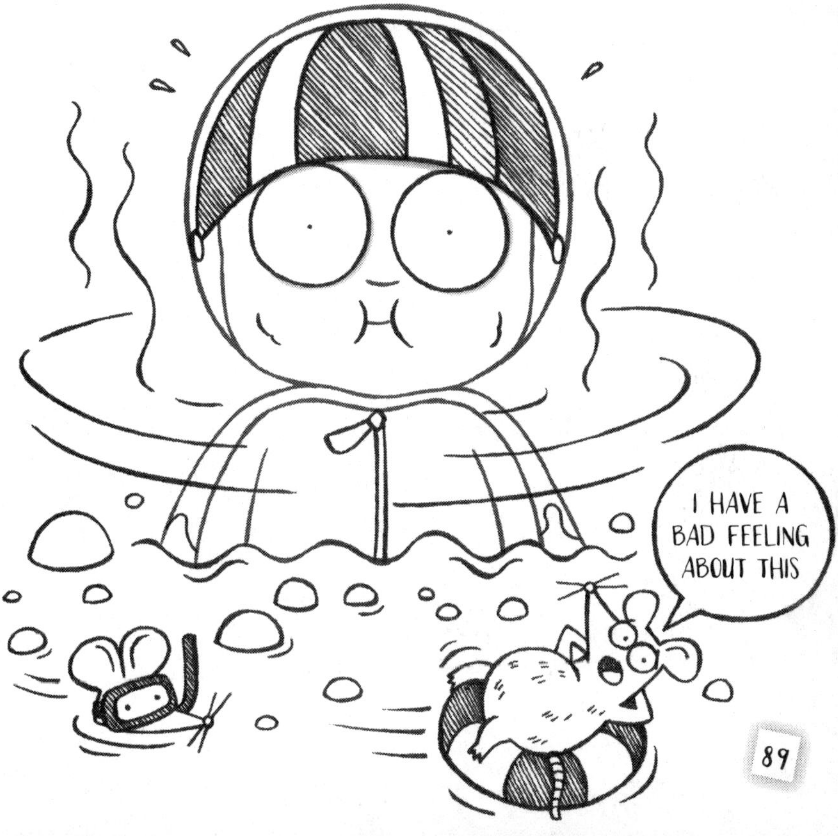
I HAVE A BAD FEELING ABOUT THIS

In no time, Little Stunt Riding Hood blew up into a million pieces! There was cheese and guts everywhere! And as it so happened, the cheesecutter had fallen in the pot with them, so she went boom-boom too!

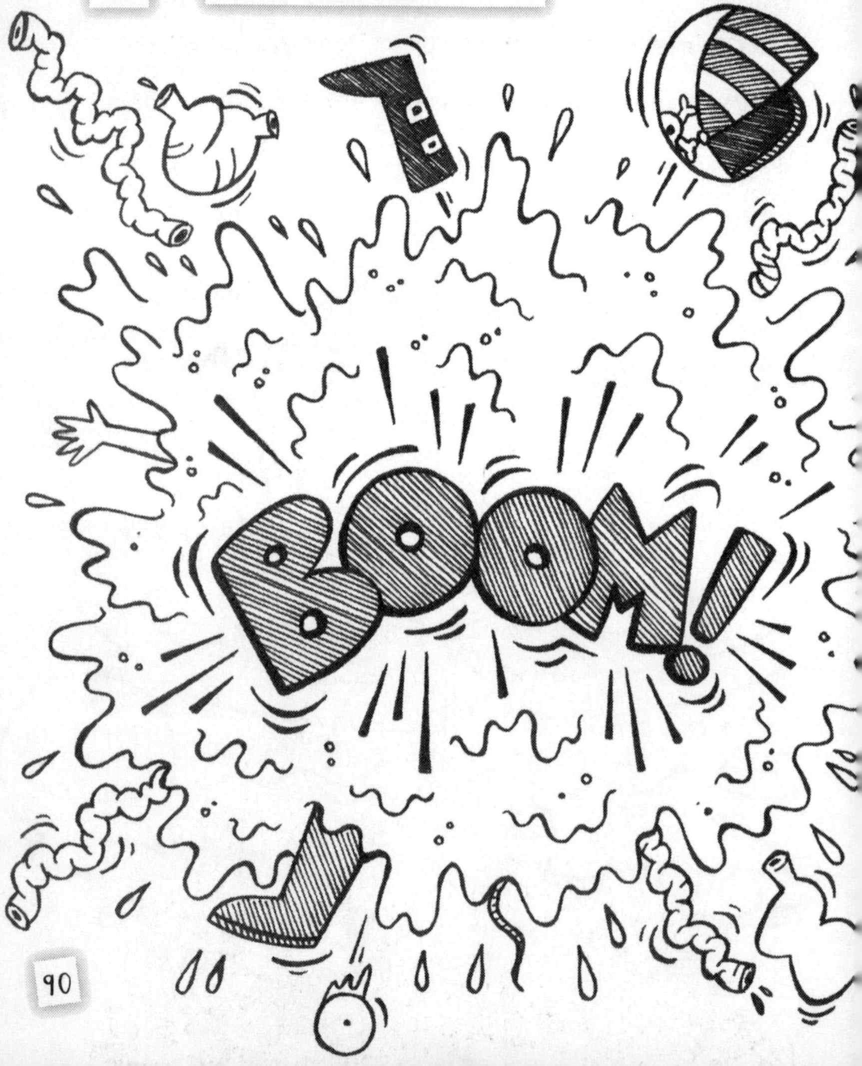
BOOM!

The racing rivals were crispy cheese chunks, but the Grandmaster lived (only just) and took over Mr Stinky's World of Cheese global empire.

Meanwhile, Little Stunt Riding Hood's manager was loaded now too, because her documentary about poor Hoodie and the cheesecutter's fateful, last race, "The Tragic Cheesy Tale of Terror on Two Wheels" was a box office smash!

The elderly manager and the Grandmaster got together and became one of the world's richest power couples ...

... and they watched the movie together

happily, every after**noon**!

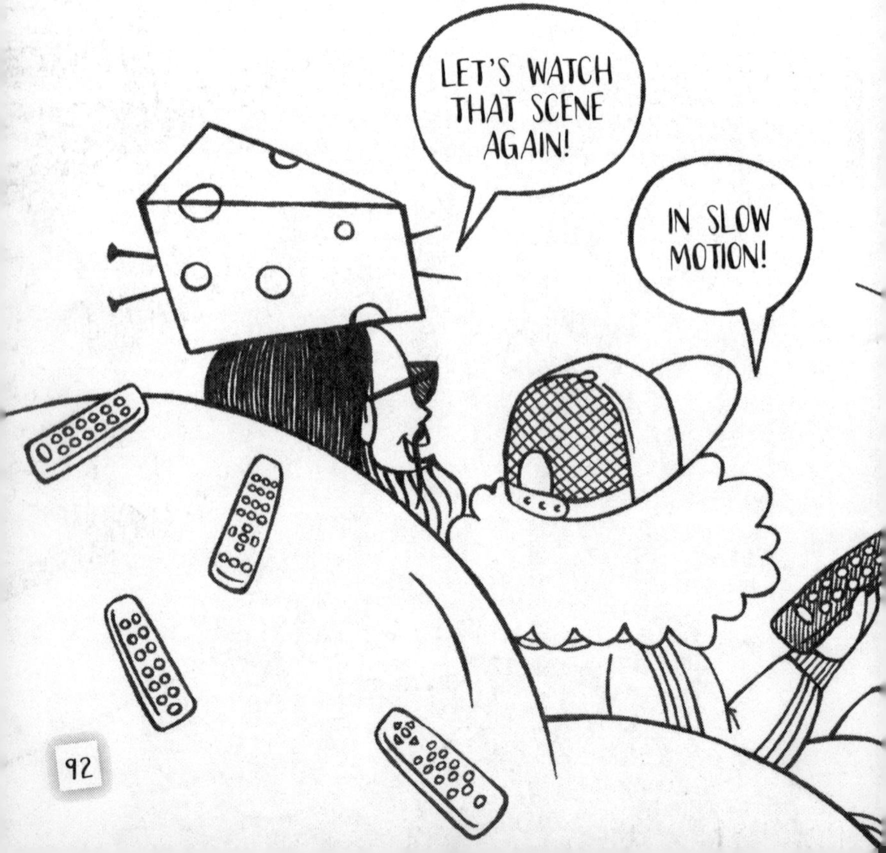
LET'S WATCH THAT SCENE AGAIN!
IN SLOW MOTION!

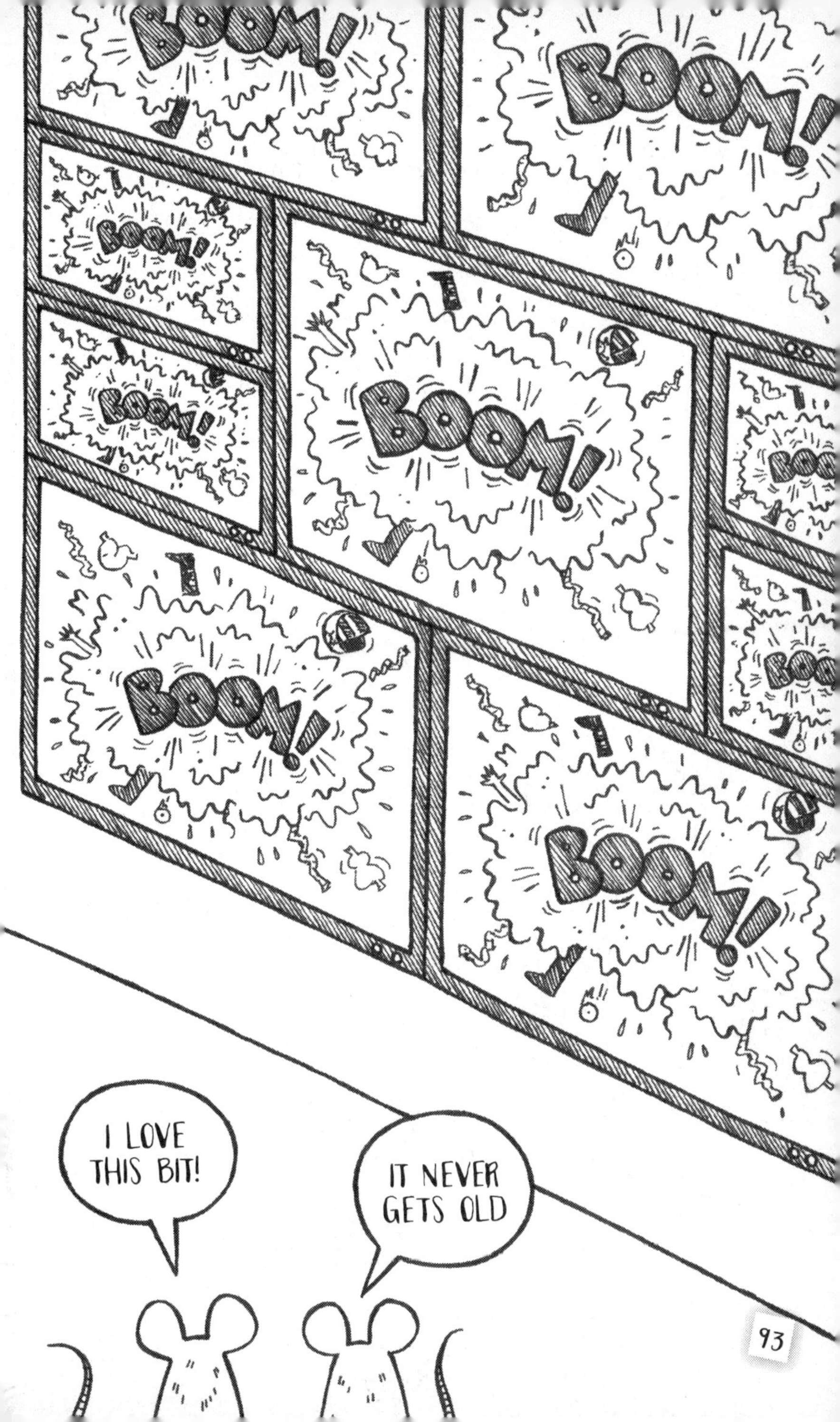
BOOM!
BOOM!
BOOM!
BOOM!
BOOM!
BOOM!
BOOM!
I LOVE THIS BIT!
IT NEVER GETS OLD

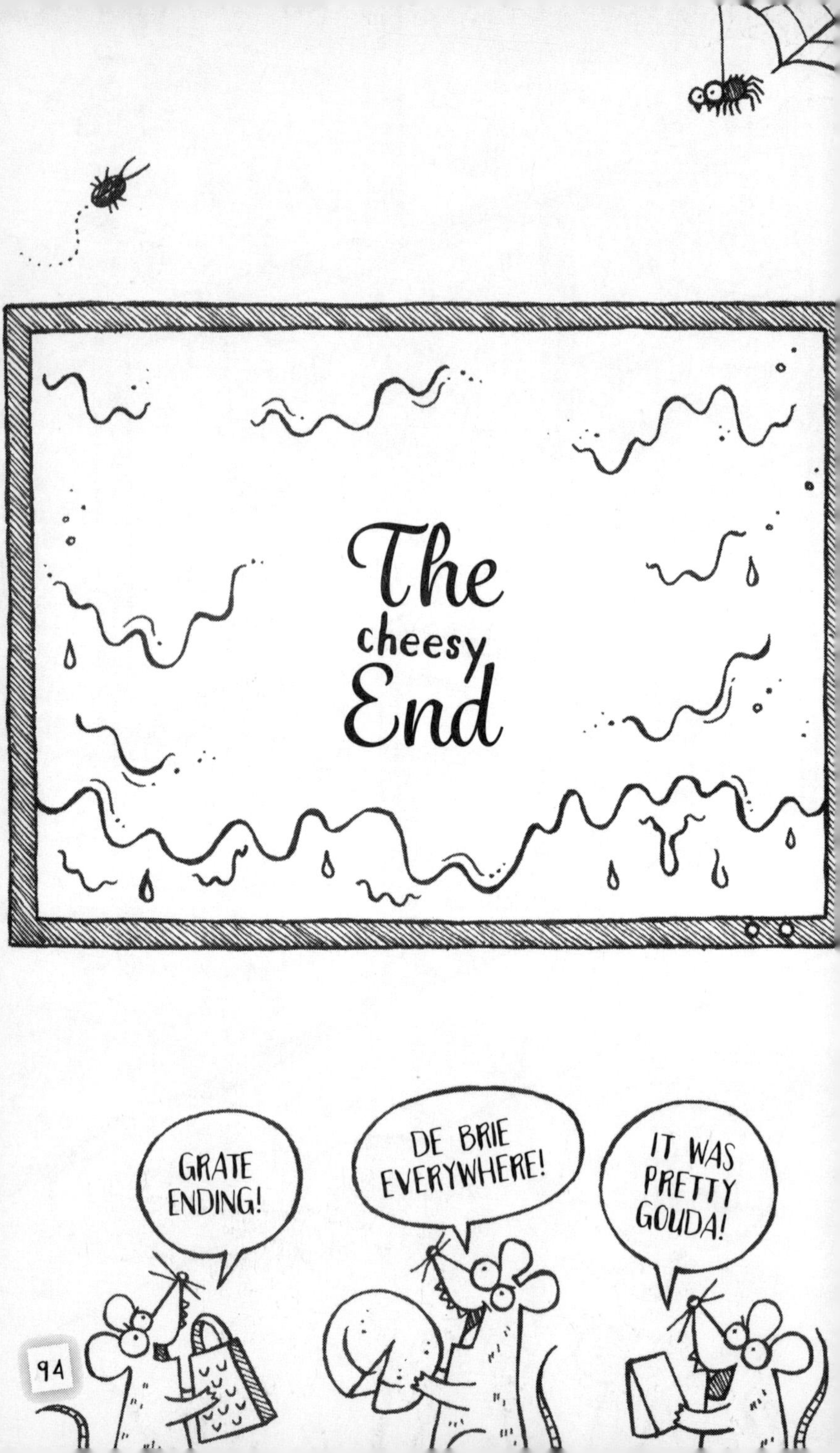
The cheesy End
GRATE ENDING!
DE BRIE EVERYWHERE!
IT WAS PRETTY GOUDA!

The Moral of the Story:
1. Never trust someone who cuts the cheese.
2. Watch out for full moons.
3. Food allergies are no joke!

I'VE SEEN FETTA

HOW DAIRY!

I CAMEMBERT IT!

How to Draw Little

STEP 1   Start with a boring old pic of Little Red Riding Hood.

STEP 2   Turn the hood into a helmet and cover the face with a visor.

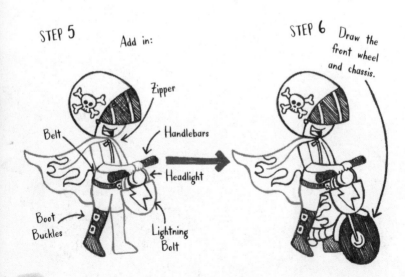

STEP 5   Add in:

Zipper

Belt

Handlebars

Headlight

Boot Buckles

Lightning Bolt

STEP 6   Draw the front wheel and chassis.

Stunt Riding Hood!

STEP 3 Add a skull and crossbones to the helmet!

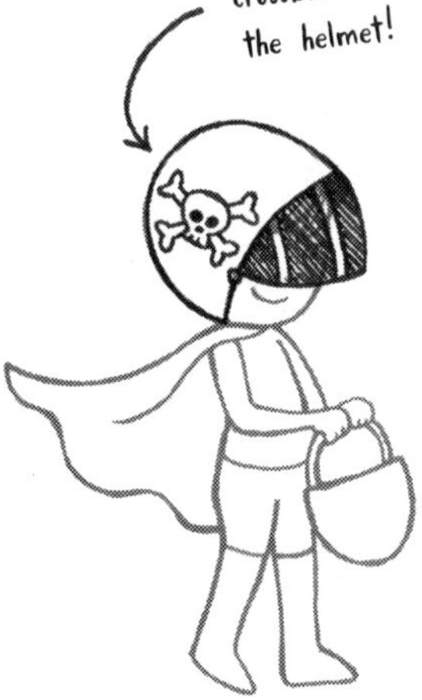

STEP 4 Draw some flames on the cape.

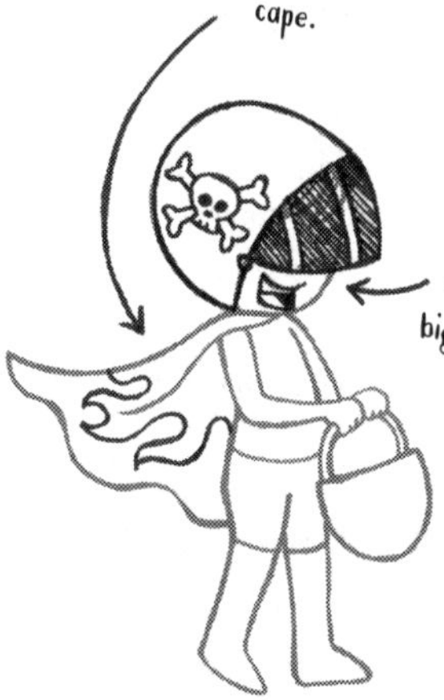

Add a big smile.

STEP 7 Add the back wheel and exhaust pipe.

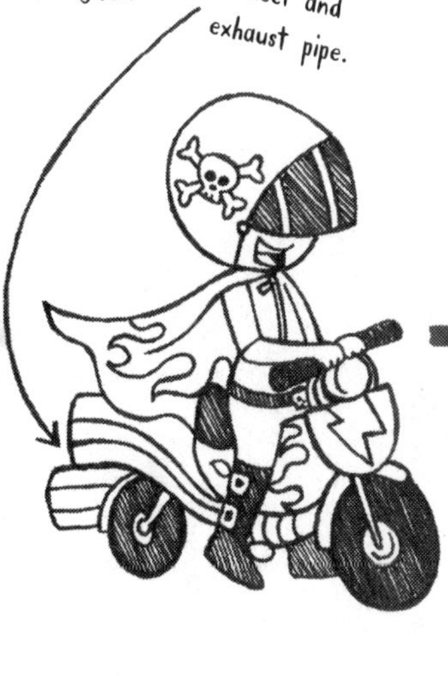

STEP 8 Finishing touches of flames and speed lines.

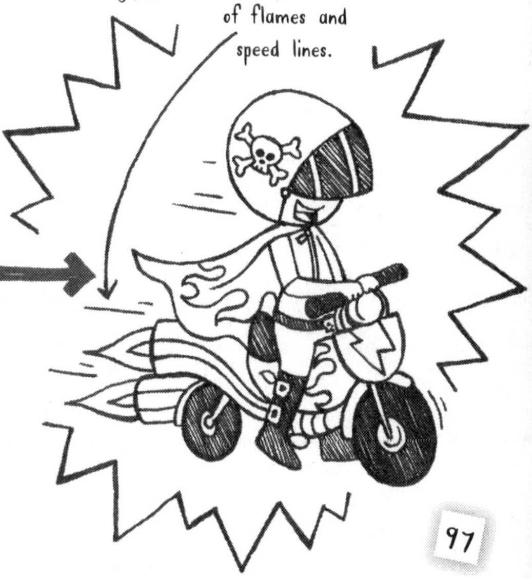

BEST BONUS STORY EVER CONTINUED!!!*

$\longrightarrow$

*I know the suspense has been killing you!

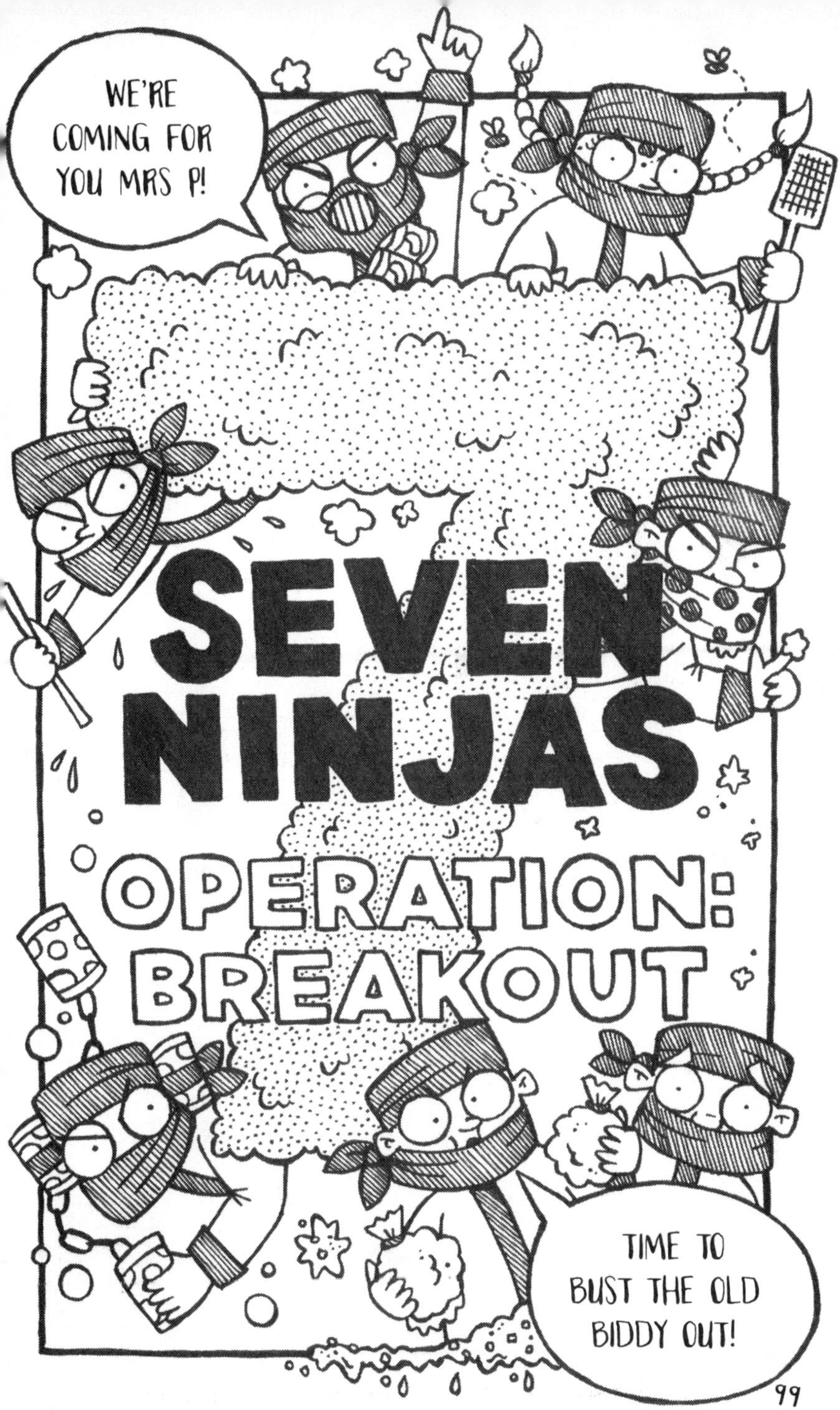
WE'RE COMING FOR YOU MRS P!
SEVEN NINJAS
OPERATION: BREAKOUT
TIME TO BUST THE OLD BIDDY OUT!

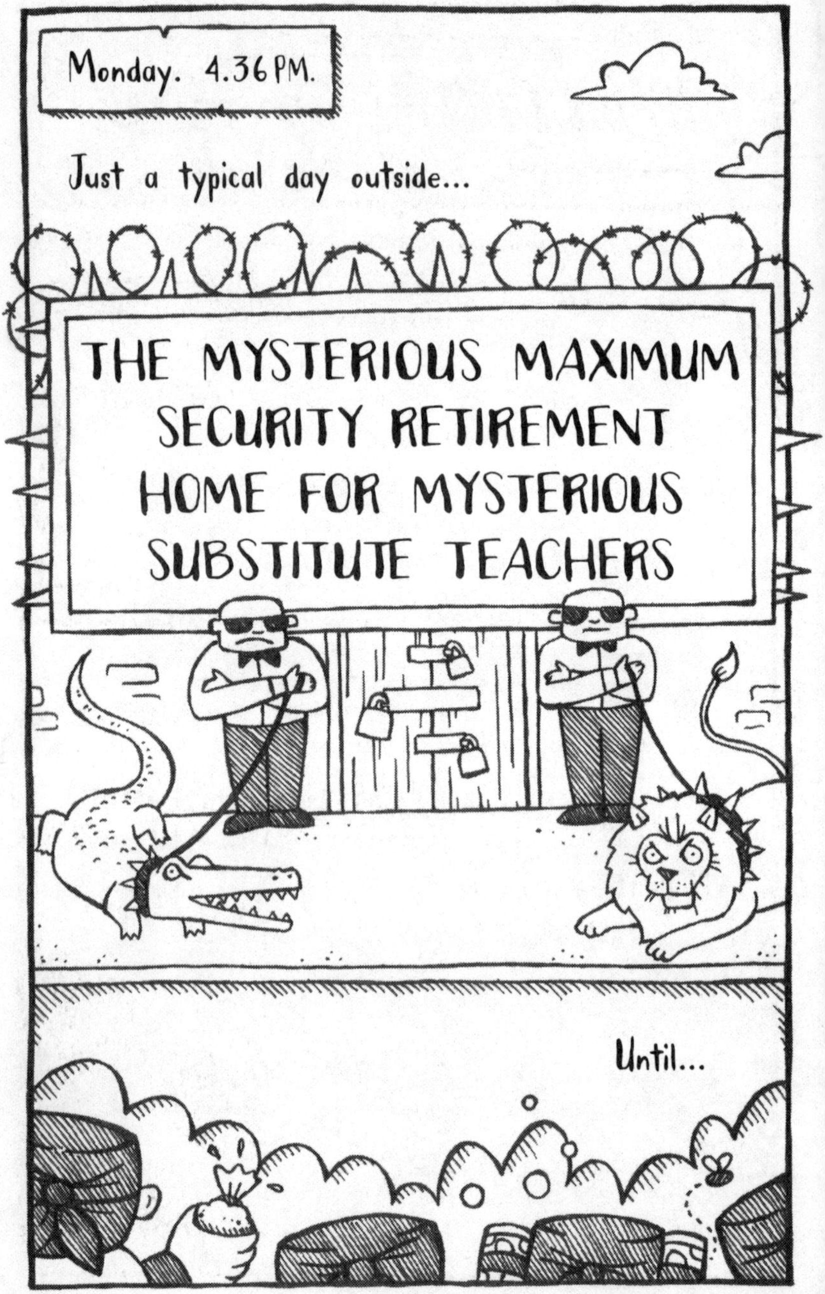
Monday. 4.36 PM.
Just a typical day outside...
THE MYSTERIOUS MAXIMUM SECURITY RETIREMENT HOME FOR MYSTERIOUS SUBSTITUTE TEACHERS
Until...

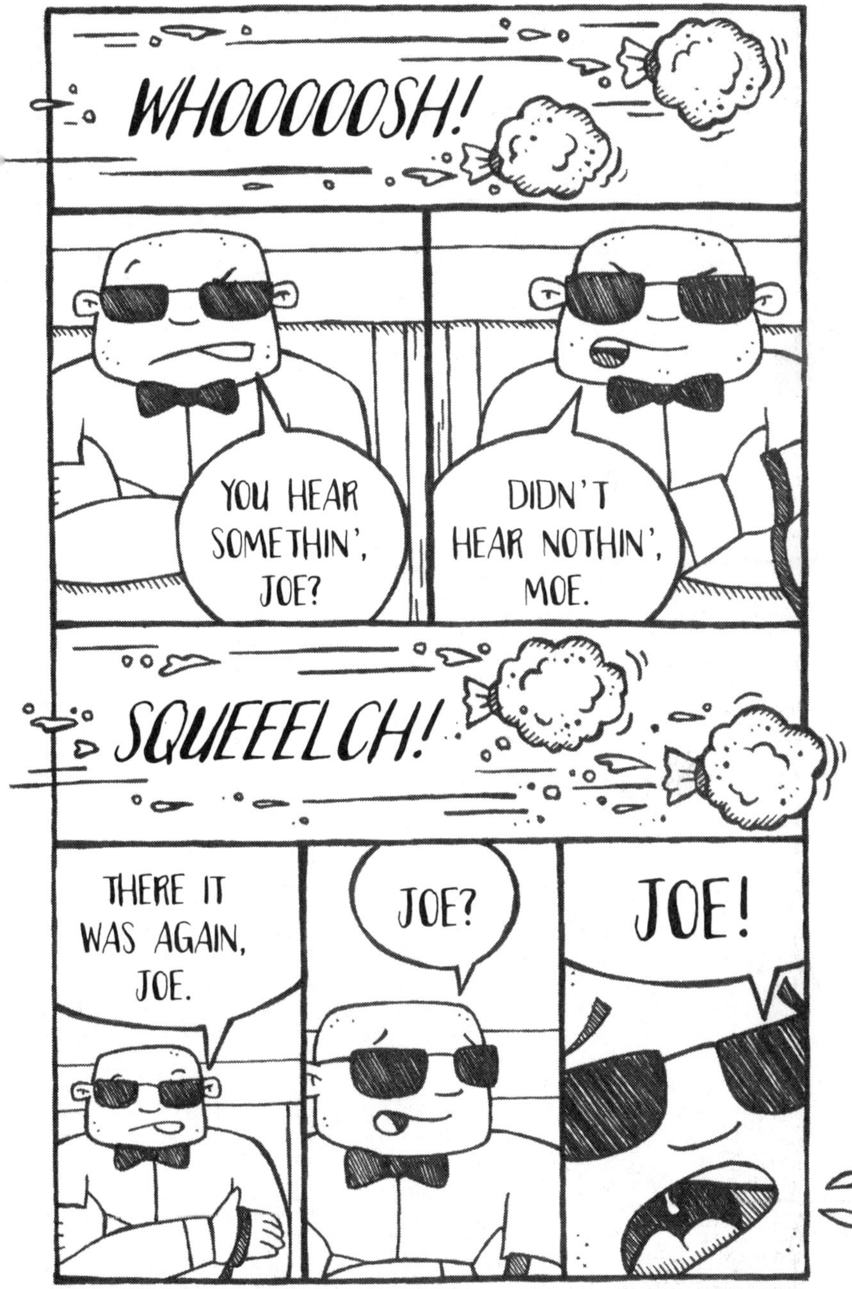
WHOOOOOOSH!
YOU HEAR SOMETHIN', JOE?
DIDN'T HEAR NOTHIN', MOE.
SQUEEELCH!
THERE IT WAS AGAIN, JOE.
JOE?
JOE!

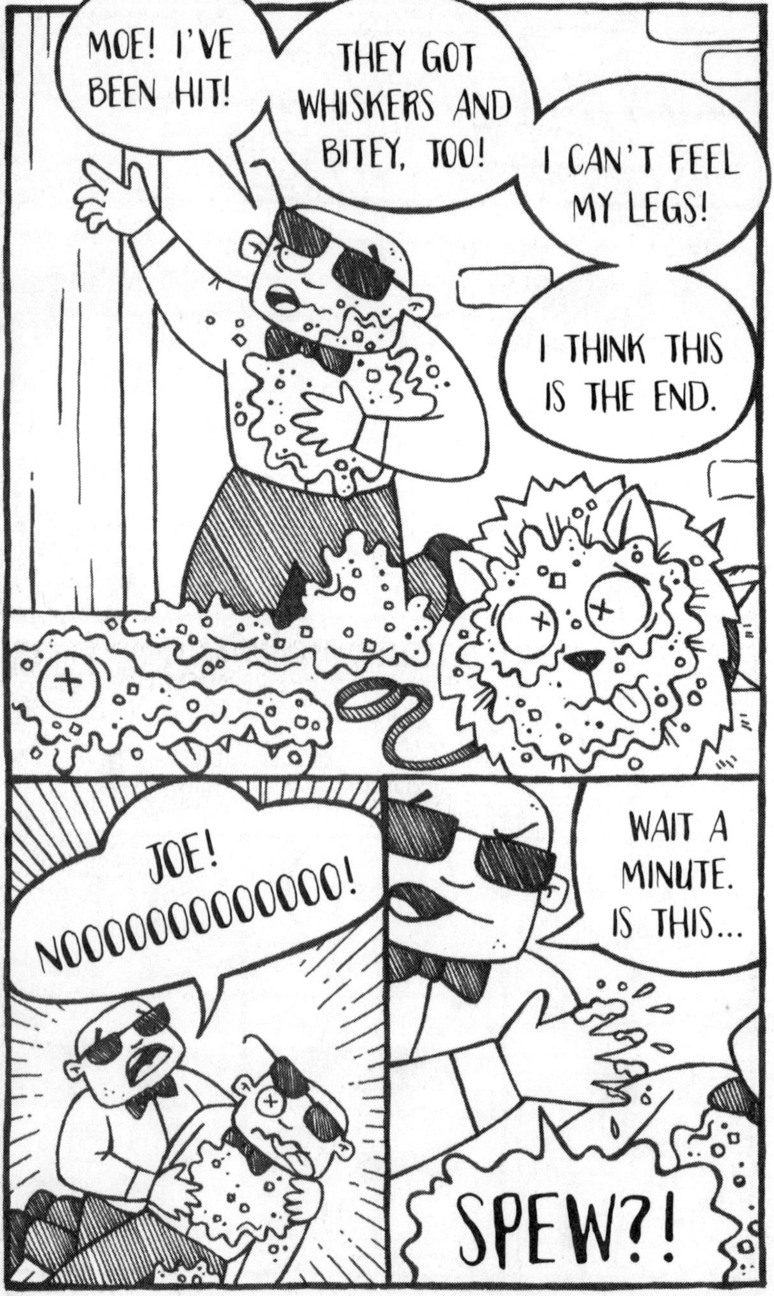
MOE! I'VE BEEN HIT!
THEY GOT WHISKERS AND BITEY, TOO!
I CAN'T FEEL MY LEGS!
I THINK THIS IS THE END.
JOE! NOOOOOOOOOOOOOO!
WAIT A MINUTE. IS THIS...
SPEW?!

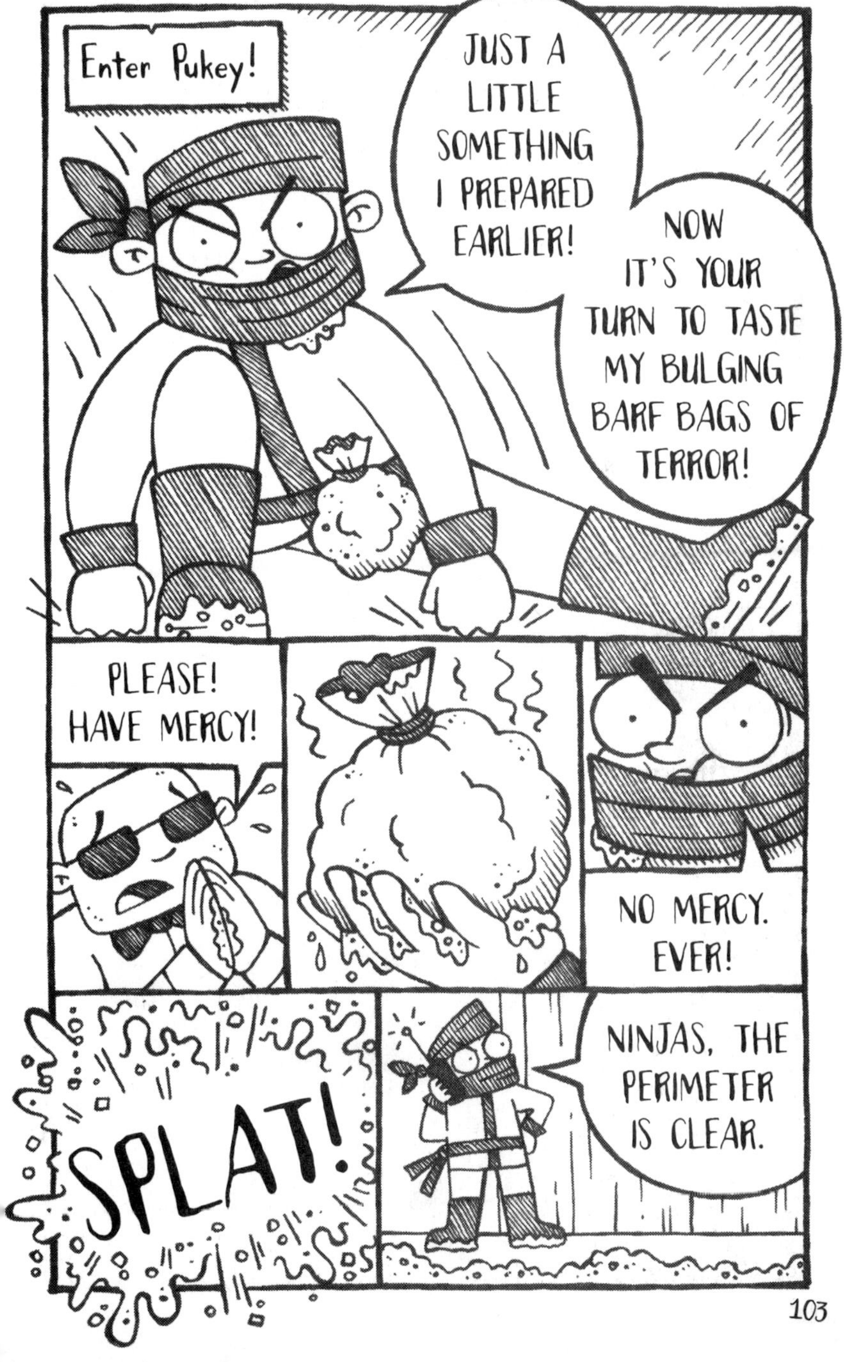
Enter Pukey!
JUST A LITTLE SOMETHING I PREPARED EARLIER!
NOW IT'S YOUR TURN TO TASTE MY BULGING BARF BAGS OF TERROR!
PLEASE! HAVE MERCY!
NO MERCY. EVER!
SPLAT!
NINJAS, THE PERIMETER IS CLEAR.

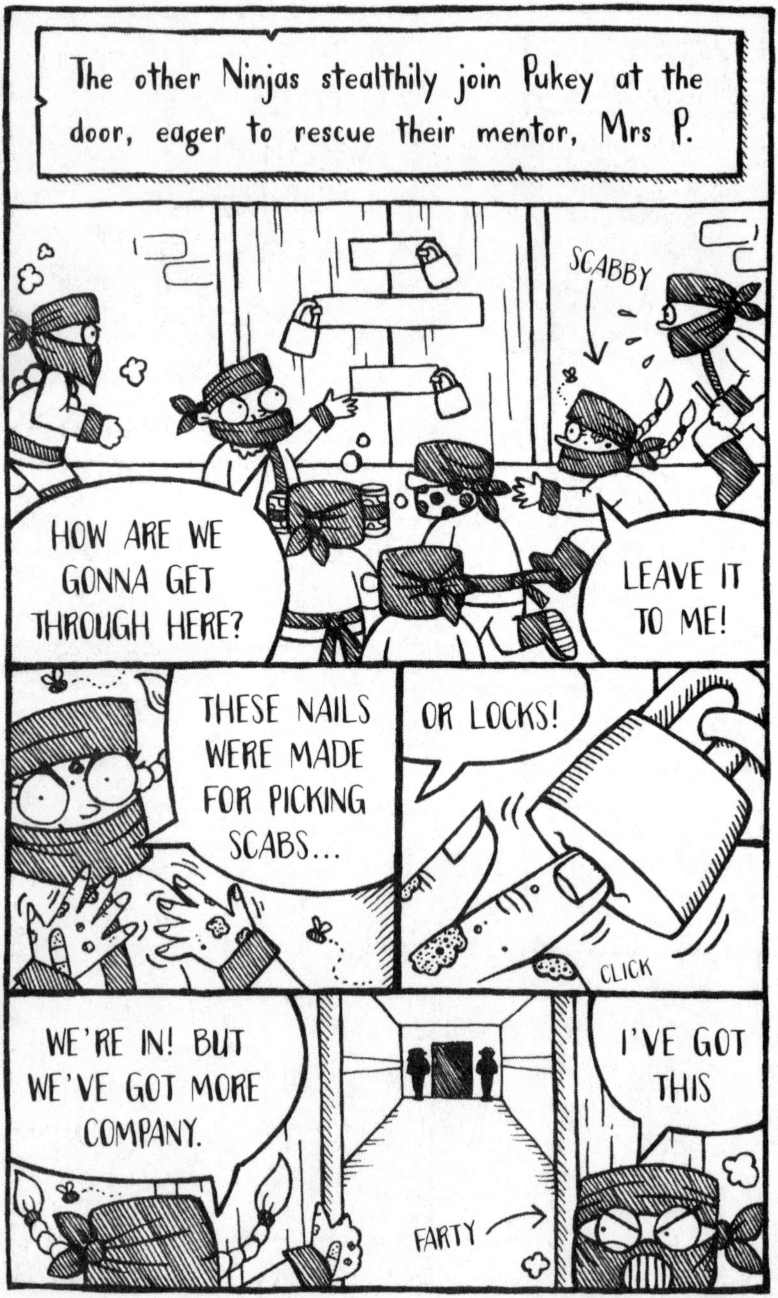
The other Ninjas stealthily join Pukey at the door, eager to rescue their mentor, Mrs P.
SCABBY
HOW ARE WE GONNA GET THROUGH HERE?
LEAVE IT TO ME!
THESE NAILS WERE MADE FOR PICKING SCABS...
OR LOCKS!
CLICK
WE'RE IN! BUT WE'VE GOT MORE COMPANY.
I'VE GOT THIS
FARTY

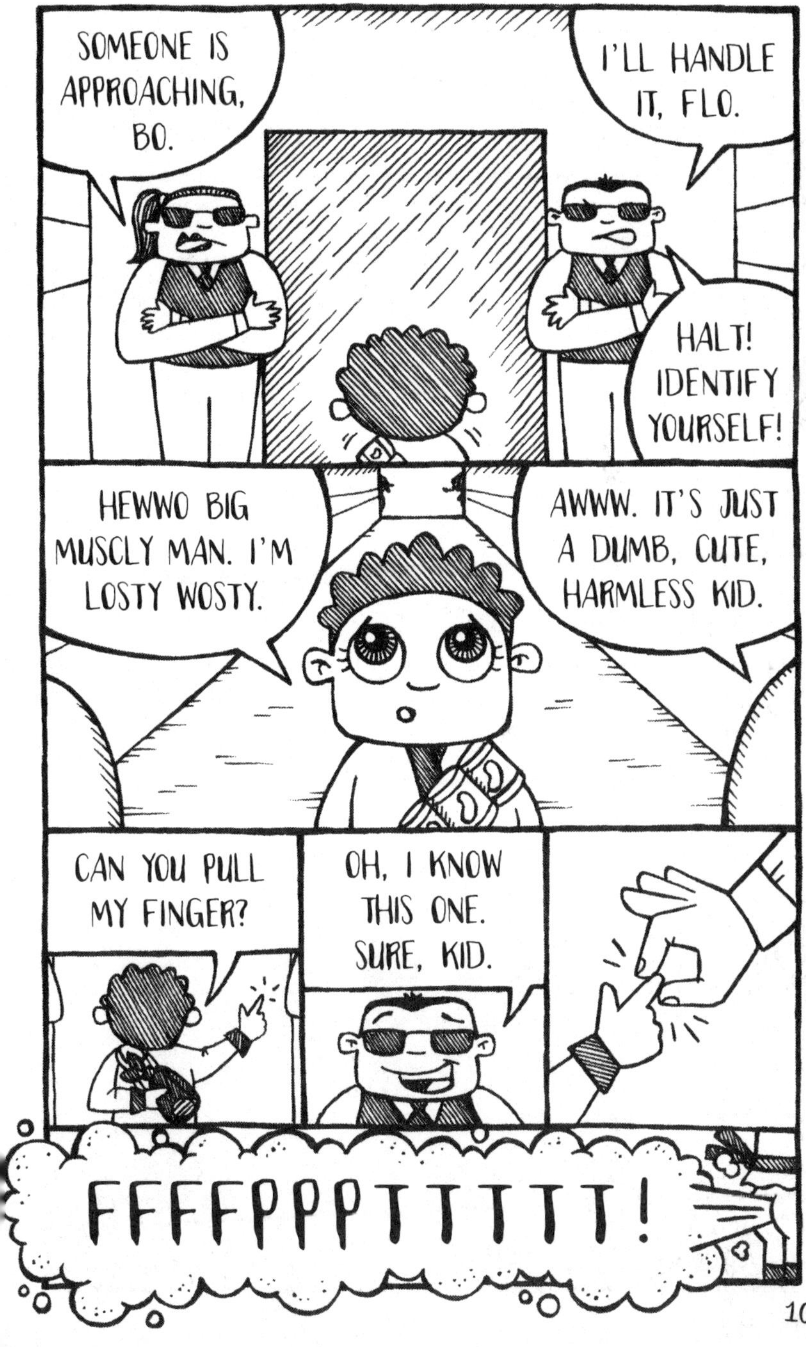
SOMEONE IS APPROACHING, BO.
I'LL HANDLE IT, FLO.
HALT! IDENTIFY YOURSELF!
HEWWO BIG MUSCLY MAN. I'M LOSTY WOSTY.
AWWW. IT'S JUST A DUMB, CUTE, HARMLESS KID.
CAN YOU PULL MY FINGER?
OH, I KNOW THIS ONE. SURE, KID.
FFFFPPPTTTTTT!

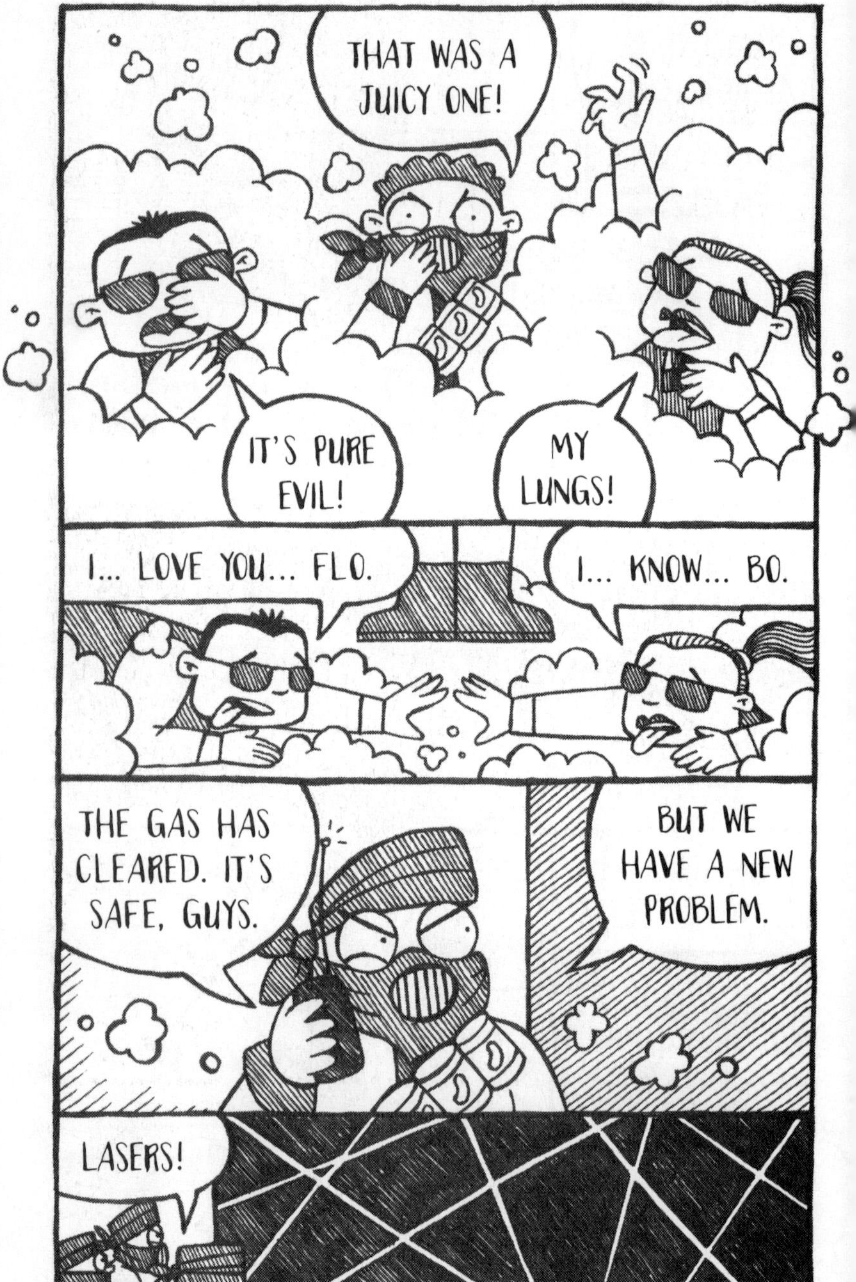

THAT WAS A JUICY ONE!
IT'S PURE EVIL!
MY LUNGS!
I... LOVE YOU... FLO.
I... KNOW... BO.
THE GAS HAS CLEARED. IT'S SAFE, GUYS.
BUT WE HAVE A NEW PROBLEM.
LASERS!

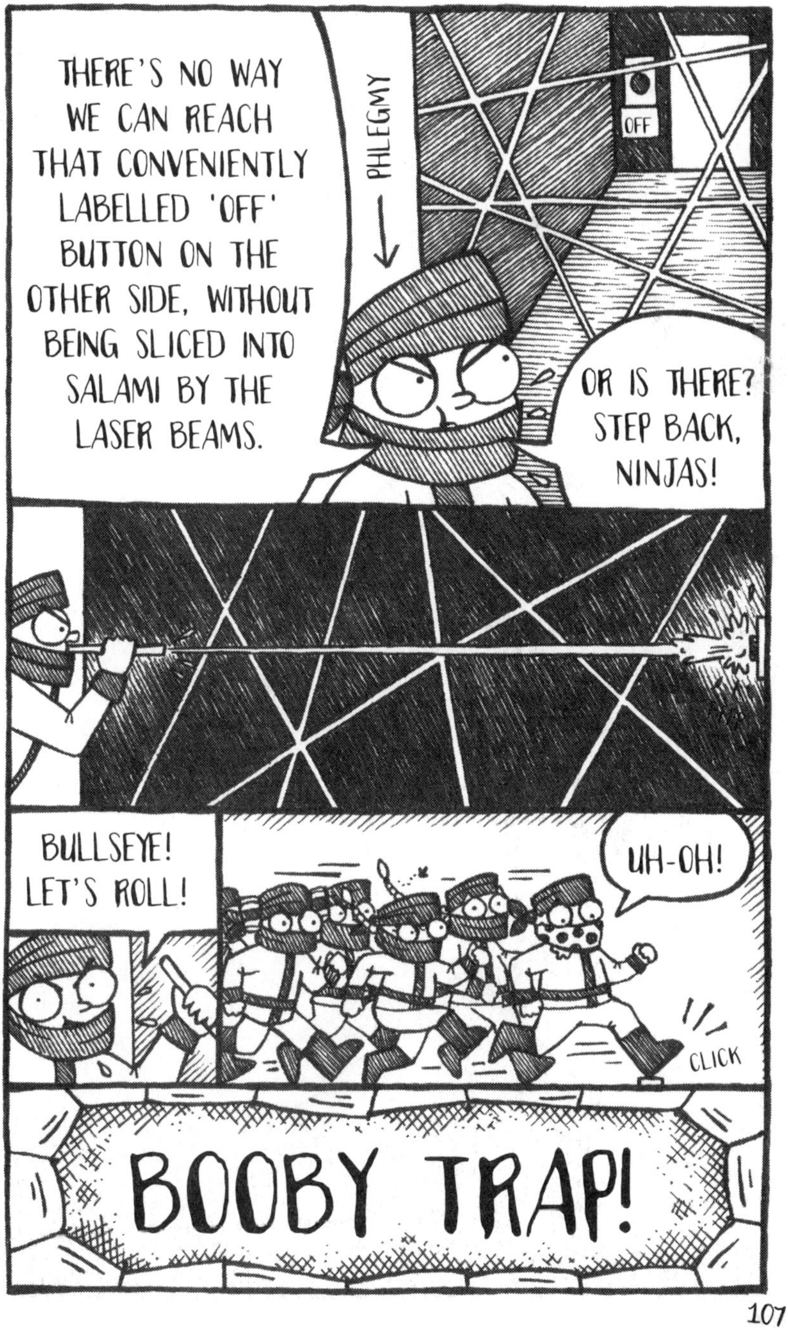
THERE'S NO WAY WE CAN REACH THAT CONVENIENTLY LABELLED 'OFF' BUTTON ON THE OTHER SIDE, WITHOUT BEING SLICED INTO SALAMI BY THE LASER BEAMS.
PHLEGMY
OFF
OR IS THERE? STEP BACK, NINJAS!
BULLSEYE! LET'S ROLL!
UH-OH!
CLICK
BOOBY TRAP!

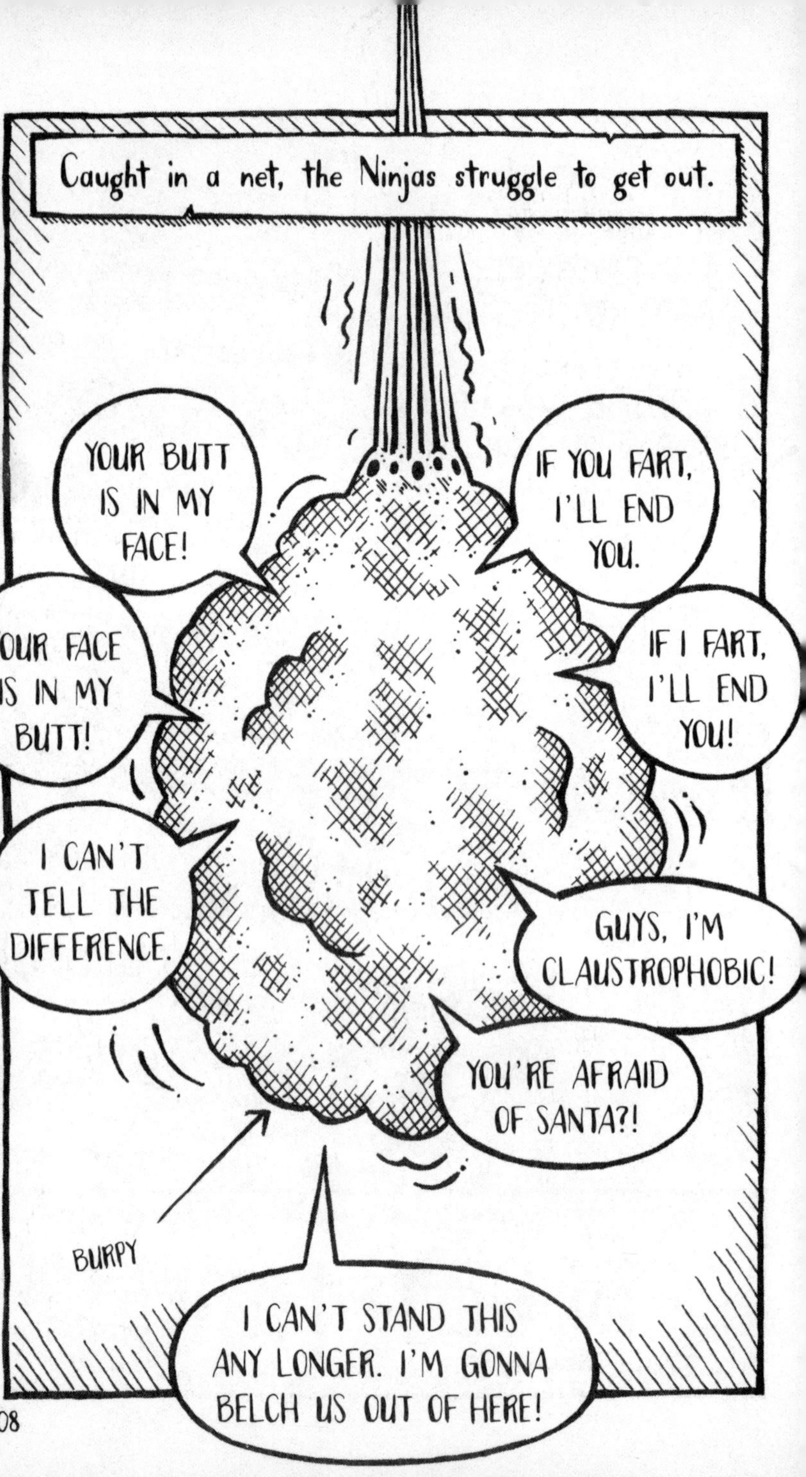
Caught in a net, the Ninjas struggle to get out.
YOUR BUTT IS IN MY FACE!
IF YOU FART, I'LL END YOU.
YOUR FACE IS IN MY BUTT!
IF I FART, I'LL END YOU!
I CAN'T TELL THE DIFFERENCE.
GUYS, I'M CLAUSTROPHOBIC!
YOU'RE AFRAID OF SANTA?!
BURPY
I CAN'T STAND THIS ANY LONGER. I'M GONNA BELCH US OUT OF HERE!

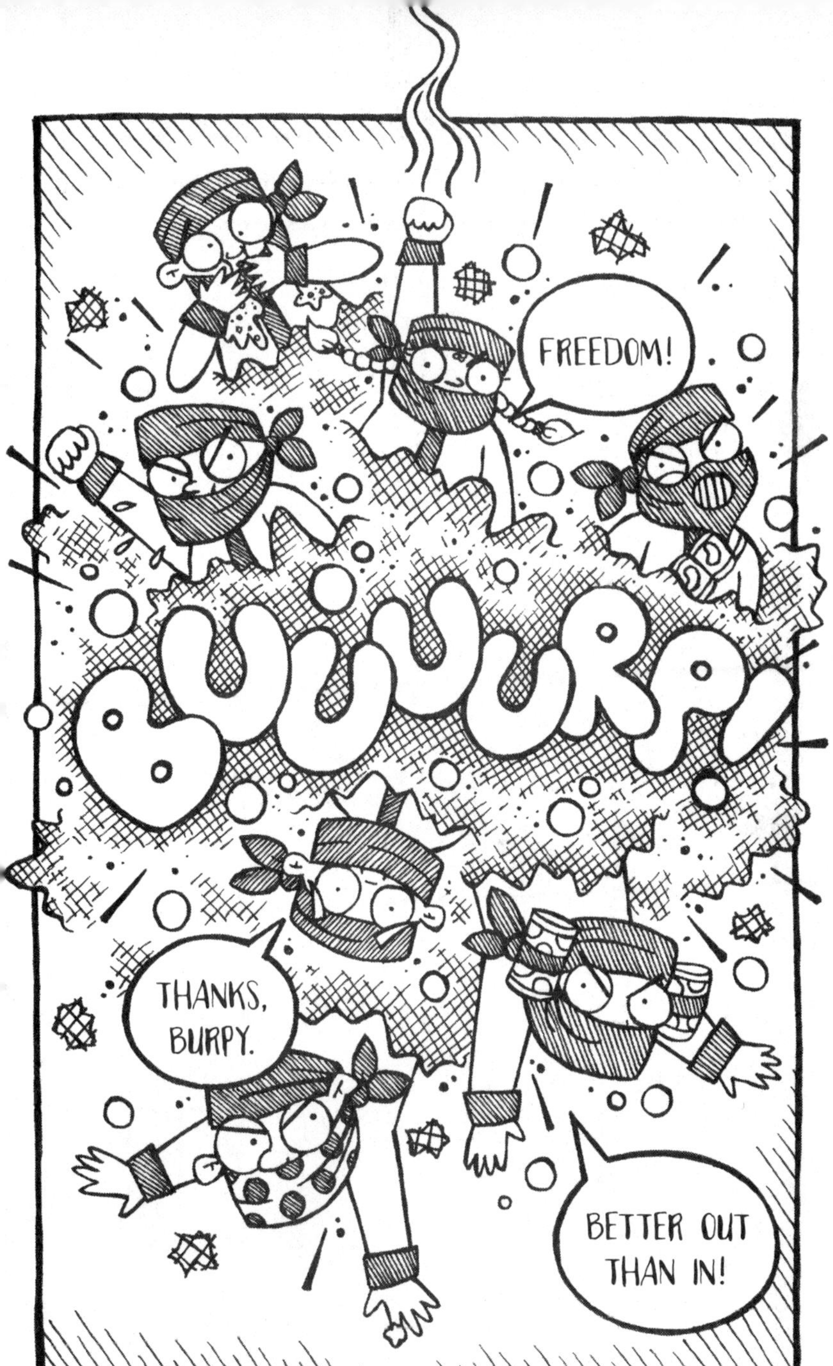
FREEDOM!
BUUUURP!
THANKS, BURPY.
BETTER OUT THAN IN!

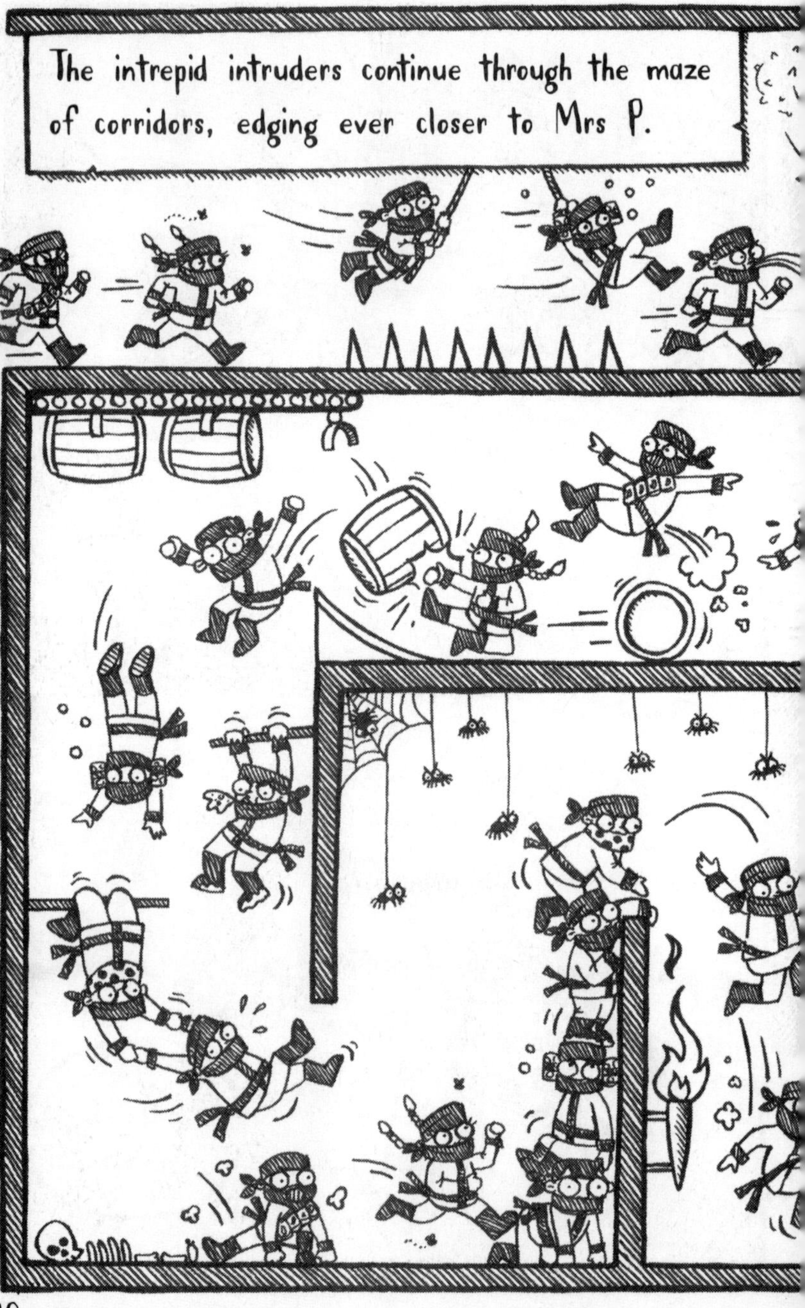
The intrepid intruders continue through the maze of corridors, edging ever closer to Mrs P.

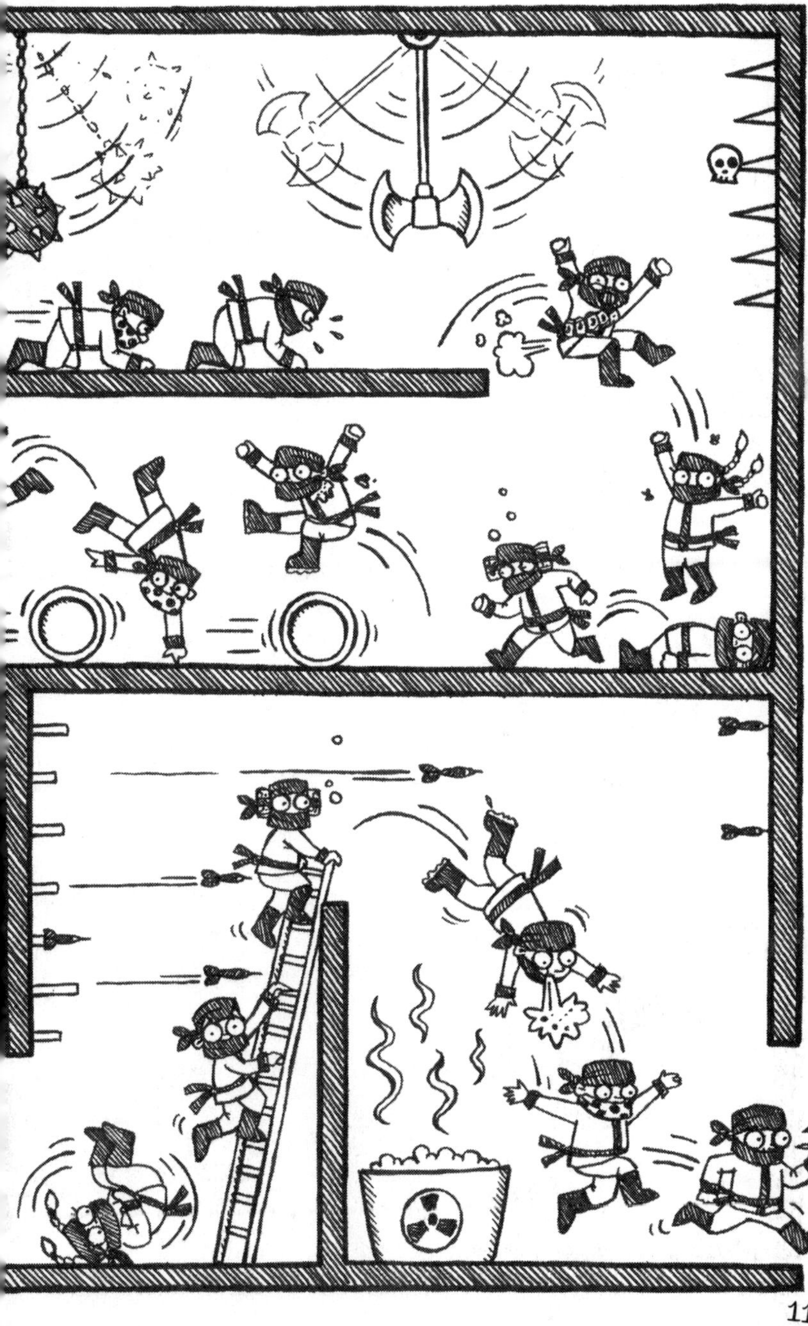

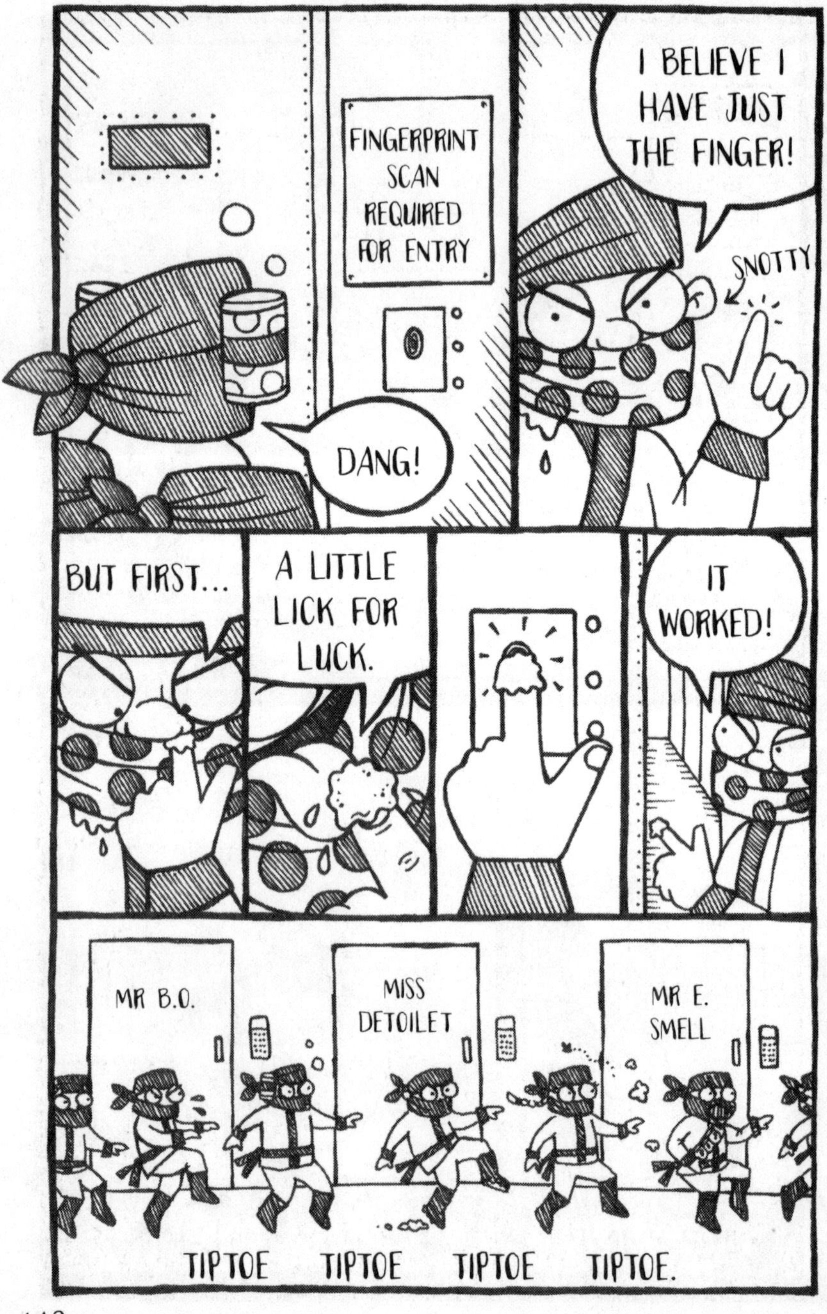
FINGERPRINT SCAN REQUIRED FOR ENTRY
DANG!
I BELIEVE I HAVE JUST THE FINGER!
SNOTTY
BUT FIRST...
A LITTLE LICK FOR LUCK.
IT WORKED!
MR B.O.
MISS DETOILET
MR E. SMELL
TIPTOE TIPTOE TIPTOE TIPTOE.

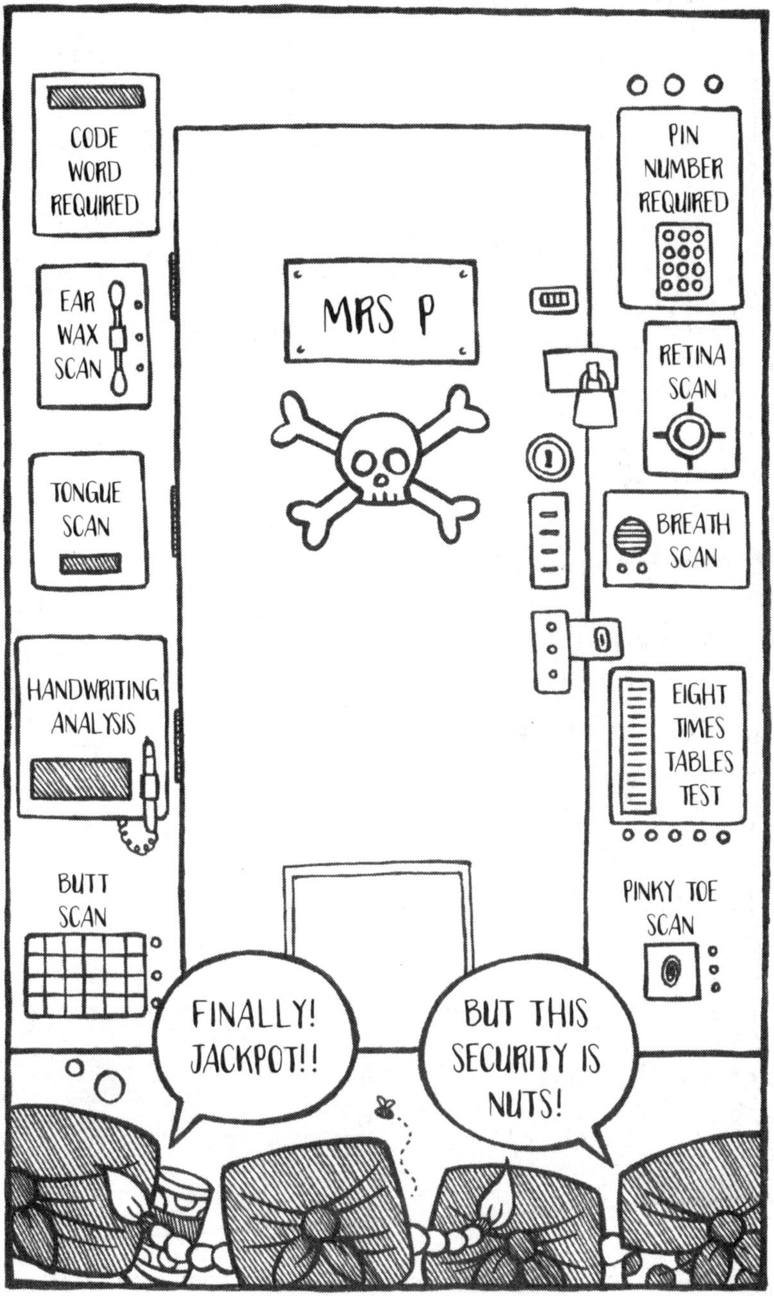
CODE WORD REQUIRED
PIN NUMBER REQUIRED
EAR WAX SCAN
MRS P
RETINA SCAN
TONGUE SCAN
BREATH SCAN
HANDWRITING ANALYSIS
EIGHT TIMES TABLES TEST
BUTT SCAN
PINKY TOE SCAN
FINALLY! JACKPOT!!
BUT THIS SECURITY IS NUTS!

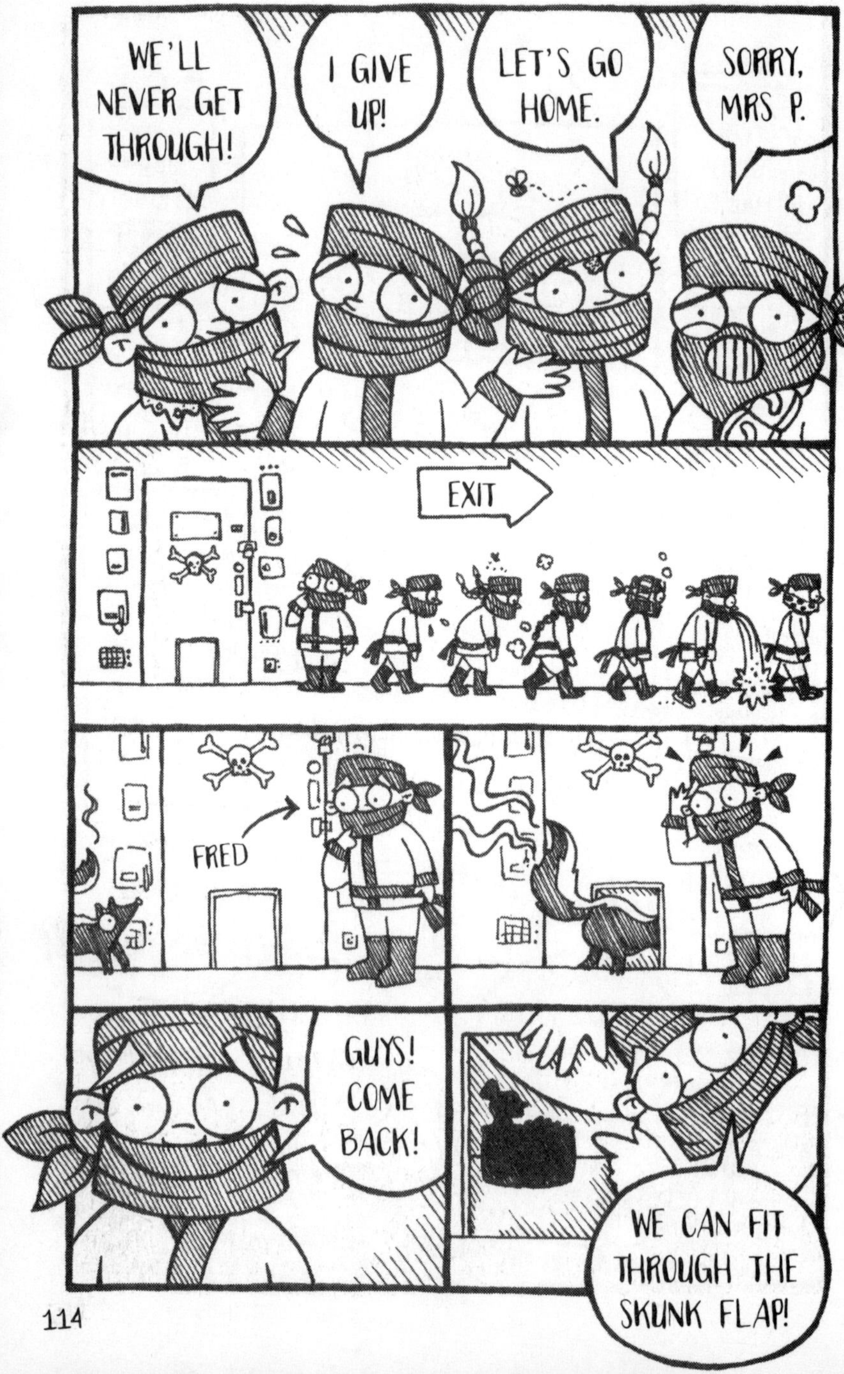
WE'LL NEVER GET THROUGH!
I GIVE UP!
LET'S GO HOME.
SORRY, MRS P.
EXIT
FRED
GUYS! COME BACK!
WE CAN FIT THROUGH THE SKUNK FLAP!

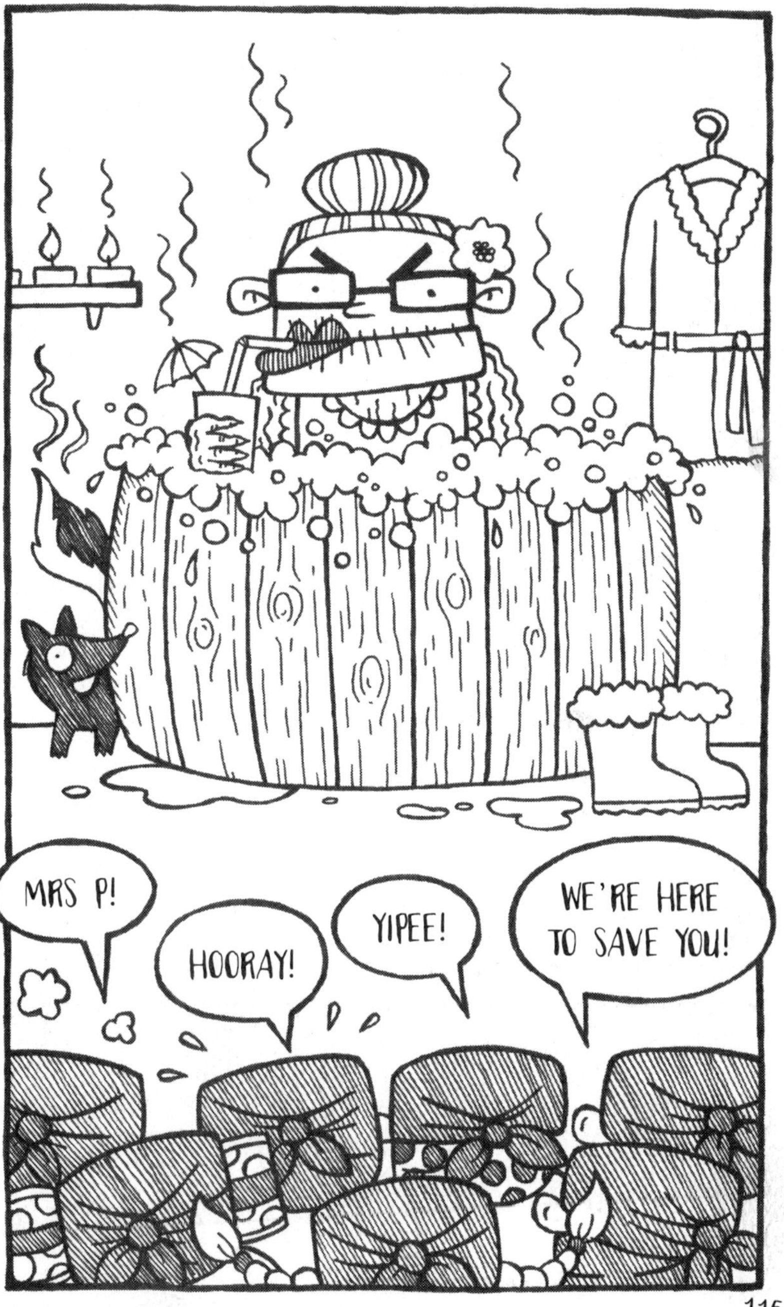
MRS P!
HOORAY!
YIPEE!
WE'RE HERE TO SAVE YOU!

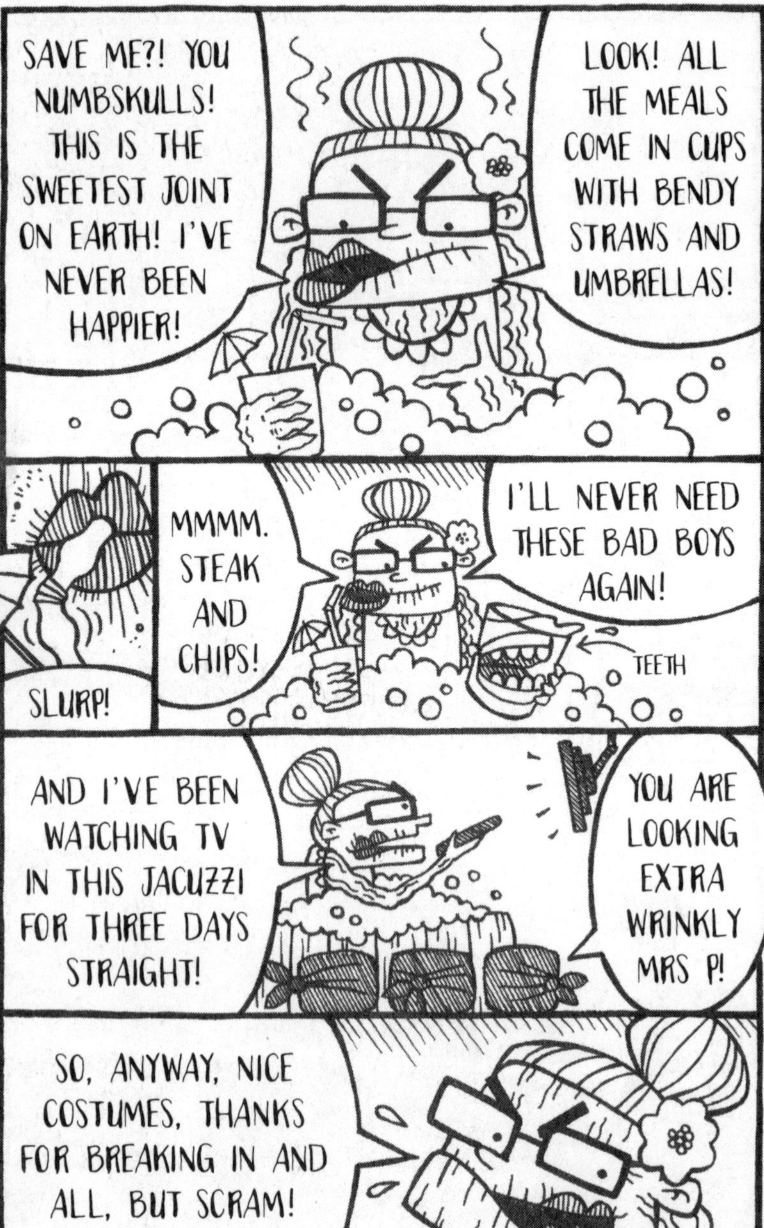
SAVE ME?! YOU NUMBSKULLS! THIS IS THE SWEETEST JOINT ON EARTH! I'VE NEVER BEEN HAPPIER!
LOOK! ALL THE MEALS COME IN CUPS WITH BENDY STRAWS AND UMBRELLAS!
SLURP!
MMMM. STEAK AND CHIPS!
I'LL NEVER NEED THESE BAD BOYS AGAIN!
TEETH
AND I'VE BEEN WATCHING TV IN THIS JACUZZI FOR THREE DAYS STRAIGHT!
YOU ARE LOOKING EXTRA WRINKLY MRS P!
SO, ANYWAY, NICE COSTUMES, THANKS FOR BREAKING IN AND ALL, BUT SCRAM! I'M NOT LEAVING!

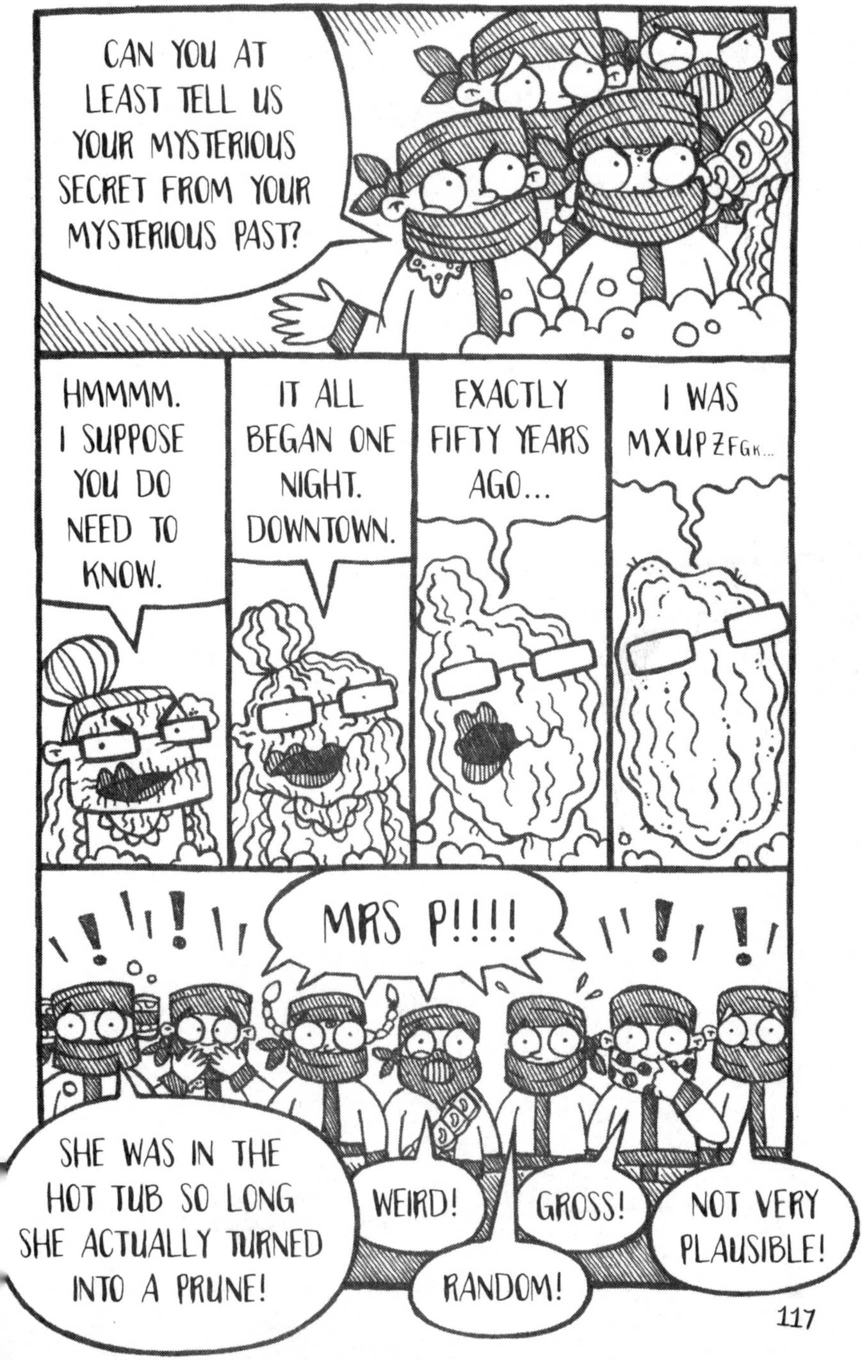
CAN YOU AT LEAST TELL US YOUR MYSTERIOUS SECRET FROM YOUR MYSTERIOUS PAST?
HMMMM. I SUPPOSE YOU DO NEED TO KNOW.
IT ALL BEGAN ONE NIGHT. DOWNTOWN.
EXACTLY FIFTY YEARS AGO...
I WAS MXUPZFGK...
MRS P!!!!
SHE WAS IN THE HOT TUB SO LONG SHE ACTUALLY TURNED INTO A PRUNE!
WEIRD!
RANDOM!
GROSS!
NOT VERY PLAUSIBLE!

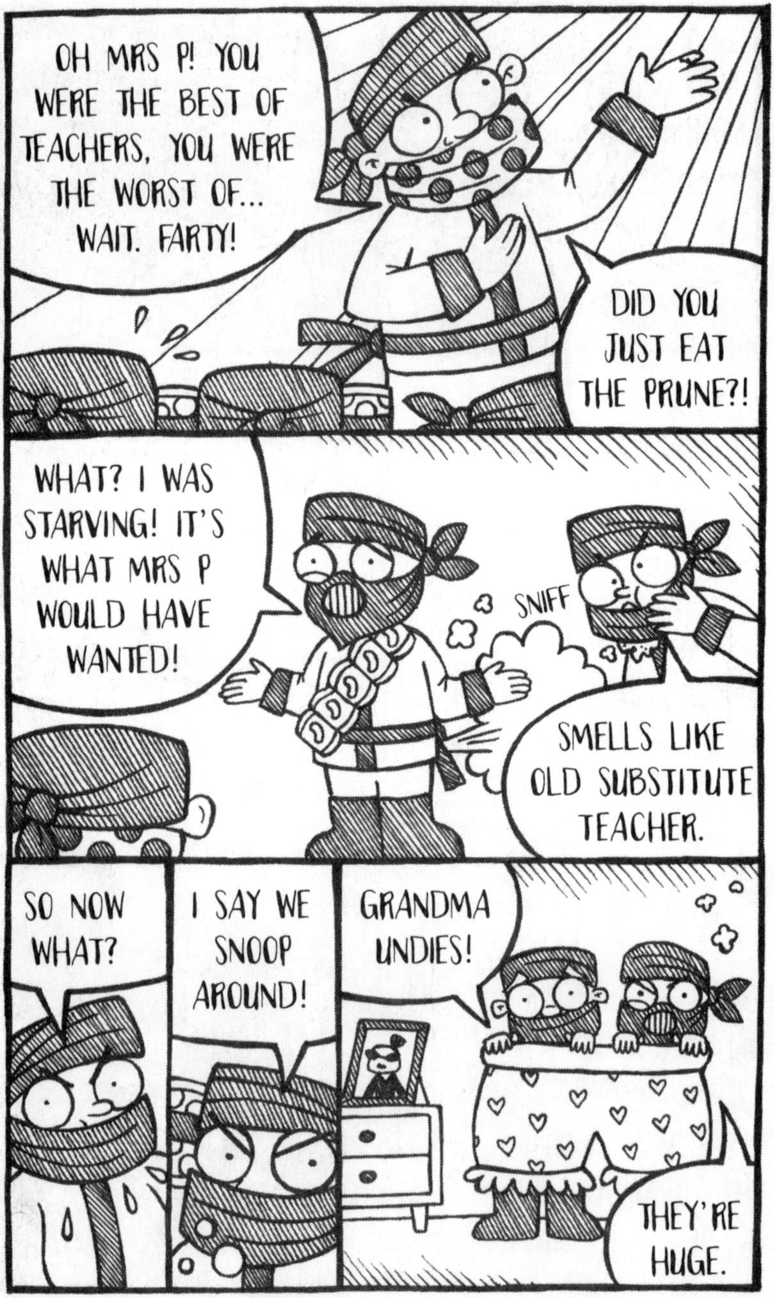
OH MRS P! YOU WERE THE BEST OF TEACHERS, YOU WERE THE WORST OF... WAIT. FARTY!
DID YOU JUST EAT THE PRUNE?!
WHAT? I WAS STARVING! IT'S WHAT MRS P WOULD HAVE WANTED!
SNIFF
SMELLS LIKE OLD SUBSTITUTE TEACHER.
SO NOW WHAT?
I SAY WE SNOOP AROUND!
GRANDMA UNDIES!
THEY'RE HUGE.

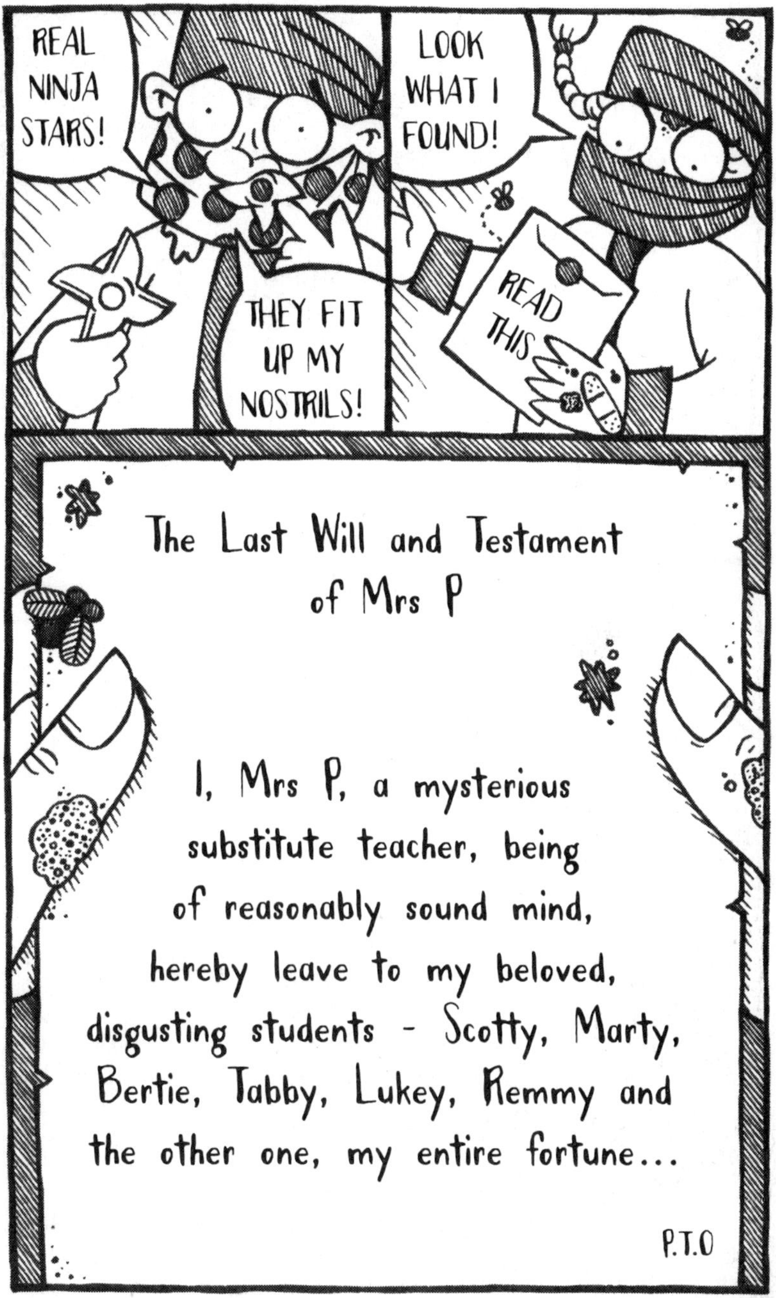
REAL NINJA STARS!
THEY FIT UP MY NOSTRILS!
LOOK WHAT I FOUND!
READ THIS
The Last Will and Testament of Mrs P
I, Mrs P, a mysterious substitute teacher, being of reasonably sound mind, hereby leave to my beloved, disgusting students - Scotty, Marty, Bertie, Tabby, Lukey, Remmy and the other one, my entire fortune...
P.T.O

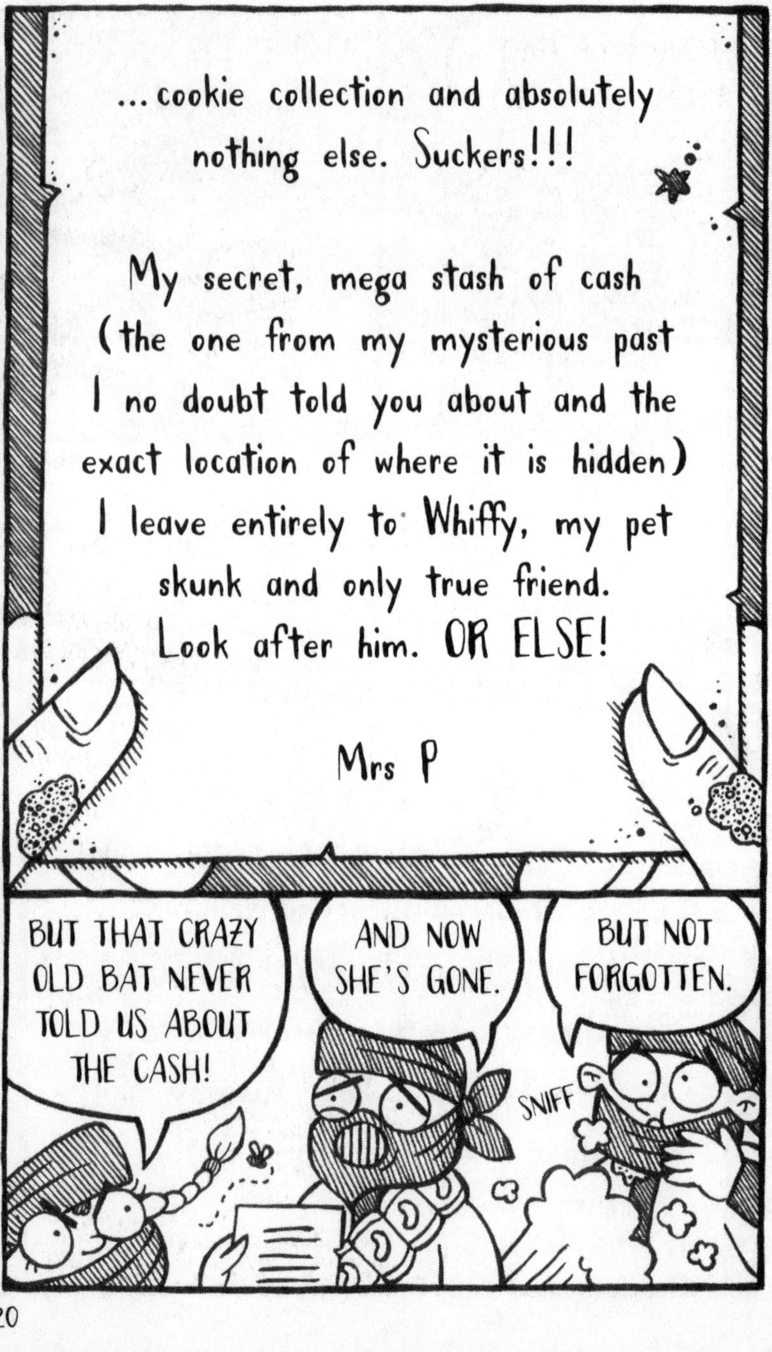
...cookie collection and absolutely nothing else. Suckers!!!
My secret, mega stash of cash (the one from my mysterious past I no doubt told you about and the exact location of where it is hidden) I leave entirely to Whiffy, my pet skunk and only true friend. Look after him. OR ELSE!
Mrs P
BUT THAT CRAZY OLD BAT NEVER TOLD US ABOUT THE CASH!
AND NOW SHE'S GONE.
BUT NOT FORGOTTEN.
SNIFF

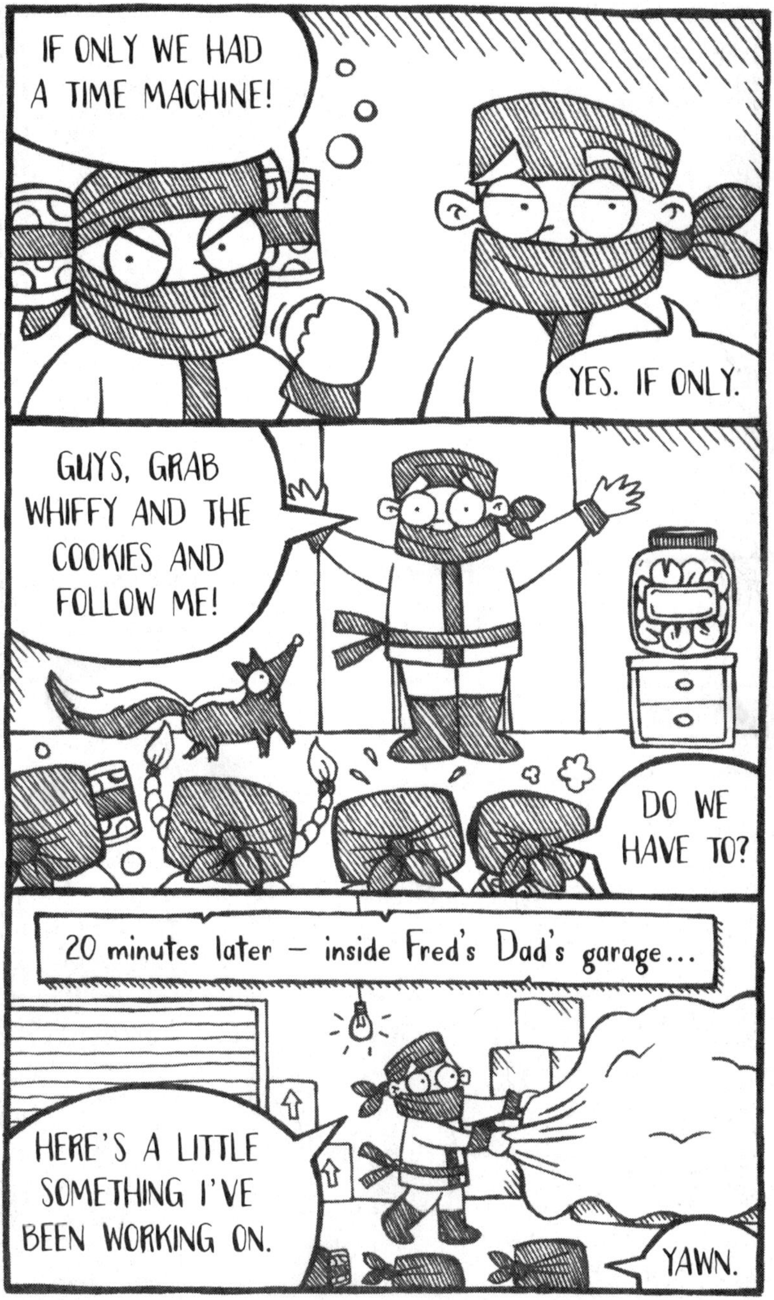
IF ONLY WE HAD A TIME MACHINE!
YES. IF ONLY.
GUYS, GRAB WHIFFY AND THE COOKIES AND FOLLOW ME!
DO WE HAVE TO?
20 minutes later – inside Fred's Dad's garage...
HERE'S A LITTLE SOMETHING I'VE BEEN WORKING ON.
YAWN.

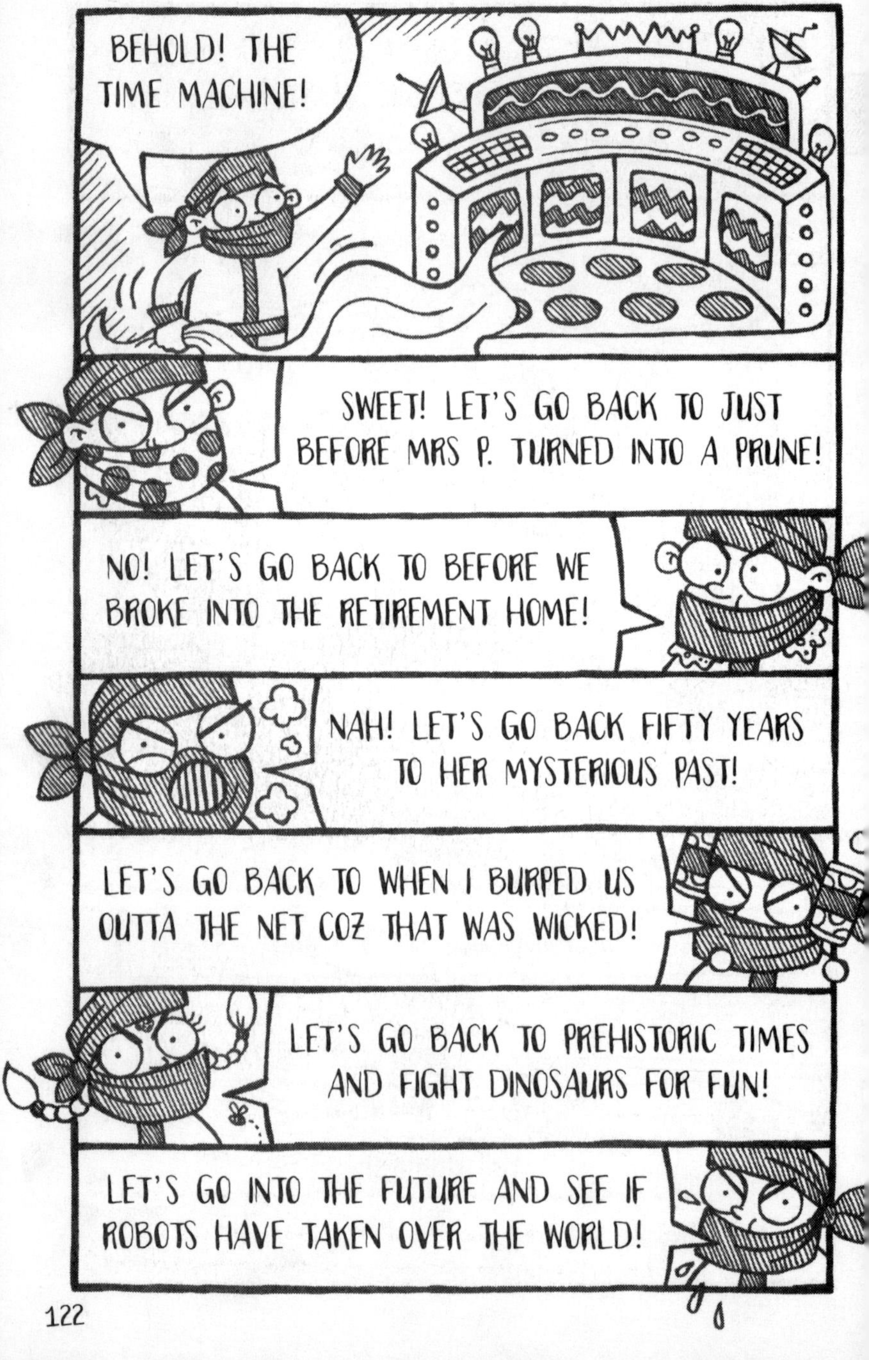
BEHOLD! THE TIME MACHINE!
SWEET! LET'S GO BACK TO JUST BEFORE MRS P. TURNED INTO A PRUNE!
NO! LET'S GO BACK TO BEFORE WE BROKE INTO THE RETIREMENT HOME!
NAH! LET'S GO BACK FIFTY YEARS TO HER MYSTERIOUS PAST!
LET'S GO BACK TO WHEN I BURPED US OUTTA THE NET COZ THAT WAS WICKED!
LET'S GO BACK TO PREHISTORIC TIMES AND FIGHT DINOSAURS FOR FUN!
LET'S GO INTO THE FUTURE AND SEE IF ROBOTS HAVE TAKEN OVER THE WORLD!

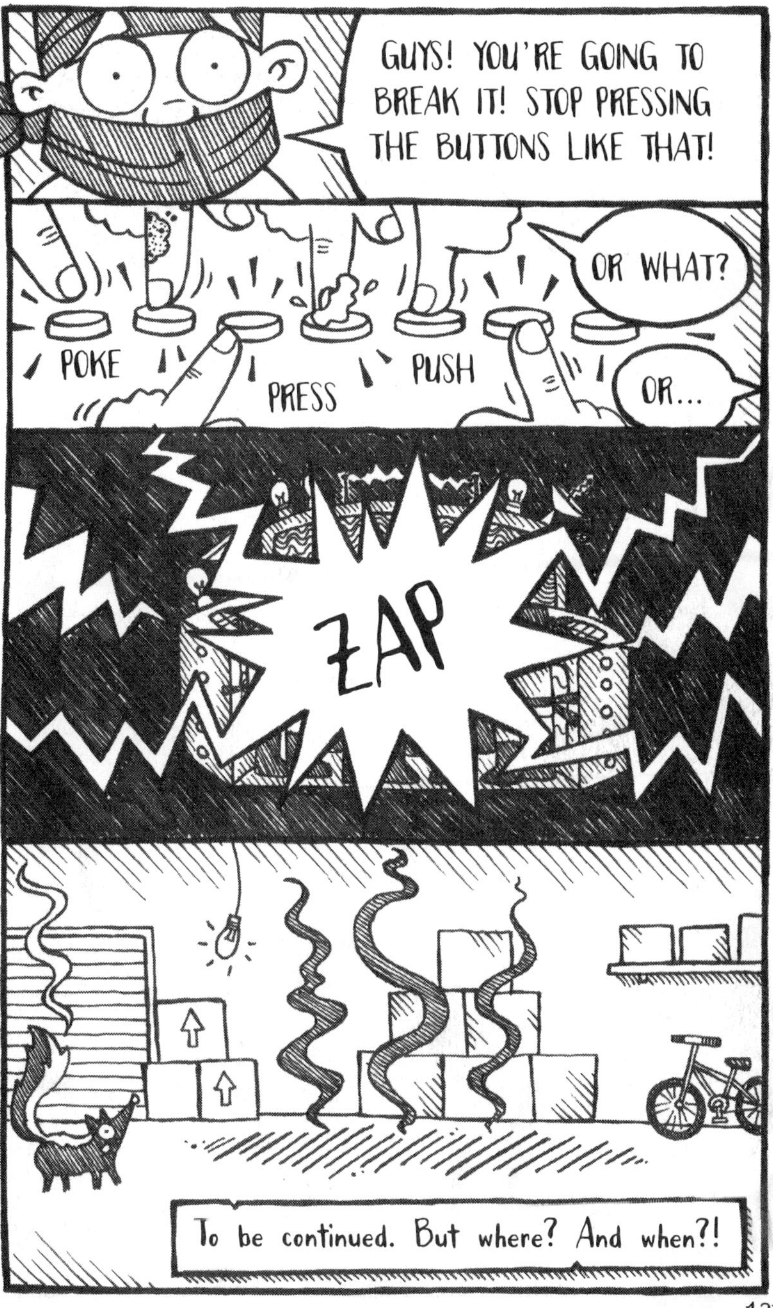
GUYS! YOU'RE GOING TO BREAK IT! STOP PRESSING THE BUTTONS LIKE THAT!
OR WHAT?
POKE
PRESS
PUSH
OR...
ZAP
To be continued. But where? And when?!

Also available
for parties and weddings...

SNOW MAN AND THE SEVEN NINJAS

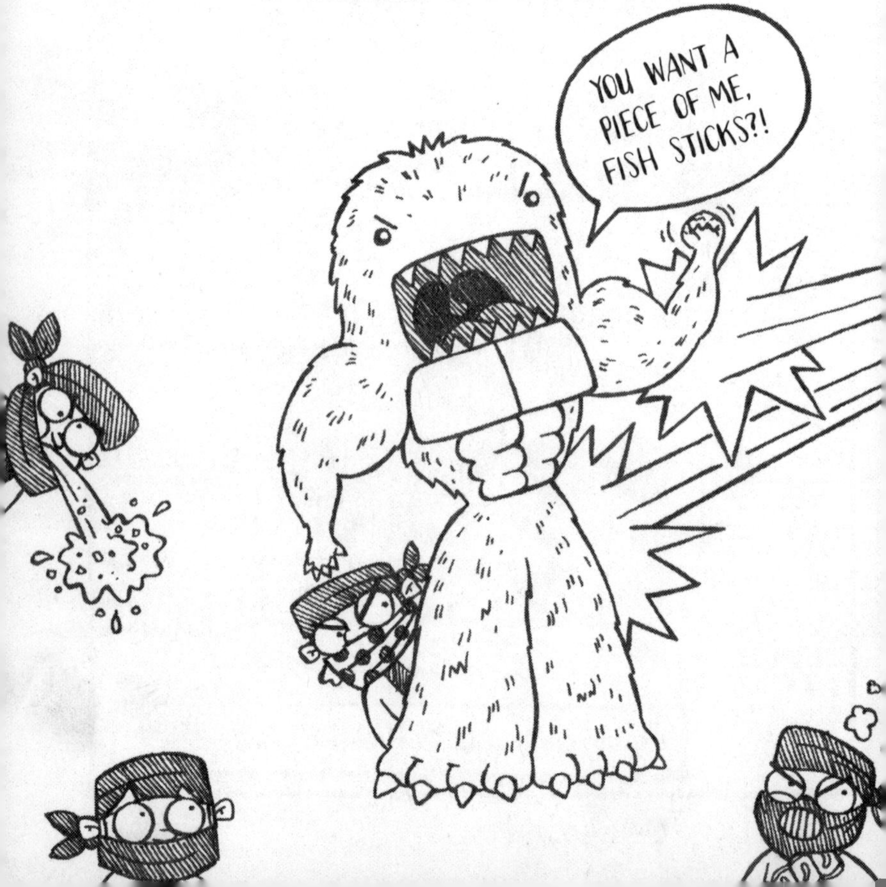
YOU WANT A PIECE OF ME, FISH STICKS?!

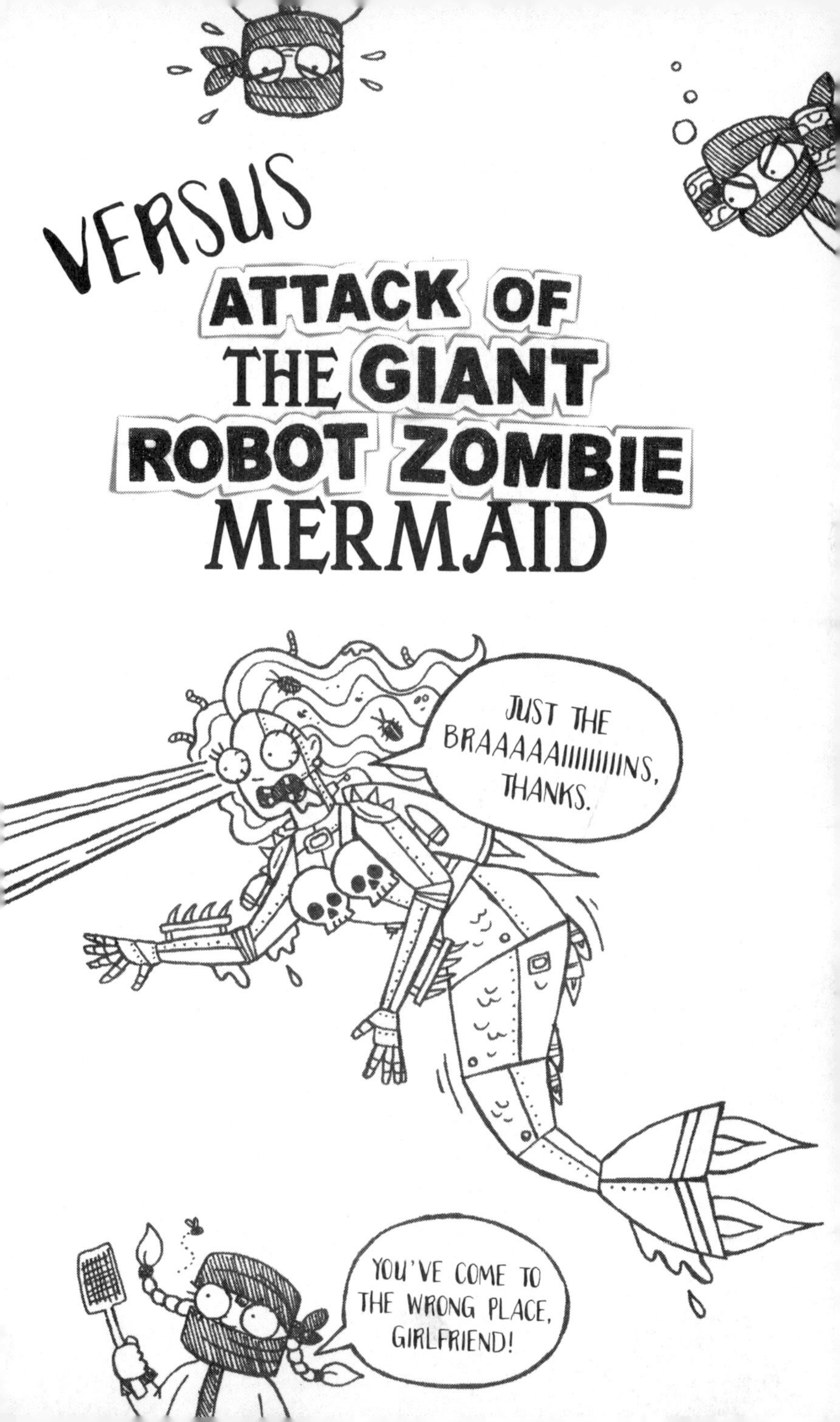
VERSUS
ATTACK OF THE GIANT ROBOT ZOMBIE MERMAID
JUST THE BRAAAAAIIIIIIIIINS, THANKS.
YOU'VE COME TO THE WRONG PLACE, GIRLFRIEND!

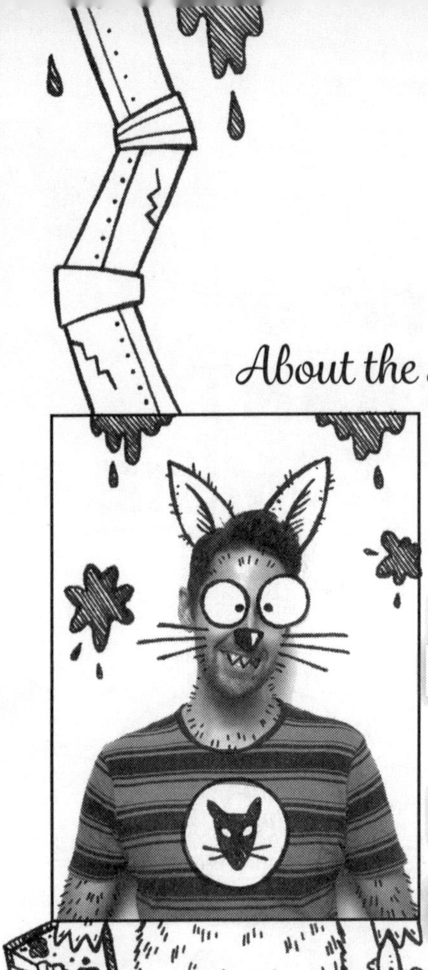

About the Author

Ratt Cosgrove is an awful and oversized hairy, mutant rodent who lives in the slimy sewers with his smelly teddy and two crocodiles.

He spends his days plotting world domination and loves making mouldy, toasted cheese sandwiches.

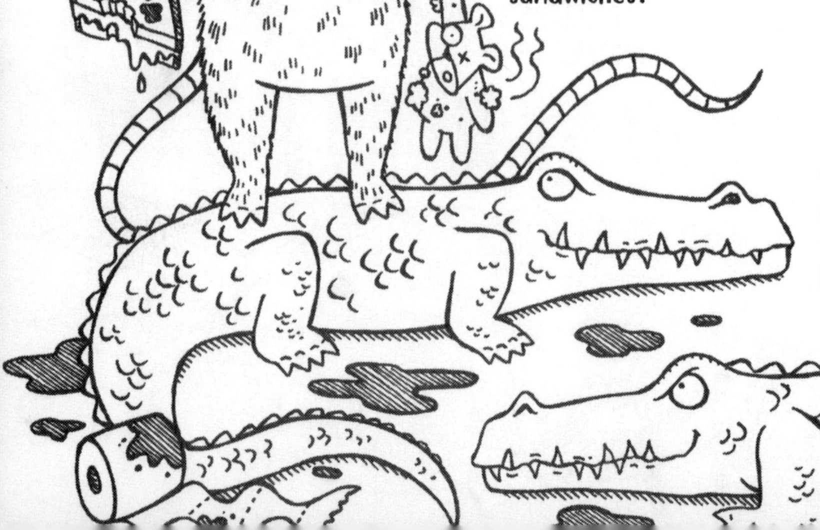

Photo: Eva Amores

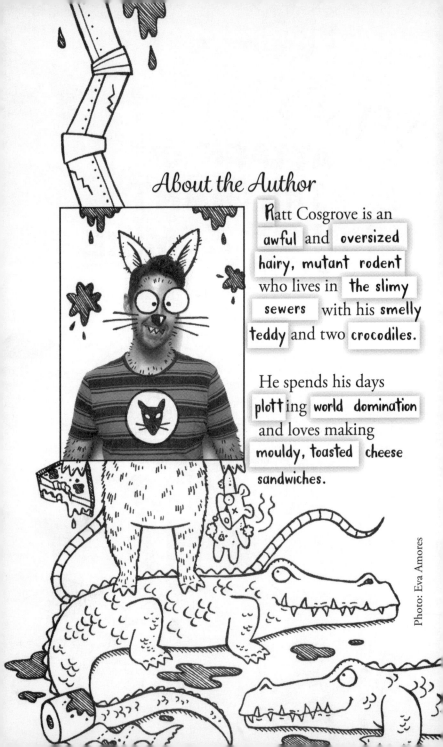